Dabblings

A JOURNEY OF HORROR AND HOPE

Dabblings

A JOURNEY OF
HORROR AND HOPE

STEVE JAMES

Vision House Publishing, Inc.
Gresham, Oregon

DABBLINGS
© 1994 by Vision House Publishing, Inc.

Published by Vision House Publishing
1217 NE Burnside, Suite 403
Gresham, OR 97030

Cover design by Multnomah Graphics/Printing

Printed in the United States of America.

94 95 96 97 98 99 00 01 — 08 07 06 05 04 03 02 01

*To
my loving
and
supportive wife.*

Foreword

The occult is exploding into our society. Bumper stickers proudly proclaim the driver to be a witch. Saturday morning cartoons are peopled with magic users. Role-playing games have gone far beyond Dungeons and Dragons as they come onto computers with full video simulation and worldwide network access. Electronic bulletin boards offer thousands of files on paganism, satanism, anarchy, and the occult. Schools and museums teach paganism and Wicca as alternative religions. Even TV uses occultic symbology to sell its wares. But many of us deny this dark reality, thinking it's only harmless entertainment and idle amusement.

Dabblings will grip your imagination as it uncovers the frightening dangers hidden behind innocent appearances. For all of us, it will guide to a deeper respect for the power of darkness while reminding us that God will ultimately prevail.

Dabblings is not entertainment. It is real and may be happening in your neighborhood. Some will think it's absurd, others overstated. But, in fact, it's just the tip of the iceberg. Our prayer is that this book will enlighten you to the devilish strategies going on in our society and warn people to leave no room for Satan's foothold in their lives.

Gary Breshears, Th.D.
Professor, Western Seminary

John VanDiest, Th.M.
Publisher, Vision House Publishing, Inc.

Preface

It was late. Everyone had gone home, but I was still in my office finishing up paperwork. The phone rang and I picked it up. Someone was on the line, but refused to speak. I hung up and another line rang. I picked it up. Same silence.

"What do you want?" I asked firmly into the receiver.

The caller hung up.

Immediately a third line rang and again all I heard was silence.

It was a strange game and I'm not sure why I kept playing, but I did. The fourth and fifth calls were the same. By the sixth call, I was angry. I picked up the receiver and said, "If you have something to say, then say it. But if I receive one more silent call, I'm notifying the police."

I heard a cough at the other end of the line. Then a muffled voice replied, "If you say or write anything about satanic cult activity, we will destroy you." *Click.*

I hung up the phone. I felt a mixture of shock, anger, and fear. Should I call the police? No, they couldn't do anything about it. I waited at the office for another fifteen minutes, but the phone rang no more. As I walked out of my building to my car, I looked around for strangers. My heart was beating quickly. Once in my car, I placed the key in the ignition and stopped. Weren't most car bombs connected to the ignition? I'd seen it in the movies. The driver turns the key and KABOOM—a giant explosion.

"This is ridiculous," I said to myself. "I can't let a phone call make me paranoid."

I turned the key and the car started. I breathed a sigh of relief and thanked God for His protection.

I'd spoken publicly about satanic cult activity for the previous five years and had even mentioned to friends that I'd like to someday write a book on the subject. However, a part of me was still skeptical. I'd interviewed hundreds of people, many who claimed to have been abused, tortured, threatened, and stalked by satanic cults. I'd listened to their horrific stories, but couldn't believe such things were happening in America.

The phone call shocked me from my skepticism. I'd talked to a number of people who had worked on satanic cult cases and who warned me to be careful. One person told me a satanic coven was trying to kidnap her. She later vanished and has not been found. A police officer told me to check my car before driving it and be sure to take a different route home each night. Another police officer suggested I either stop speaking on the subject or hire a bodyguard when I spoke publicly. Writers, psychologists, social workers, priests, and pastors all had advice for me. I heard one admonition repeatedly: Write down what you've learned, but don't use your real name. I was also warned to never write about actual people or real incidents. If I did, I'd be in danger.

Ten months after my unsettling phone call, I decided to start this book. Something about the caller's threat challenged me. So I wrote, and this is the product of that effort.

Some have asked: Why write a book about satanic cults? I would answer: To illustrate truth. I want to expose the dark side of life for what it is, thereby educating people in the roots and reality of evil. It is only as we know our Enemy, that we become aware of how he works.

This book is a novel, but it could have happened. All the

people presented here are fictional except for Goya, the Marque de Sade, Aliester Crowley, and the historical individuals described in chapter 16.

The following story is based on four simple premises commonly held since the dawn of human history. They are:

Satan is real.

Demons are real.

Witchcraft is real.

Satanic covens are real.

In considering evil and its agents, we face two opposing dangers: denial and paranoia. Denial disbelieves in the existence and reality of supernatural evil. Satan and his demons are reduced to superstition. Many churches no longer believe in Satan as an actual being, but as only a symbol of evil; demons are symbols of psychological trauma and pain. Meanwhile witchcraft and satanic covens are seen as fantasies or, at their worst, harmless pranks. A brief survey of historical data will show the naiveté of such a position.

Paranoia exaggerates the activity and power of evil. Satan and demons become inescapable gods who secretly orchestrate every act of pain, perversion, and failure in the universe, while those involved in witchcraft and satanic covens lurk around every corner.

I believe the truth lies somewhere in between these two extremes. However, if you lean toward denial, please suspend your disbelief as you turn the following pages. If you lean toward paranoia, please read this book with the lights on and in the company of a friend.

Acknowledgments

To my extended family,
who has always been there when needed.

To my friends and colleagues,
who encouraged me to keep writing.

To those who read this manuscript
and provided invaluable feedback.

To my publisher,
who has the vision and courage to take risks.

WARNING

Read with caution.
Included within are quotes from books of sorcery,
historical information about black magic,
and portrayals of demonic activity.
These scenes may be upsetting to some.

The purpose of this book is not to offend or sensationalize, but to expose and educate. My goal is accuracy without magnifying or minimizing the nature of evil. I pray the following story will encourage thinking, promote truth, disclose danger, and remind you that there is hope. Here the truth is presented without apology.

However, this book is not for everyone. It is not recommended for you if you are:

1. Highly sensitive. The content may be emotionally disturbing and result in anxiety, paranoia, and/or nightmares.

2. A ritual abuse survivor, unless in a therapeutic relationship with a trained professional. If this material triggers flashbacks, repressed memories, physical abreactions, or dissociation, discontinue reading immediately.

3. Too fascinated with evil. This material may feed an unhealthy obsession, slowly drawing you into forms of dabbling, which in time could threaten both your physical safety and your very soul.

4. A child or an early adolescent. Young minds are simply not psychologically prepared to face concrete portrayals of evil. Exposure at a young age risks phobias, anxiety, insecurity, and nightmares.

For those of you who choose to go ahead: Do not be afraid, for, to paraphrase the Holy Scriptures, you shall know the truth and the truth need not bind you, but set you free.

"We must ultimately belong either
to God or the devil."
—*Scott Peck*

"Resist the devil
and he will flee from you.
Draw near to God
and he will draw near to you."
—*The Holy Bible*

Prologue

The Vow
(October 31, 1929)

A full moon cast eerie shadows across the circle of thirteen men in white robes. They stood near the edge of an isolated cliff with wheat fields to the north and a mighty river to the south. The wind blew through the wheat and water—each moved with the breeze. But the men on the cliff stiffened against the October blast. Nothing moved them.

In the center of this circle two bronze dishes rested in the fine sand, small fires in each. One of the thirteen figures stepped forward and stood between the two dishes. His face was painted black except for a silver star on his forehead. His eyes glowed red in the reflection of the fire as he yelled above the wind.

"Tonight there exists a crack in time. Tonight the gates of the underworld will be opened. Tonight a pact will be sealed with the great-horned god." The twelve disciples repeated the sacred triad.

The leader lifted both hands above his head. His palms were painted black with a silver star, and on each star was drawn a dark horned goat.

"Let us call forth the Ancient serpent. Let us awaken the eternal black cat. Let us worship the almighty baphomet." The leader raised his voice and spoke the mighty words that opened the gates of hell. "Zazas, zazas, nasatanada, zazas."

The twelve knelt and spoke in unison, "Oh, come to us Rex Mundi."

One hundred feet from the ceremony twenty-four-year-old Vincent trembled in the shadows and awaited his turn. His hands were shoved deep into the pants pockets of an expensive black suit. He listened to the incantations, carefully memorizing each line, mesmerized by the ritual. Behind him loomed a life-size replica of Stonehenge: thirty twelve-foot monoliths encircled five twenty-foot inner arches and in the center stood the altar. Before him thirteen sorcerers called forth Satan.

The white robes parted and Vincent stepped slowly, hesitantly into the flickering circle. The brisk wind slapped his face and pushed him closer to the fire. The leader pulled out a silver-handled knife from a leather sheath at his side, forced it into Vincent's left hand, and said, "Before the full moon falls, an evil sorcerer will be initiated and his heart will be darkened forever."

The twelve drooled and pointed to Vincent asking in unison, "What will you give as a token of your secrecy?"

Vincent's mouth opened. He cleared his throat and whispered, "My blood."

Vincent fingered the handle of the sacrificial knife, staring at the ornate carvings of a cat with its mouth wide open. Sharp teeth pointed toward the blade and blended into its cutting edge. Thirteen sets of wicked eyes watched, waiting for his act of obedience to the underworld. Vincent gripped the cat's neck and took a deep breath.

The twelve spoke in unison, "What will you give to gain the infinite knowledge from the tree of good and evil?"

Vincent said, "My life."

Vincent shuffled his feet, pulled a neatly-folded red handkerchief from the breast pocket of his suit and wiped the sweat from his forehead. Two of the twelve stepped forward until they stood directly in front of him, inches from his face. One handed him a deep red apple, the other motioned him to eat. Vincent looked around the circle nervously, lifted the apple to his lips and bit. He held the fruit in his mouth for a second and then gagged—it was laced with a bitter drug. He squeezed his eyes shut and swallowed hard. Stones and white robes swirled around him.

The twelve stared at Vincent. "What will you give to gain the everlasting power?"

"My future progeny."

The leader set a golden cross between the two fires. Vincent spit on the cross three times and repeated the Lord's Prayer backward.

The leader raised his hands and yelled, "Blessed is he who reaches deep into the earth, who draws down the moon, who bequeaths his seed to the evil baphomet. Dear Vincent, this is a night you will never forget."

Chapter 1

Slowly the silver Mercedes drove by the old Victorian house. Heather watched both the car and her daughter from the front window of her new home. The suntanned little girl sat on the porch steps in her sundress, her bare feet crossed in front of her. A stack of picture books sat beside the five-year-old and one rested awkwardly on her lap. As she read aloud, her head bobbed up and down.

Ten minutes later the car passed again. The driver studied the house this time and Heather could guess what the driver was thinking: built about 1895, no sign of a basement, painted gray and white, small front yard with no fence, large oak tree in back, probably no security system. Again the silver car disappeared, only to return ten minutes later. It drove up to the curb, the car door silently opened, and a graceful woman slipped out from behind the steering wheel. Heather hid behind the curtains so she could watch without being seen. The sleek lady walked lightly across the driveway in a cream-colored linen blouse, designer jeans, and leather flats. Jennifer was still absorbed in her reading and wouldn't have noticed the woman's approach if it hadn't been for the slight metallic sound of her long, dangling cat earrings.

"Grandma, Grandma!" The little girl jumped up and threw her arms around the woman who didn't look old enough to have grandchildren.

"Hi, Jennifer," she said.

"This is our new house, Grandma. Do you like it?"

"Yes, it's very pretty."

Taking her grandmother's hand, Jennifer said, "Would you please read me a book?"

"Why don't you read one to me?"

"I can't read," Jennifer insisted.

"But I watched you sitting here reading all these books."

Jennifer laughed. "I was just pretending. I look at the pictures and make up stories."

"If you want me to read a book, I'd love to." The grandmother sat down on the porch, Jennifer crawled into her lap, and together they read an old Dr. Seuss tale. As the story ended, Heather, an attractive woman in her early thirties, stepped through the screen door and onto the porch. The door slammed behind her and the grandmother jumped.

"Oh, it's you Heather."

"Mom, I didn't expect you to drop by so soon. The house is a mess. Everything's still in boxes."

"That's why I came." Heather's mother stood up. "I thought you might need some help putting things in order. And since your father's gone again, I have extra time on my hands."

"Let's go inside." Heather opened the screen door. Turning to Jennifer, she said, "Your grandmother and I need to talk. Why don't you play out here for a while?"

Jennifer wrinkled her nose but said, "Okay."

Heather and her mother walked into the front entryway. "What happened to Dad?" Heather asked.

"My guess is your grandfather ordered a meeting. Someone called in the middle of the night and the next thing I knew he was gone—no explanation, no goodbye, nothing. That was three days ago."

Heather shifted her weight from one foot to the other. "What sort of meeting and where?"

"I can't talk about the agenda, but I think Grandfather was going to be at Chichén Itzá about now. So I'm sure they'll gather in the caves."

"Where's that?"

"Don't you remember?"

Heather shook her head.

"Maybe that's best." Her mother paused. "We visited there when you were seven or eight. It's on the Yucatan Peninsula in eastern Mexico."

"When do you think he'll be back?"

"Something significant is about to happen here in town . . ." Her eyes glazed over and her voice sounded strange. "The passing of the vow . . . the inclusion of the last generation . . ."

"Mother, what are you talking about?"

"Your father . . . I don't think he'll be gone for more than a week or two." She shook her head and refocused. "In the meantime, I'm here and I'd like a tour. These old houses have such character."

"Let's go upstairs and I'll show you the bedrooms first." Heather guided her mother through the three bedrooms and one oversized bath.

After walking back downstairs, Heather showed her mother the living room, parlor, half-bath, and the large kitchen with its cozy breakfast nook.

"Once you get organized," her mother said, "this place will be very nice. Where do you want me to start?"

"Well . . ." Heather studied the boxes. "Let's move all the boxes labeled 'Jennifer' up to her bedroom and unpack them."

"Why don't I take care of Jennifer's room and you go about with whatever you were doing before I arrived?"

Heather's mother picked up a box and headed up the stairs. Heather went into the kitchen and finished putting everything in place. An hour later she climbed the old staircase to see how her mother was doing. The door to Jennifer's room was shut. Heather turned the knob and pushed. "Mom? What's in front of this door?"

"Jennifer's dresser. Hold on for a minute and I'll move it."

Heather waited in the hallway for what seemed like fifteen minutes before the door opened. "What took you so long?" she asked. "Why did you . . ."

"How do you like it?" her mother asked.

Heather was dumbfounded. Her mother had made the canopy bed, arranged the closet, and filled the dresser. The room was completely unpacked except for a few boxes tied in twine.

"Mother, this looks perfect."

"Do you have a knife handy? I need to cut the twine on these two boxes and then I'll be finished."

"Sure, let me get you one." Heather ran down to the kitchen, grabbed a steak knife off the counter and ran back upstairs. "I'm sorry, but this is all I could find."

"That's okay, I'm sure it will work."

Her mother placed the knife beneath the twine and pulled. The string snapped. Her mother cried out and dropped the knife. Blood flowed quickly from a jagged cut on her thumb. Heather stared at her mother's thumb, eyes frozen and stomach nauseous. Images of red hands flooded her vision. All sizes and shapes of hands crowded her and every one was red—petite feminine hands with long nails that scratched and clawed; large rugged masculine hands that grabbed and punched; old wrinkled hands, too gnarled to hold their prey; tiny frightened hands that tried to escape. They all moved closer until Heather couldn't breathe. Suddenly the room went from red to black.

When Heather opened her eyes she was lying on the floor with a wet washcloth on her forehead. Her mother knelt beside her with a glass of cold water.

"I'm sorry. I didn't mean to faint, but when I . . ."

"That's okay, just relax."

". . . saw your thumb . . ." Heather breathed deeply. "I could never stand the sight of blood. It gives me the creeps." Heather sat up and drank the water. "I feel back to normal now. How's your cut?"

"It isn't very deep. If I put a Band-Aid on it, it should be fine."

"They're in the bathroom. Let me get you one."

"No, you take it easy. I'll get it." Heather's mother left the room and returned a few minutes later with a brightly-colored Band-Aid on her thumb. "Let's finish these boxes and then I need to get home just in case your father, or maybe even your grandfather, calls."

While her mother unpacked the open box, Heather carefully cut the twine on the other. Half an hour later, both boxes were unpacked and put away. Her mother left in a hurry and Heather moved downstairs to work in the living room.

Out the window Heather watched Jennifer on the front porch as she arranged brightly colored wildflowers into two small bouquets. She carefully counted out the different colors—light blue, pink, white, yellow—and organized them into bunches. She reached into the pocket of her gingham sundress, pulled out two ribbons, and wrapped them around the flowers. Her brown eyes concentrated as she crossed, twisted, and looped each ribbon in an exercise of creative knot-tying. When finished, she patted each tangled ribbon and called, "Mommy, I need you."

Heather opened the screen door and peeked out. "What's up?"

"I picked you flowers. The blue ones are my favorite. They're so pretty. These are for you . . ." Jennifer handed the bundle to her mother. Heather smiled and kissed Jennifer on the forehead. The little girl held up the second bundle, " . . . and these are for Daddy."

"Oh, Honey." Heather sat down beside Jennifer and held her closely. "I love you so much. Your daddy would be proud of you."

"Can I give these to Daddy?"

"You mean at the cemetery?"

Jennifer lowered her head and nodded. "Mommy," she whispered into her mother's ear, "I miss Daddy. Are you sure he can't come back?"

Heather held her daughter's hand and shook her head. "When you die, you can't come back."

"But I want him. I want him so bad."

A tear ran down Heather's cheek. "I want him, too."

The two hugged and Heather stroked Jennifer's light brown hair. Suddenly Jennifer pulled away. "Is Daddy in heaven?" she asked.

"I don't know, Sweetheart."

"Brittany says that dead people go to heaven."

Heather stood up. "I need to get these flowers into water and finish some unpacking. Maybe we can go to the cemetery tomorrow."

Inside, Heather tried to distract herself by unpacking another box. But she couldn't stop thinking about Chuck and the day he died. Involuntarily, she began to tremble. Something was wrong. No matter how many times she examined the details, they never fit together quite right. Even the police said it was an "unusual" place to have an accident. But if it wasn't an accident, what was it? Heather turned up the radio in an attempt to drown out her thoughts.

An hour later, Heather heard a faint noise upstairs. It couldn't be Jennifer; she'd just seen her in the front yard playing with a neighbor's kitten. "Jennifer?" she called. She crept up the narrow staircase and across the hall to Jennifer's bedroom. Listening at the door, all she could hear was the thump, thump, thump of her heart.

Then, behind the door, a little girl giggled. Heather sighed. Jennifer must have come up while she was moving boxes to the garage. Heather quietly opened the door and peeked in to see Jennifer dressing one of her dolls. *What a precious little girl,* she thought. *If anything ever happens to her . . .*

Jennifer wrapped her dolly in a blanket, held her closely, and began to sing to her. Heather closed the door and returned to the living room. What was wrong with her? She was so jumpy. Everything startled her. She paced back and forth, talking to herself. "Is it the dreams? Maybe, but there's something else." She went to the kitchen and got a cold drink of water. "The date. Could it be the date?" Yes, it was June 20th, but she was so sure the anniversary wasn't going to bother her. It appeared she was wrong.

Heather burst into tears.

The telephone rang and she jumped. She wiped away her tears and tried to ignore it. It rang again. She picked it up.

"Hi. This is Carolyn. Brittany was wondering if Jennifer could come over to play."

"Of course, she'd love that."

"Heather, are you okay?"

"No, not really."

"What's wrong?"

"I don't know—I think I'm depressed. In two days it's both summer solstice and the one-year anniversary of Chuck's death."

"Oh, I'm so sorry. Is there anything I can do?"

Heather paused, wondering how much she should tell. "I'm not sure."

"Why don't you bring Jennifer over and the two of us can have a cup of coffee?"

Heather agreed and went to get Jennifer. She liked Carolyn. They'd both gone to the same high school. They hadn't known each other well in school, but now, as she had gotten to know her, Carolyn seemed like the sort of person Heather could trust. Once next door, the two women sent their daughters to the backyard to play and then sat down at the kitchen table to talk.

"Are you unpacked?" Carolyn asked.

"Almost. It's hard to concentrate. My life has just been so miserable since Chuck was killed." Her mind flashed to the white Volvo half submerged in a shallow part of the river. She would never forget how the sun sparkled on the muddy water that day.

"It must be awful," Carolyn said. "I don't know what I'd do if anything happened to Dale."

"It was especially hard on Jennifer." Heather hesitated and then the words gushed out. "About six months ago I started having trouble sleeping. I had these weird premonitions— black cats clawing at Jennifer and red hands choking her. I live in fear every day that something's going to happen to her." It felt so good to finally be able to talk to someone about this.

"Wow . . ." Carolyn leaned forward. "Why would you be afraid of that? I mean, dreams are just, well, dreams."

"I don't know." Heather blushed and played with the handle of her leather purse. "Everything's been so crazy lately. Chuck dies, the dreams start, and then my father disappears. Oh, I'm probably just being paranoid."

"Your father disappeared? What do you mean?"

"Every so often, Dad gets restless and takes off. My mother wakes up one morning and he's gone, just like that. About a week or two later he shows up and acts like nothing's happened. It doesn't seem to bother my mother, but I think it's really strange."

"That is strange. Do you think he's having an affair or something?"

Heather laughed, thinking about it. "No, not my dad. My mother thinks he's meeting my grandfather somewhere in Mexico."

"Why? What about?"

Heather suddenly realized how crazy this must all sound to Carolyn who had a perfectly normal life with a perfectly normal family. Still, she continued. "I've tried to figure my family out for years, but I get nowhere. In fact, I can't even remember that much about my childhood. I'm an only child. My father was a salesman. He's a quiet, easygoing sort of guy. Every summer when I was a kid, he took a month off work in August and we'd pan for gold in Southern Oregon. It was a lot of fun. The only thing that scared me was . . ." How could she say this?

"What?" Carolyn prodded gently.

"Well, my father would build these big bonfires out in the woods. On some nights he'd build two or three different fires—huge ones that lit up the skies for miles. He loved the flames and heat and excitement. He would . . . well, . . . let's see . . ." Heather stopped again. What was Carolyn thinking?

"I—uh—I never met your father," Carolyn said, "but I remember your mother picking you up after school. She drove that silver Mercedes."

"She still drives a silver Mercedes, but not the same one. She picked me up a lot in high school. She was a third grade teacher at St. Anthony's, the Catholic school across the street from the high school. She was a devout Catholic. We went to Mass and confession once a week, ate fish on Friday, and I went to a Catholic grade school. When I got older, she decided I could go to a public high school, but she still picked me up every day."

"She sounds strict. Do you still go to church?"

"No, not since grade school. My grandfather found out that my mom had been taking us to church and he was furious. He made lots of threats to get her to stop. I think about church sometimes and how God is supposed to be everywhere. I don't know if I really believe that, though. I wish God were here. I'd feel so much safer if I weren't so alone, especially with all the nightmares and feelings I've had lately. They come, . . ." Heather cleared her throat. "They come at night, when I'm trying to sleep. I get restless and my mind races. I get up and . . ." Heather felt her mouth twist uncontrollably. "I get up and . . ." Her eyes darted back and forth and her back stiffened as she continued in a rough whisper, ". . . and I'm pacing . . . watching . . . prowling . . . ears pricked . . ."

Carolyn put her hand on Heather's arm. "Heather, what's wrong?"

Heather reoriented herself to the room. "I'm so sorry if I scared you. Every once in a while I fall into these trances. I can't seem to stop them." Embarrassed, she jumped up from the table. She had to get out of there.

"Maybe you should see a doctor." Carolyn took a step backward.

"Mommy, Mommy!" Jennifer bounced into the room. Heather picked her up and gave her a big squeeze.

"Hi, Sweetheart. I guess we'd better get back home." Heather walked to the door with Jennifer's hand in hers.

Carolyn followed. "It's Brittany's birthday in a couple of days and she's having a few of her friends spend the night. We'd love to have Jennifer join us. That might be a tough day for you. You might need some time alone."

"That's nice of you to ask. I'll bring her over." Heather stopped at the door and turned to face Carolyn. "I'm so embarrassed about what just happened. You must think . . ."

"That's okay." Carolyn patted her arm. "Don't think another thing about it."

Heather carried Jennifer home and the two spent the afternoon playing Candyland.

Later they ate supper on the back porch, enjoying the sunshine and each other's company. While cleaning up the dishes, Heather ran across the day's mail on the kitchen counter. She'd been so busy, this was her first chance to thumb through it. Two bills, three pieces of junk mail, and a plain white business envelope with her name and address neatly printed on the front. At the bottom of the envelope in large black letters three words were printed: "PERSONAL AND CONFIDENTIAL." Heather opened the letter with a mixture of curiosity and dread. Inside she found a flyer announcing an upcoming theatrical performance of Tennessee Williams's famous play, *Cat on a Hot Tin Roof.* Heather's hands trembled. What was this? Turning the flyer over she found a message scrawled in red felt pen: *Embrace the cat!*

Heather stared at each word with horror, unable to move. She felt herself begin to fade, but shook herself free of the trance. She crumpled the paper, tore it in half, and threw it into the garbage pail beneath the kitchen sink. She wasn't about to let this message scare her.

Chapter 2

That evening, Heather carried sleepy-eyed Jennifer up the stairs on her back. She helped her into her nightgown and squeezed toothpaste onto her teddy bear toothbrush. Together they giggled, side by side on Jennifer's pink canopy bed, as Heather read story after story. Somehow in her subconscious she knew she was prolonging this moment in an effort to put off going into her own bedroom . . . and her own night dreams—alone.

But finally Jennifer was asleep. Heather kissed her on the forehead and crept out of the room.

She decided to relax in the parlor before going to bed. The sun had set through the French windows and darkness had settled on the room. She yawned, kicked off her shoes, and strolled through the house turning on antique light fixtures. Hardwood floors creaked under her bare feet and shadows disappeared. She studied each lighted room with its high ceilings and meticulous woodwork. She loved this old house perched on a hill in Oregon City. She hadn't wanted to sell their custom-built home on the west side of Portland, but it held too many memories. Chuck, an architect, had designed that house. Every nook and cranny reminded her of how much she loved him and the depth of her loss.

She paced her new house. Glancing here and there, she stared at the walls and listened. Something didn't feel right.

She stopped, her hands trembling. Cats fought and screeched in the neighbor's backyard. Her ears perked and her pacing accelerated. She held her hands over her ears, but she could still hear them. Wild pictures ran through her head—images of furious cats slashing, biting, cutting. What was happening? Was she crazy? She tried to push the images from her mind, tried to calm herself, tried to regain control, but it was useless. Her muscles twitched as adrenaline pulsed through her. She felt disconnected from her body. Driven by wild and primitive impulses that moved of their own accord, she was pulled along by forces beyond her understanding. She felt trapped in this body . . . in this building . . . even in this city. Nothing seemed real as her eyes flashed back and forth, scanning the room for some invisible prey. She needed to run. No! *It* needed to run and roam the wide open spaces. The inner pressure was so intense, she felt ready to explode.

Suddenly the telephone rang, breaking the spell. Heather collapsed into a chair, exhausted and confused. She stared at the phone, then slowly picked it up.

"Hi, Heather," Carolyn said. "Jennifer left her sweater over at our house this afternoon. I thought I'd just run it over, if that's . . ."

"No . . . not now . . ."

"Heather, what is it?"

"It's happening again."

"What?"

"The animal trance. I felt like a cat . . . or something. It was the same thing that happened this afternoon at your house that stopped when you touched me. Tonight it broke through and I was losing control. I'm so glad you called."

The two women talked for about fifteen minutes. After Heather hung up, she sat at her kitchen table with a hot cup of herbal tea. "What's going on with me?" she asked herself. Pondering it, small pieces of memory began to fit together.

Heather's mother loved cats and nicknamed Heather "Kitty," to her a name of ultimate affection. She believed cats were more intelligent than people, and that some of them had actually been people. White cats were once good people and black cats were bad. She tried to explain to Heather about an old Druid belief called transmigration, where a person's soul passes into the body of an animal. She welcomed every stray cat who visited their doorstep with a bowl of fresh milk, especially black cats. She once told her daughter, "Someday if you're very lucky, maybe you can be a cat." Heather laughed it off at the time, but she never forgot it.

When Heather was ten, her mother came home one day with a large oil painting of three wild cats: a majestic lion and a lioness stood over an albino lion cub. Her parents hung the picture in the front hallway and every time Heather came or went, she felt the two larger cats following her with their piercing brown eyes. They leaned forward, ready to pounce, watching every move with human eyes which held her in their gazes. The cats pursued her tirelessly, it seemed, and late at night, she often awoke screaming with bad dreams. Sitting up in bed, she saw the four shining eyes crouched in the corner, waiting.

"Can we please get rid of the wild cats?" Heather asked her mother one morning. "I hate that picture. It gives me nightmares."

"Kitty, how can you say such a thing? After all, it's a portrait of our lovely family."

On Heather's sixteenth birthday, her parents threw a surprise party for her. All her friends were invited. They ate, played games, danced, and then at midnight, Heather's mother ushered Heather and a few of her closest friends into the dining room where the lights were turned low. A lady in a long black dress sat at the head of the dining room table. Everybody was seated and asked to hold hands.

Heather giggled. "This is too spooky. Let's go back to the party."

"No," the medium spoke sharply. "The spirits have called us together."

"What spirits? This is weird." Heather turned to one of her friends. "Let's go."

"Oh, don't be silly," her friend said. "This is exciting."

"There's a message to be given tonight," the medium said as she closed her eyes. "A message from the underworld to Kitty so that she . . ."

"I don't like this," Heather interrupted.

"Shhhhh!" her friends hissed.

". . . so that she can meet her destiny." The medium put her head face-down on the table and groaned. Heather's stomach tightened and her heart raced. The room felt warm and she desperately wanted a glass of water, but she didn't want her friends to get angry with her again. She stayed glued to her chair.

The medium slowly raised her head and opened her eyes, glowing eyes which stared into nothing. "Listen closely my dear," the medium spoke in a raspy male voice. There was a long, uncomfortable pause before the medium continued.

"Your father is a lion
Who loves to roam and roar.
Your mother is a lioness
Watching at your door.
And you were born to darkness;
A lion from the start,
With a family of heritage
And blackness at its heart."

Heather couldn't remember what happened after that, but the poem had always haunted her. As she thought about her problem now, these memories all seemed to fit together. Viewed separately they were eccentric pieces of childhood trivia; when placed side by side they appeared to be much more.

Several days later Heather was still confused about what was happening to her. She telephoned her mother's brother, her Uncle George, a Catholic priest and a Rhodes scholar. He taught theology and philosophy at a small Catholic Seminary in a remote area of the Pacific Northwest, but he also lectured throughout the world. Uncle George was a bit of a pedagogue with two doctorates and a half dozen honorary degrees.

He lived on the seminary grounds with twenty-seven other priests who had become his friends and family. Before dawn, each morning they gathered in a simple chapel and sang praises to God. Each evening they gathered again to close their day with vespers. Uncle George lived in a simple one-room apartment in the rectory complex. It was sparsely furnished with a twin bed neatly made with two plain wool blankets, a lamp, a small bookcase (most of his books were in his office), a well-worn overstuffed chair, and a wooden dresser with an old-fashioned porcelain pitcher and basin on top of it. The room was rectangular with a door on one end and a small window on the other. The walls were bare except for two pictures: one of Jesus kneeling in the Garden of Gethsemane, sweating blood and looking toward heaven; the other of his mother, young and beautiful and innocent and angelic-looking.

Whenever Heather thought of her uncle she imagined him surrounded by books in his office, reading dusty volumes and scribbling notes for his next lecture. She hadn't seen him in several years, but she remembered his face clearly. It was thin with high cheekbones, a straight nose, and a solid jaw. His skin was taunt, except for a few crowsfeet and a wrinkled brow. If it weren't for his thinning gray hair, which he always ran his right hand through while thinking, people would have guessed him to be twenty years younger than those meted out by sixty-one cold and rainy winters. Bushy eyebrows accented brown eyes that were constantly moving, analyzing, evaluating, correlating, and assimilating everything within sight. Small, wire spectacles magnified this process, giving him an intellectual look. Yet the spectacles were often a distraction as they slipped down his nose. Uncle George, who was usually lost in thought or lecture, ignored the slippage until all those around him had mentally pushed them up his bridge at least two or three times.

Heather loved her uncle and had great respect for him. Yet their conversations were frequently more academic than personal. Uncle George may have been eccentric, but Heather knew he would do anything for her. Besides, he was the smartest person she'd ever known.

"Uncle George, may I ask you a few questions?" she began when her uncle answered the phone.

"Yes, of course." His voice was deep and rich.

Heather explained the resurfacing memories of her mother, the cats, and the medium. She even recited the medium's poem.

Her uncle didn't answer right away, then he said, "I'm not sure you're ready for what I'm going to say."

"Maybe not, but I have to know."

"Well, to put it briefly, your mother has one foot in the faith and the other in sacrilege," Uncle George said in his usual enigmatic way. "A person can't stand for both God and demons. Sooner or later you'll end up on one side or the other. Simply put, your mother flirts with the Devil. I'm sorry, Heather, but the sins of the father and mother visit the children to the third or fourth generation."

Heather closed her eyes and let the phone hang limply in her hand. She was the third generation; Jennifer was the fourth.

"Heather, are you okay?"

"Just stunned." She swallowed hard and forced herself to ask the next question. "What about the lions?"

"Some cultures consider cats as holy and believe they hold the spirits of human beings."

"My mother would agree with that."

"So would your grandfather. That's why he gave your parents the cat picture. He even believes some cats are actually demons."

"That's ridiculous."

"It gets worse. There's an old family story that your grandfather made a deal with the Devil and Satan appeared to him in the form of a black cat."

"That can't be true. Do you think he's mentally ill or something?"

"That would be the easy explanation. But I don't think we should write this family rumor off too quickly. Every day people all over the world deal with the Devil without even knowing it. And if anybody's going to align himself with Satan, it would be your grandfather."

"I kind of wish you weren't telling me this. It's just going to make my nightmares worse. But I guess I feel like I have to know, even if it scares me to death." Heather paused for a moment, pulling together her courage. "Back to the lions . . ."

"I'm not sure what sort of deal was struck," said Uncle George, "but it had to do with cats becoming our family totem or something like that."

"So that's why Mother is obsessed with cats. Even if the rumor isn't true, she might still believe it."

"I hope I haven't said too much."

"Thanks, Uncle George."

Heather was trembling uncontrollably before she even hung up the phone. She'd tried so hard to be rational about all of this but her walls of objectivity were cracking. She had wanted answers, but Uncle George had simply added more pieces to Heather's puzzle. The more she thought about Satan and his demons, the more nervous she became. She felt cold shivers move up her back. She went though the house locking the doors, turning on all the lights, and wishing it wasn't night. She was suddenly terrified and the object of her terror was Satan . . . Lucifer . . . the Lord of the Flies . . . the Deceiver . . . the Devil . . . the Adversary . . . the Evil One . . . Beelzebub . . . the Father of Lies . . . Mephistopheles. Wasn't this like admitting she's afraid of the bogeyman or the monsters under the bed? It was all Uncle George's fault. If he hadn't mentioned the family legend . . .

Rap. Rap. Rap. Her bedroom window shuddered. Now every unexpected noise startled her. Heather clung to her pillow and held her eyes tightly closed. *Rap. Rap. Rap.* The glass echoed the request to enter. Heather dreamt she was awake and moving toward the window, curious as to who would beckon her so late at night. Gazing through the transparent barrier, all she saw was black. Heather turned and started back to bed. *Rap. Rap. Rap.* She swung around. A large man in a black robe with devilish eyes knocked on the window. He laughed at her terror and smashed the glass with his twisted claws. Heather screamed and sat up in her bed. The nightmare vanished, but slivers of glass lay on the floor and her window was a memory.

Chapter 3

"It's 73 degrees with an expected high of 88 on this summer solstice, the longest day of the year. It's 7:15 and . . ."

Heather rolled over and turned off her clock radio. She hadn't slept since last night's dream. It kept replaying itself in her mind, crossing and recrossing the thin line between nightmare and reality. She stared at the glass shattered on the floor, not really comprehending it. How did that happen? Could the dream possibly have been real? She shook herself to alertness and dragged her body from the bed.

The jagged hole in the window was real. Splinters of glass shimmered on the hardwood floor. She tried to look away, but it pulled her back. Her imagination ran wild and she began to panic. A slight breeze blew through the broken window and brought her back to reality. Men in black robes don't crawl around rooftops in the middle of the night. It was just a crazy dream. The window was probably shattered by a branch from the backyard oak tree or a disoriented bird. She tiptoed across the room and pulled the curtain shut. Maybe if she couldn't see the window, it wouldn't make her so uneasy.

A few minutes later, she stepped into the shower. As the hot water streamed down her face, a chilling memory surfaced. Exactly one year ago today a police officer stood at her door.

"Are you Heather Davis?"

"Yes."

"Do you own a 1986 white Volvo with Oregon license plate number SRD 166."

"Yes, that's my husband's car."

"Do you know who was last driving the vehicle?"

"My husband took it up the Columbia Gorge to The Dalles on business." She felt a tightening in her throat. "What is it? Has something happened to Chuck?"

"There has been an accident and . . ."

"Oh, no. Is my husband okay? What's wrong? Please tell me."

"We aren't sure. We found the car in the Columbia River about an hour ago, but there was no body."

Three hundred and sixty-four days later, there was still no body. And even now, Heather found herself waiting for Chuck to drive the white Volvo into the garage. It had taken her several painful months to finally accept that he was gone, but the accident still didn't make any sense. It was a bright sunny day on a straight stretch of highway with light traffic. The police department had asked her opinion on a number of theories. Could he have fallen asleep? It was the middle of the day. Was he intoxicated? Chuck never drank. Maybe he'd had a heart attack or some other medical problem. But he was in perfect health with no history of medical difficulties. Those theories just didn't work. The only clue was an anonymous phone call to the state police on the day in question reporting a white Volvo headed west on Interstate 84 driving erratically.

The mystery lingered and Heather's love for Chuck refused to fade. Each day she missed him—his strong arms and deep laugh. They had achieved everything they had ever wanted: a great marriage, a darling daughter, and a beautiful new home. Life is fragile. One car accident changed everything.

Heather rinsed the shampoo from her hair and stepped out of the shower. Today would be tough. She was glad she had to work; it might distract her from the memories. She slipped into a silk fuchsia blouse and a white linen suit jacket with a matching fitted skirt. She checked her outfit in the bedroom mirror and then finished putting on her make-up and jewelry. The gold earrings and bracelet were from her mother. The emerald mounted on a simple gold band was from Chuck. She thought of him each time she slipped it on her finger. She pulled on her white pumps and went downstairs where she found Jennifer helping herself to a banana and a box of cereal.

On the way to work, Heather dropped Jennifer off at Sunshine Day Care and reminded her of the party at Brittany's house that night. Then she drove on to Specialty Travel. About three months ago she started filling in periodically at the travel agency. Chuck had left a hefty insurance policy when he died, so she really didn't need the job. Yet, it kept her busy and she liked the travel benefits.

At 5:30 Jennifer and Heather stood on Carolyn's front porch with an overnight bag in one hand and a brightly wrapped present in the other.

"Now I want you to remember your manners," Heather said as she straightened her daughter's floral party dress, "and be sure to obey Brittany's mother. Have a lot of fun and I'll see you in the morning."

Heather rang the doorbell.

"Hello! Come on in," Carolyn said. Heather fidgeted with her purse. The family room was decorated with balloons, streamers, and a banner reading HAPPY BIRTHDAY! Heather's vision blurred and beads of perspiration formed on her forehead. On the coffee table sat a pink cake with five candles.

Heather gasped for air. "I have to go. I'll pick her up at 9:00 tomorrow morning." She rushed out the front door and headed for her car.

Parties. Heather had always hated parties. They felt evil to her. Heather grabbed onto the car door and caught her balance. Once inside the car, she put her head on the steering wheel and breathed deeply. The world spun and her vision went black. When she opened her eyes she was in her parent's living room. She was thirteen and they were throwing another party.

The room was hot and crowded. Heather's mother nudged her toward the fireplace where a group of men were clustered around a large man in his late sixties. He had silver hair with a neatly trimmed beard and mustache which he stroked as he spoke. He wore an expensive dark gray three-piece suit accented with a red tie, matching silk handkerchief, and a white rose in his lapel. When he spoke everyone listened. His voice sounded hollow and seemed to echo about his chest before escaping his mouth.

"I'm attracted to the desolate locales—the rugged fjords of Northwest Iceland . . ."

"Heather, go greet your grandfather."

". . . the loch's and moors of the Scottish Highlands, the ancient mountains of Nepal—that's where . . ."

Heather leaned back as her mother pushed her forward. "Please," the child whispered. "I don't feel well. I want to go. I want out of here."

" . . . the mystic grows and the magician finds his solitude."

Heather was now three feet from her grandfather. "Be polite and say something." Her mother stood directly behind her, blocking her escape.

Grandfather Vincent leaned forward on his walking stick and shifted his full attention to the trembling girl. "Congratulations! I hear you've reached puberty."

Silence fell over the room. Heather refused to look at her grandfather and stared instead at his walking stick. Something about his gaze was hypnotic. His piercing gray eyes seemed to focus beyond the object of his interest. Heather always felt he was looking right through her and into her soul. She studied the ornate carvings on the stick. Her grandfather's wrinkled hand gripped the head of a black cat with its mouth wide open. Its sharp teeth pointed down and blended into the wood. Two diamonds were embedded in its eye sockets.

"Kitty? What's wrong? Cat got your tongue?"

Heather's eyes didn't move and the silence continued. Everybody watched as Grandfather Vincent bent down and whispered in her ear, "Embrace the cat!"

Heather shuddered. She ducked around her mother, ran from the room, and crept downstairs to the basement.

Suddenly Heather found herself in a more primitive world where strobe lights pulsing to loud psychedelic music slashed the darkness. The air was heavy with incense and distorted by marijuana smoke. Teenagers in faded jeans and tie-dyed shirts huddled in small groups.

"Hi, Kitty. Nice party," each group called out as she walked across the room.

Heather sat in a corner, and watched the children of her parents' friends. A couple kissed passionately on the sofa. A circle formed in the center of the room and a joint moved slowly from mouth to mouth. Three or four individuals danced in the jerky flashes of light.

Why are my parents allowing this? Heather asked herself. They had to know what was going on down there.

About midnight somebody brought out a giant Ouija board. Heather's face flushed and shivers crept up her spine. Everybody gathered around the board. Heather tried to leave, but a hand grabbed her arm and wouldn't let go.

"I don't like this."

"Relax, it's just a game," someone said.

"No, it's not," Heather cried. "Please let's do something else, anything else. Please leave the board alone."

Nobody listened. The ritual proceeded and Heather was forced to join. At her turn, the Ouija board spelled out: "You are purfect."

Everybody laughed. "The spirits can't spell," someone joked. But Heather knew it was spelled the way it was meant to be spelled.

Heather opened her eyes and lifted her head from the steering wheel. The flashback had felt so real—she'd seen the dimly-lit Ouija board, heard the laughter, smelled the sweet aroma of marijuana smoke. Her stomach was tight and her teeth were clenched. She had managed to repress this scene from her childhood until now. But it was coming back to her in full force. Her parents threw a party each summer solstice. She dreaded these yearly rituals and was ill for three to four days afterward. She hated Ouija boards. They should all be destroyed.

Those last five words repeated themselves in her mind as she started the car and drove toward Portland. They should all be destroyed. A few moments later, she parked in front of an English Tudor house with a perfectly manicured lawn in the northwest hills of the city. She knew her parents weren't home. Her father was still gone and her mother had left for their special meeting place in hopes that he'd left Mexico and was back in the Pacific Northwest.

Heather unlocked the oak front door. The omniscient eyes of the two adult cats watched as she entered. She looked away and tip-toed down the hall, feeling the eyes follow her. She searched through the game cupboard but came up empty handed. Then she remembered that her mother always kept the Ouija board on the top shelf of her bedroom closet. She entered her parents' bedroom and found it right where she remembered it to be. She pulled it down and a stack of four dusty books dropped on top of her. She swore and rubbed her head. The books were old and well-worn but nicely bound in leather or pigskin with gold lettering on their broken spines.

Heather gathered the books from the floor and studied their curious titles: *Threefold Harrowing of Hell by Dr. Faust*, *One Hundred and Twenty Days of Sodom* by the Marque de Sade, *Magick in Theory and Practice* by Aliester Crowley, and *Key of Solomon*. The last was the largest volume; it had fallen apart and was tied together with a thin strip of leather. Heather picked it up and opened it to a place marked by a scrap of paper. The thick, yellow pages were smudged with fingerprints. Certain passages were marked with pencil. On one page Heather was drawn to these words:

> When you want to make your pact with one of the principal demons that I have just named, you will begin, on the evening before the pact, by cutting, with a new knife that has never been used, a wild nut-tree twig that has never borne fruit . . . at the exact moment that the sun appears on our horizon.
>
> This being done, you will fortify yourself with a blood stone and consecrated candles, and you will then choose a spot for the operation where nobody will disturb you . . .
>
> After which, you will trace a triangle with your bloodstone. . . . Then you will set the two candles on the side, placing the sacred name of Jesus behind you, to prevent the spirits from inflicting any harm on you.
>
> Then, you will stand in the middle of the triangle, with the mystic wand in your hand, with the great invocation to the demon . . .

Heather set the book down and took a deep breath. These must be Grandfather's books. She was frightened to read more, but something pushed her forward.

> Having performed scrupulously all that is indicated, you will begin to recite the following invocation: "Emperor Lucifer, Master of all the rebellious spirits, I beg you to be favorable in the invocation that I make to your great Minister Lucifuge Rofocale, as I wish to make a pact with him. I beg you also Prince Beelzebub, to protect me in my enterprise.
>
> "O Count Astorath! Be propitious, and bring it to pass that, this very night, the great Lucifuge appear to me in human form and without any evil odor, and that he grant me, by the means of the pact that I shall offer him, all the wealth that I need.

"O great Lucifuge! I beg you to leave your abode . . . to come and speak to me . . .

"So come forth instantly! Or I shall torture you endlessly by the force of these powerful words of the Key . . ."

This was followed by twenty-three strange and eerie words; some looked Hebrew while others looked Latin or Greek. Heather studied the letters carefully and tried to pronounce the odd syllables. The words seemed to move, calling to her, and the color of the ink changed from black to red. She looked up at the big picture window. The sun was setting and shadows filled the room. It was her imagination of course. Heather's hands shook. She slammed the book shut and quickly retied the leather strap. She sensed that she could have called forth demons by simply looking at the words. Flushed and breathing hard, she placed the four volumes back on the upper shelf. She grabbed the Ouija board and fled the house. Four glowing eyes followed her out the door and into the twilight.

Speeding away, Heather drove onto the Columbia Gorge Highway and headed east. She didn't know where she was going, but she had to escape. Half an hour later she turned north off the main highway toward the Bridge of the Gods. Halfway across the water Heather stopped and climbed out of the car, the Ouija board under her arm. Leaning on the railing, she stared down at the black waters of the Columbia River and for a split second thought about jumping. Instead, she flung the board off the bridge, and watched it turn and twist to the water below. It hit the river with a tiny splash, floated down stream a few hundred feet, and slipped beneath the surface. Destroyed. She sighed and headed back to her car.

Heather shook her head to clear away the sleepiness that was making it hard to concentrate. She felt a compelling force calling her to the meeting place. She wondered if her mother had found her father. She started the car and stared trance-like through the front windshield. She must join them at their secret hide-away.

Her mind drifted up the gorge, to an isolated bluff overlooking the river, where a replica of England's famous Stonehenge stood. Massive rocks and twenty-foot-tall arches formed a circular temple. At the center was the simple altar where Heather's parents first met. She had heard the story many times. It was a midsummer night in 1956 when they stared through infinity—watching Orion, the hunter, stalk the speckled sky. Their magic circle protected them from the wind as they spoke of Druid enigmas and Celtic rituals. Huddled in the blackness, they welcomed the sun as it kissed the heel stone and enflamed their open-air cathedral.

"No," Heather yelled at herself, "I won't join them." Images of her grandfather standing before the altar at Stonehenge haunted her. In one hand he held his stack of wicked books and in the other, a black cat. Heather breathed deeply, turned on the radio, and pulled away from the bridge toward home. In the rearview mirror she saw flashes of four glowing eyes following her through the darkness.

Chapter 4

Early the next morning, before picking up Jennifer, Heather called Uncle George and told him about the four books she'd found at her parents' house.

"You're right," Uncle George said. "Those books belong to your grandfather. I wonder what happened to the rest of them. He had a sizable library of occult books and medieval grimoires."

"What's a grimoire?"

"It's a manual of magic, usually black magic. It's full of rituals, incantations, and information about demons. The *Key of Solomon* was one of the most popular grimoires of the middle ages. Casanova owned a copy and it strongly influenced Aliester Crowley."

"I read some of it." Heather shuddered. "It gave me the creeps."

"That book is black magic incarnate. The Catholic Church thought it was so dangerous that they prohibited it way back in 1559."

"But I thought King Solomon in the Bible wrote it."

"That's the claim," Uncle George said, "but it's highly unlikely."

"Then who wrote it?"

"Probably some unknown heretic trying to cash in on all the folklore surrounding this famous king."

"Uncle George, you're amazing. You know about everything. Have you ever heard of any of the rest of these books?"

"Each has an interesting history. *The Threefold Harrowing of Hell* is a German grimoire from the 1500s. It says you can have anything you want—riches, wisdom, glory—if you seek it from the Devil."

"Why do people write these kinds of books? What about the *One Hundred and Twenty Days of Sodom*? What's that about?"

"Marque de Sade wrote that one. It's about sexual perversion and murder. It's sort of a pornographic encyclopedia."

"What's wrong with Grandfather? Why does he have these books?"

Uncle George grunted. "I remember he once said, 'The three grandest hobbies of all are witchcraft, pornography, and drugs. I'm a master of all three.' "

"That's sick," said Heather.

"You're right, but your grandfather is proud of his sickness. He's even boasted of being friends with Aliester Crowley."

"Who's that?"

"He was a poet, a sorcerer, and a heroin addict," Uncle George said. "He promoted what he called 'sexual magick' and claimed to be the reincarnation of several powerful magicians from the past. He said his number was 666 and he was 'the Great Beast.' He believed it was his job to usher in the age of the occult and to destroy Christianity. The newspapers of his time called him the wickedest man in the world. He led demonic rituals saturated with sex and blood and claimed to have performed 150 human sacrifices per year between 1912 and 1928."

Heather mentally calculated. "That's over two thousand sacrifices. How could he get away with that?"

"He didn't always. In 1923 Mussolini kicked him out of Italy and shortly afterward he was expelled from France. He was an arrogant braggart and nobody knew when to take him seriously. He was definitely evil enough to perform human sacrifices, nobody doubts that."

"So how did Grandfather meet him?"

"After graduating from high school, your grandfather traveled to Europe. He spent a lot of time in Paris, the center of satanic worship at that time. That's where he met Crowley and became interested in witchcraft, pornography, and drugs. He joined Crowley's Order of the Silver Star and studied ancient Gnostic writings. He even went with Crowley to the deserts of Tunsia to call forth demons.

After this, your grandfather became obsessed with making a deal with the Devil. He returned to the states in 1925 with a trunk full of Gnostic writings, medieval grimoires, pornographic books, and manuscripts on the occult. I'm sure all the books you found came from that trunk, except for *Magick in Theory and Practice* which was published later. Your grandfather and Crowley kept up a lively correspondence until Crowley's death in 1947. He even went to England for the funeral and participated in a black mass for Crowley at the crematorium in Brighton, much to the chagrin of the local townsfolk. In fact, do you remember the silver urn in the front room next to the fireplace at your grandfather's house?"

"The one with the stars that he gave to my mother?"

"Yes, that's the one. Those stars are pentagrams, and inside the urn are some of the ashes of Aliester Crowley."

"You have to be kidding." Heather shook her head with a pained look. "This is so disgusting, I can hardly believe it. I knew Grandfather Vincent was odd, but I never imagined anything like this. Why didn't anybody ever tell me about this? I've never even heard the name Aliester Crowley until now."

"Your mother was trying to protect you and Jennifer."

"Protect us from what?"

"From your grandfather's pact with the Devil."

"What does that have to do with us?"

"Heather, there's more, but I don't think you're ready to hear it."

"That isn't fair, Uncle George. If it has to do with Jennifer, I need to know what it is."

"When I was young and asked too many questions, your grandfather would bend down and whisper, 'Remember, curiosity killed the cat.' "

Obviously Uncle George had said all he was going to say. While walking next door to get Jennifer a few minutes later, the words hit her again: "Remember, curiosity killed the cat."

Chapter 5

The evening was cool and Heather curled up in front of the cozy fireplace, daydreaming and watching the glow. She was hypnotized by the colors and movement of the flames. Suddenly the fire crackled and spit sparks into the room. A few landed on a bundle of dry kindling stacked beside the hearth. Poof! The wood exploded and flames quickly spread across the room. She tried to stamp it out, but it was out of control. She ran to the door. It was locked. She jiggled the handle, pounded on the door, and screamed for help. She hurried to the window and found wrought iron bars on it. She grabbed the bars and pulled with all her might, but they didn't budge. The heat burned into her back as she broke the window and yelled until she was out of breath. She slid to the ground, coughing and crying. "Help me, I don't want to die. Oh, God, please help me."

"God cannot help you," a gruff voice spoke out of the fire. "You are mine. You are purfect. Now you must be marked by the fire . . . eaten by the fire."

Sparks flew at Heather as she huddled on the floor. Sweat ran down her face and mingled with her tears. "No. No. I hate fire," she moaned.

"Just relax. Let the fire take you. Lay down with it. You have been given to the fire. In the end, you and the fire must become one."

Heather's throat burned and smoke stung her eyes. She pulled herself to her feet once more and ran toward the door. Before she reached it, the flames attacked her and swallowed her.

Heather sat up in bed and tried to scream. She couldn't. She needed water, milk, anything wet. She made her way to the bathroom, drank two cups of water and toweled off her sweaty body. She went back to bed but couldn't sleep. She got up and checked on Jennifer who was sleeping calmly, cuddled up with her favorite doll and blanket. Heather stood in the doorway and watched her sleep. "If I could only do the same thing," she said to herself as she returned to her bedroom.

The next morning, Heather went to Carolyn's for coffee.

"What do you think of dreams?" Heather asked her friend after a few minutes of small talk.

"Well, in college I read a book that said dreams are the gateway between the conscious and the unconscious. Sometimes they remind us of things we've forgotten. Sometimes they let us know what we're really feeling. Sometimes they help us solve problems."

"Can I tell you about a dream I had last night?"

"Sure, go ahead."

After describing her dream, Heather asked, "What do you think it means?"

"I don't know, but it's sure full of powerful symbols and images. Somewhere I read that the dreamer is the best interpreter—that's you."

"I wouldn't even know where to start."

"Are you afraid of fire?"

"Yes, terrified."

"Why? Did something happen? In your past?"

"I can't think of anything." Heather forced her mind to concentrate. Suddenly her face grimaced as she cried, "Oh, yes, I remember." Heather stared inward to a childhood memory. "It was a big fire . . . burning and crackling."

"Where?" Carolyn probed.

"Outside in the woods. It was autumn. It was night."

"What happened?"

"My grandfather was there, and my mother and father, their friends, and lots of grown-ups and little kids. They all stood in a circle, watching this fire, laughing, telling jokes."

Heather froze, her mouth open, her face ashen. Carolyn grabbed her hand. "What else do you remember?"

"Mother disappeared. I knew something bad was going to happen. I wanted to go home."

"That must have been scary." Carolyn held Heather's hand tighter.

"She showed up again on the other side of the fire." Heather felt sick, thinking about it. "She was wearing white furry animal skins. Her face was painted black with white whiskers. She walked back and forth around the fire, growling and hissing. My grandfather stood behind her, chanting and howling, orchestrating her every move. The others watched. No more laughing. Everybody was quiet." Heather buried her face in her hands.

"Nothing can hurt you now," Carolyn said gently.

"She had a burlap bag. She took out a tiny white kitten. Everybody cheered. She held it over the fire by the scruff of the neck. The kitty squirmed and tried to get away. I heard it cry . . ." Heather began to sob.

Carolyn placed her arm around Heather's shoulders. "You're not alone. Not now."

"She let go. The kitty screamed and disappeared into the flames. I hate her for that. My father put his arm around me. But I didn't want him to touch me. He pushed me toward my mother. There was no place to hide. I was sure I'd be next. I felt the heat of the fire on my face. I didn't want to die." She buried her head in Carolyn's shoulder.

"Heather, it's okay. It's just a memory. You're safe."

Heather's face felt hot and she gasped for breath. "I feel like I'm burning up."

"Would you like a glass of water?"

"Please."

After drinking the full glass, Heather said, "I wonder why I never remembered this incident until now?"

"Maybe you didn't want to admit it actually happened."

"I still don't want to admit it happened. If it's true, what does that say about my mother?"

"If it's true, she's not exactly who you think she is."

"Carolyn, do you think there is a real Satan?"

Carolyn nodded. "My church just had a class on the nature of evil and we talked a lot about Satan."

"I hear people talk about the Devil, but I don't know much about him."

"In the Bible he was called Lucifer," Carolyn began. "He was the most beautiful and powerful angel in heaven. But he got greedy and power-hungry. He wanted to dethrone God, so he led something like a third of all the angels in a revolt. The coup failed and Satan was banished from heaven. Later, he showed up as a serpent and tempted Adam and Eve."

"Anything else?"

"The Bible calls him the ruler of this world and says he prowls about like a roaring lion, looking for someone to devour."

Heather shuddered. "Sounds painful."

"Some people think that God and Satan are equal, but God is stronger than the Devil and all his demons put together."

"Can't Satan control people?"

"Only if they let him. Satan's a liar. He makes lots of promises, but it's all smoke and illusion. At the end of the world, he'll be thrown into the lake of fire and be tormented for eternity."

"My uncle told me that my grandfather made a deal with the Devil."

"You're kidding. What kind of person is he to do something like that?"

"He was into witchcraft and hung out in the desert trying to summon demons. About seven or eight years ago he moved out of this country to some old castle in England, but he left some sort of demonic curse on the family. My uncle won't tell me the details, but I think Jennifer and I are in danger. I'm scared and I don't know what to do. I think they're following me."

"Who?"

"I don't know. Eyes . . . cats . . . nightmares . . . demons."

"Heather, relax. You've been through a lot of stress in the past year and you just had a powerful flashback. Nobody is following you."

"I thought you believed in demons."

"I do, but I don't think they hide around every corner, waiting to attack someone. Maybe your grandfather did make a deal with the Devil, but he was crazy. He probably didn't even know what he was doing. If Satan listened to every lunatic who tried to send demons after people, he'd be exhausted."

"You're probably right. Maybe I've watched too many late-night horror movies and my imagination is running away with itself."

"Heather, don't misunderstand me. I believe demons exist, but I've never actually seen or felt one. So, when people tell me about demonic activity, I'm a little skeptical."

"Well, I know something weird is going on and I'm scared. I'd feel much better if I knew God was protecting us. Could we come to your church sometime? I'd like Jennifer to learn more about God."

Chapter 6

The next day, Heather's brain swirled with images of fires and cats and demons, but foremost on her mind was her mother. Carolyn's statement, "If it's true, she's not exactly who you think she is," echoed over and over again. Each time she heard it she asked herself, "Who is she then?"

That afternoon Heather sat at her desk and pulled out a ragged diary. She hadn't written in it for a long time, but she felt it might help her sort out her thoughts. She turned to an empty page, and began to write.

My Mother

My mother was kind and gentle and loving. She sat beside my bed when I was sick, reading me books and taking my temperature. If I scraped my knee, she had a Band-Aid. If I did poorly on a math test, she had encouragement. If some guy broke my heart, she had a shoulder on which to cry. She was always there when I needed her. When she squeezed my hand and kissed my cheek, I knew everything would be okay.

I always thought my mother was the epitome of holiness. As a child, she taught me that God was good and sins must be confessed. On Sunday afternoons, she sat for hours telling me stories about the saints and their amazing acts of faith. She had a great respect for the church and anything Christian. She was so proud that Uncle George was a priest. She never swore or lied or took anything that wasn't hers. She gave to strangers in need, always carried a rosary, and prayed before every meal. I remember thinking that if she didn't make it to heaven, nobody would.

Mother was also a bit eccentric. She loved the Catholic mass, and her favorite was the Requiem for the dead. Every time a person passed away, she went to the Cathedral. She knelt in the back row, bowed her head, and hummed along with the dark reverberations of the giant pipe organ. She had the full mass memorized and whispered the chants along with the priest. The tall lines of the sanctuary drew her upward; the music, candles, and incense lifted her beyond the arched ceiling. On her way home she repeated the prayers for the dead and then we'd kneel beside my bed and she'd chant pieces of the Requiem mass in Latin. With her eyes closed and a rosary clutched in her hand, she spoke each phrase with such intensity, it scared me. It was as if her own soul depended on the sincerity of her words. When finished she lit a candle and tucked me into bed with "Jesus bless you. Mary protect you. Angels guard you well."

This first glimpse into my mother's dark side triggered others. She was modest. I never saw her in a swimsuit or a tight dress. One day I came home from a shopping spree with a bikini and she was furious. She yelled and screamed at me, using language I'd never heard from her before. She grabbed the bikini, ripped it apart and said, "If you wish a life of seduction, talk to your grandfather. But if I ever see something like this in my house again, I'll kill you." I was shocked and hurt. An hour later, she came and apologized. She said she didn't know what had gotten into her.

Then before my first date, she lectured me for two

hours on proper conduct with boys. As I left the house, she pulled me aside and said, "Beware of the kiss of a Templar." Strange sayings like this were not uncommon to my mother. Her reaction to sexual issues was usually extreme. This served as a perplexing contrast to the terrible innuendoes and rumors I'd heard from relatives as I was growing up, stories I had forgotten until the last few days. Now I wonder if they might be true. The whispered tales suggested that Grandfather was a producer of pornographic films and that his favorite naked starlet was my mother. I was told she had been in many, many films during her teens and twenties.

Heather put down her pen and stared at what she'd written. Carolyn's statement echoed in her mind once again, "If it's true, she's not exactly who you think she is."

Heather remembered the mysterious silver urn with three pentagrams. When her mother received it, she placed it in the front hall underneath the picture of the cats. Surely, she must have known it held Aliester Crowley's ashes. Why would she keep such a black and morbid thing? Heather remembered the carefully etched image inside each of the three stars. In one was a cat, in the next was a rattlesnake, and in the third was the upper body of a great horned goat. These images reminded Heather of a poem her mother had recited to her as a child:

Three things we love the most—
the Father,
the Son,
the Holy Ghost.
Three things we can't forget—
the black cat,
the poison snake,
the unholy baphomet.

Heather had always wondered what a baphomet was and now part of the riddle was solved. A baphomet must be a great horned goat. But why does the poem say "we can't forget?"

And exactly what is the significance of a baphomet? She decided these were questions for Uncle George, but the most important one was: From what was Heather's mother trying to protect Heather and Jennifer? She picked up her pen and continued writing.

Mother had always tried to protect me, but sometimes she made me nervous. There was an eerie aspect to my mother that didn't fit her general portrait. Late at night, once or twice a month, something came over her—something wild and unpredictable. As I tried to sleep, I'd hear growling and scratching below in the living room. Trying to ignore it, I'd squeeze my eyes shut and hum to myself.

One night curiosity got the best of me. I crept out of bed, slipped down the stairs, and stood in the shadows of the hallway. Quietly peeking around the corner to the living room, I watched my mother pace back and forth in a cat-like manner. Her eyes darted, her lips were pulled tight, and her hair was tangled and windblown. She sensed my presence and stared into the shadows. I didn't move. She snarled in my direction and bounded out of the house. I was terrified and confused. Who was this lady in the living room? She looked like my mother, but she didn't. I ran back up the stairs to bed and awoke early the next morning thinking it was all a bad nightmare. At breakfast, I asked my father where she was. Nonchalantly, he replied that she had gone out for a while and hadn't returned yet.

Heather had written enough for today. The more she thought about her mother, the more convinced she became that there was only one valid conclusion. She had two mothers, both sharing the same body; one was good and caring, the other evil and cat-like. It was like Dr. Jeckyl and Mr. Hyde. But if she accepted this hypothesis, it raised more questions. How did her mother get this way? Was she dangerous? And again, most importantly, why did she need to protect Jennifer and Heather?

Late Sunday night Heather lay in bed reading a book. At midnight, she turned out her bedside lamp and closed her eyes. She was almost asleep when a cold breeze blew through the room and she sat up, suddenly alert. What was that? Shivers ran through her body. It wasn't only cold, it was freezing. Her senses were keen—every sound was amplified. She flipped on the bedside lamp and looked around the room—everything seemed in order. Even the door and windows were closed. The cold was gone. But where had it come from?

Heather looked around one more time. All was quiet, except her heart. She left the light on and crawled deep beneath her covers. Her body was tense; her mind sensed danger. She could smell it. But what was it? Where was it? Whatever it was, she knew it would come again.

Heather curled up tightly in a fetal position and tried to convince herself this was just her imagination. Several minutes later, the cold breeze returned. Heather shot out of bed and started for the door, but her instincts stopped her. An evil presence lurked in the shadows by the door. She felt it watching her. She wanted to run, but she was trapped. Adrenaline flooded her body. Her thoughts raced. What was stalking her? Why?

Heather gritted her teeth and stared more intently into the shadows. Something flickered: a small spark of light, maybe two. She screamed, lunged forward, and ran madly out the door. Jennifer, startled by the commotion, began to cry. Heather rushed into her daughter's room, heart pounding and hands shaking. She pulled Jennifer into her arms. "It's okay, Sweetheart," she said more for herself than for Jennifer. "You're safe. God's watching over us. He won't let anything bad get us. I know he won't." The cold was gone and Heather hoped it wouldn't return, but her confidence was fragile. She held Jennifer closely and rocked her until they both fell into a deep, dreamless sleep.

Chapter 7

Bright sunlight peeked into Jennifer's bedroom and nudged Heather awake. For a moment she felt as if someone or something was watching her—but just for a moment. As she pulled herself from sleep, she found her arms still wrapped around her daughter, protecting her from some invisible terror. Heather watched Jennifer sleep peacefully, her chest rising and falling with each gentle breath. Her face was soft and innocent with the hint of a smile.

Heather brushed a wisp of Jennifer's hair from her forehead and saw a small red mark. Suddenly images of last night flooded her mind and her heartbeat quickened. Heather's fingers darted to the round impression—it looked like a thumbprint. Could Grandfather have somehow marked her? She jerked forward to study it. With a sigh of relief she saw it was just a mark where Jennifer had slept on one of Heather's pajama buttons. Heather wanted to hug her closer but didn't want to wake her. She offered up a silent prayer. *Thank you, God, for protecting this little angel. Please forgive my family for all they have done. Help me to be a good mother and to teach Jennifer how to follow you.*

Jennifer stretched and said, "Mommy, you're still with me!"

"I sure am," Heather said, "and I have a great idea for something to do today."

"What is it?" Jennifer rubbed her eyes.

"Let's go to church with Brittany and her parents."

Jennifer jumped out of bed and danced about her room. "I want to wear my new flower dress."

"Okay, but first I need to call Brittany's mother." Heather went downstairs and called Carolyn.

"Carolyn, I was wondering . . . could we go to church with you this morning?"

"Of course! Would you like to ride with us?"

"No, we'll take our own car and follow you."

"Great. Sunday school begins at 9:45, so we leave about 9:15. Brittany will be so excited."

Later that morning Heather found Riverside Community Church—a friendly congregation of about two hundred people. Pastor Freedman, a large, burly man, greeted Carolyn and her husband at the door with a hearty handshake and a sincere smile.

"This is Heather and her daughter, Jennifer," Carolyn's husband, Dale, told the pastor.

"I'm glad you could join us this morning," he said as he shook Heather's hand. Then he leaned down and said to Jennifer, "My, my, what a lovely dress."

Jennifer smiled shyly. "Thank you."

Brittany led Jennifer to the preschool class, while the adults stepped into the main sanctuary. The room had tall ceilings, wooden pews, and stained-glass windows. Heather silently followed Carolyn to a front pew. Colored lights surrounded her and pulled her eyes to the illuminated windows—four giant pictures, two on each side of the room. Heather sat in awe. Each scene transported her to a spiritual reality deeper and truer than the hard wooden pew on which she sat. She was moved, her spirit stirred. She studied each window and absorbed its translucent meaning, remembering the Bible stories her mother had told her as a child. On her right, Noah built a massive ark and Moses parted the Red

Sea. On her left, David killed Goliath and Daniel stood safely in a den of lions. The pictures comforted her. They each seemed to say, "Do not be afraid. For if you have faith, God will guide and protect you."

"Do you like the windows?" asked a faraway voice.

"Yes, they're beautiful," said Heather.

"After a while you get so used to them you hardly even notice," said Carolyn.

Pastor Freedman stepped to the pulpit and the room grew silent. He looked over the congregation, made a few introductory comments, and quickly moved to the core of his lesson. "These are difficult times. Evil surrounds us and wickedness is our neighbor. It disguises itself in hatred and selfishness, sexual abuse and immorality, sorcery and witchcraft . . ."

Heather's ears perked and her heart raced. The pastor stared at her. Did he know her grandfather? The pastor continued his lesson, but it took Heather a moment to make out the words. She played with her right earring and concentrated on the pastor.

"We've all grown accustomed to evil and have become numb to its dangers. We close our eyes, apathetic to the growing darkness. The prophet Amos said, 'Love good and hate evil.' To do this we must take action. We must protect the good and root out what is evil. This isn't always easy and it may not be popular. But to do anything else is to give in to the darkness. Let me tell you a story . . ."

Heather leaned forward. She wanted to fight her grandfather's wickedness, but she didn't know how.

"Long ago when the world was young, children laughed and ran barefoot through sunny meadows. Adults sat beside still waters, listening to the birds and watching the playful wildlife. Life was so carefree and perfect that some called the place Paradise, others simply called it Eden. Then one day a shadow crossed the sun, the laughter ceased, the earth shook, and a dark seed fell into a field of white daisies. All nature held its breath as storm clouds brought rain and the seed sprouted into a bramble of angry thorns. The daisies trembled when they saw the sharpness of the thorns. In time the briars multiplied, choking the flowers and claiming the meadow as its own. Word of the strangled daisies spread and with it a warning: *Beware of the dark seed.*

"Yet people didn't listen to the warning. They were too busy, and besides, they'd never seen the desperate thorn. Even if it did exist, they doubted it would ever threaten their carefully tended fields.

"As the years passed, birds dropped the seeds of the tangled briar on many faraway fields. The brambles grew and all that was good was choked by the dangerous thorns. Not only were flowers and plants destroyed by these dark intruders, but so were people. If anyone wandered too close to the hungry briars, they grabbed at arms and legs, searching for a place to leave a vicious scratch. Yet the viciousness wasn't in the scratch itself, it was in the poison within each thorn. This poison attacked the senses, leaving some deaf and others blind. However, the worst symptom was the confusion and madness. The poor victims groped about their private hell, babbling for relief and praying for death.

"With such a serious threat one might expect people to battle the brambles, but they didn't. They simply ignored the dark thorns, pretending they didn't exist. So the briars grew, claiming more of the earth and driving people mad. Soon the world was one giant bramble, except for one small meadow where a faithful farmer lived with his family. The farmer and his wife were honest, hardworking folks who knew goodness must be cherished and evil must be destroyed. Their meadow was lovingly tilled and divided into an orchard and two fields. The orchard produced apples, cherries, peaches, pears, and plums. In the first field grew a basic assortment of garden vegetables. The second field held a hundred varieties of flowers, but the most beautiful were the sparkling white daisies. From the kitchen window the farmer gazed at the healthy meadow and smiled. A quotation from the holy scriptures hung on the wall in a corner of the kitchen and captured his philosophy: 'Do not be overcome by evil, but overcome evil with good' (Romans 12:21).

"If one asked the farmer what this verse meant, he would clear his voice and say something like: 'No one can uproot all the dark thorns in every corner of this treacherous planet. But each person, no matter how small, can weed his own field and keep it pure. By doing this, our children can smell the daisies, enjoy beauty, and walk barefoot across the clean earth.' "

These words gripped Heather and struck something deep inside her. She'd seen the darkness and felt surrounded by the poisonous bramble. Yet she didn't want to give up. Pastor Freedman's message gave her hope. Heather was determined to uproot the dark thorns and cut back the briars. She wanted her freedom, but knew it wouldn't come easily. The pastor prayed and left the pulpit. Between Sunday school and church everyone went to the fellowship hall for coffee. Pastor Freedman's words seemed to be forgotten as the people laughed and socialized. Carolyn introduced Heather to more people than she could remember.

"This is Dr. and Mrs. James. They have a little boy Jennifer's age. This is Suzie Williams. We've been old friends since college. This is Sam and Judy. They work with the young people here at the church. And this is Kent . . ."

Heather took his outstretched hand. His grip was firm and she held on longer than normal.

". . . he's a high school teacher . . ."

Something about his eyes—kind, sensitive, good—reminded her of Chuck.

". . . and for some reason he's still single."

Heather tried to look away from those blue eyes, but she couldn't. She felt herself blush and time stopped. Kent, tall and handsome, was neatly groomed and casually dressed in a brown sports jacket, Western tie, blue denim jeans, and cowboy boots.

"Glad to meet you, Heather. How long have you known Carolyn?"

"Quite a while, actually. We went to high school together. My daughter and I just happened to move next door to her last weekend."

The organ music started and they all moved toward the sanctuary. Carolyn, Dale, and Heather sat near the back and joined the hymn.

"A mighty fortress is our God. A bulwark never failing . . ."

One pew in front of them sat Kent. Throughout the rest of the service Heather couldn't keep her eyes off him. She watched the way he threw his head back as he sang, the way he ran his fingers through his blonde hair during the prayer, and the concentration of his tan face during the sermon.

The service went quickly and after the benediction Carolyn said, "Heather, would you like to go out to lunch with us?"

"Sure, that sounds like fun."

"I think I'll ask Kent to join us."

Over lunch the four adults discussed the Sunday school lesson on evil, while the two girls giggled and played with their food. When leaving the restaurant, Kent turned to Heather, "Would you mind if I called you later in the week? Maybe we could go down to Saturday Market or take Jennifer out for ice cream."

"I'd like that a lot."

Chapter 8

The black cat stalked through the night on padded paws. A careful hunter, it waited for the perfect moment to attack its prey. Crouched in the alleyway, it seemed a mere shadow. Foam formed on the sides of its mouth as it anticipated the kill. After all, the dark side always wins. Heather stirred in her sleep. She was familiar with this dream. This was when her restlessness usually began.

A white cat entered the alleyway, purring and peaceful and sometimes even playful. As the victim strolled closer, the black cat's ears laid back and its tail swished violently. A low growl began deep in its throat. The white cat stopped, ears pointed and eyes darting. Cautiously she proceeded until she reached the brick wall at the end of the alley. A snarl caused her to whirl around and face the demon. Fire burned in the black cat's eyes as its snarl became a hiss. The white cat slowly backed away as the black cat stepped forward and batted at its enemy with deadly claws. She was trapped. Suddenly the demon screamed and pounced on its victim.

Heather cried, "No!" and sat up in bed. The battle was over, but the night visions continued. The black cat licked its paws and cleaned itself. The white cat lie motionless with a fatal wound to the neck. The black cat smiled a wicked smile and lapped away the last trace of blood. Heather rubbed the sleep from her eyes and felt sick. She placed her hands on her stomach as the tears rolled down her cheeks.

Jumbled images flooded Heather's mind: the cat picture; her grandfather's warning, "Embrace the cat"; her own cat-like trances; Uncle George's statement about cats being a family totem. But what disturbed her the most was the memory of the burning of the kitten and her mother's involvement in the ceremony. Heather's head ached. She tried to push away the flashbacks, but they clung tenaciously. She decided to call Uncle George.

Heather immediately telephoned her uncle and told him everything she had remembered about her mother since their last conversation. When finished she asked, "Do you really think my mother burned that kitten, or am I going crazy?"

"It sounds bizarre, but it doesn't surprise me." Heather imagined him running his hand through his gray hair. "Your grandfather did some awfully strange things. He was obsessed with cats. Whenever he saw a dead cat on the side of the road, he picked it up, took it home, and buried it. At the back of his property, on the other side of the oak trees, he had a small cat cemetery with fifty to sixty little white crosses."

"My mother never mentioned the cemetery."

"She was probably afraid of the cat-ghosts."

"The what?"

"The cat-ghosts. When your mother was a child, she went with your grandfather sometimes to bury the cats. The two of them were very close. In fact, she was the only other person allowed in the cemetery. After the funerals, she would tell me about the cat-ghosts and that if either of us told about the cemetery, they would get us."

"So what are they and how can they get you?"

"They're supposedly the spirits of dead people. If you aren't obedient, they enter your body and try to take your soul."

"Obedient to what?"

"Obedient to your grandfather. I don't know whether he

actually believed in cat-ghosts or was just pulling our legs, but he sure spooked us."

"Do you think these cat-ghosts have anything to do with Grandfather's belief that Satan took the form of a black cat?"

"Maybe."

"My mother told me once that white cats are the spirits of good people and black cats are the spirits of bad people."

"Your grandfather used to tell a story about a white cat and a black cat caught in mortal combat. I think it was a metaphor for the struggle between good and evil, but he told it vividly. In his version, the black cat always won. It was a tragic tale."

Heather remembered her previous night's dream. "Uncle George, why would my mother burn an innocent kitten? How could she do that?"

"It was your grandfather; he controlled her. If he told her to do something, she did it—no questions asked."

"Do you suppose that what I saw as a child in the living room was a cat-ghost controlling my mother?"

"Possibly. If you believe in cat-ghosts."

"What do you believe?"

"Well I see at least three possibilities: Either your mother is psychotic, she has a drug problem, or this is a case of demonology."

"Demonology? You mean she's possessed, like in the movie *The Exorcist?*"

"Not necessarily. Demonic activity is usually more subtle."

Heather longed to tell Uncle George about her own cat-like experiences, but she was afraid he'd think the same thing about her, that she was either crazy or possessed.

"If my mother is possessed, how did she get that way?"

"It probably goes back to your grandfather's deal with the Devil," Uncle George said. "It was Halloween 1929. He made his vow and gave his heart to Lucifer. That event changed his whole life and ultimately drove him crazy."

"What exactly happened that night?"

"Things too evil to even talk about. You know, I have some of your grandfather's old diaries. One of them has his account of that evening. If I can find it, I'll send you a copy."

"Thanks, I'd like to read it. At least, I think I would. I didn't know Grandfather went crazy. What happened?"

"Drugs, pornography, and witchcraft all lead to insanity, eventually. They twist your mind and warp your sense of reality. In time, either hallucinations or delusions take hold and nothing is ever the same. That's what happened to the Marque de Sade and Aliester Crowley. It even happened to Goya." Uncle George paused and his words seemed to drift. "Each of these men were connected with the Templars in one way or another. The Marque de Sade was familiar with the Paris underground and a small group who claimed to be descendants of the original Templars. Aliester Crowley was a modern Templar. And one of Goya's mistresses was a free-mason who initiated him into Templar customs. Goya was the Spanish artist who painted *The Witches' Sabbath.* He dabbled in witchcraft and your grandfather collected his more bizarre works. I'm sure your grandfather is leaving a copy of *The Witches' Sabbath* to you in his will."

"I've never seen that painting. In fact, I didn't know Grandfather was leaving me anything."

"I'm sure he is. Before he moved to England, he willed you an old trunk and several pieces of his art collection."

"I'll have to ask my mother about it. I wonder why no one ever told me Grandfather is crazy?"

"Maybe your mother was trying to protect you again."

"Why would she want to protect me if she's possessed herself?" Heather shook her head. "I don't understand her."

"Your grandfather has become violent in recent years. He used to be a great actor. For short periods of time he would seem almost normal. But if he grew tired, strange things happened."

"When I last saw him he seemed strange, but not dangerous. What's he been like lately?"

"Your grandfather was never quite the same after he reached the rank of Ipsissimus, in about 1962. Ipsissimus was the highest level of Aliester Crowley's secret organization. To qualify for this position, you had to be free of all physical limitations and had to invoke 'insanity' itself. Shortly after that he believed he could read peoples' minds and turn them into animals. The last time I talked to him was about twelve years ago. It was during one of his psychotic breakdowns. We spoke, if you could call it that, for over an hour, but it was mostly babbling and gibberish."

"What kind of gibberish?"

"Hold on for just a minute and I'll get it. I wrote down the words I could understand." A minute or two later Uncle George returned. "It's long, but let me read it to you: 'Forbidden fruit . . . snake in the garden . . . snake in the pocket . . . sorcerers and enchanters . . . knights of the temple . . . bonfires and full moons . . . the Lord's Prayer backward . . . three times . . . 666 . . . Templestowe and sacred circles on Lammas eve . . . a crack in time lets the cat loose . . . deal with the Devil . . . witches' sabbath . . . black sabbath . . . black magic . . . black mass . . . don't let the cat out of the bag . . . taste the magician's ashes . . . kiss insanity . . . the baphomet controls the knife . . . cat-ghosts in the golden dawn . . . the new age . . . Jacques de Molay, thou art avenged.' "

"That's crazy," Heather said.

"Crazy, but not irrational. Each of these phrases have a meaning. They chart a course through his satanic dabblings and provide a history of man's fall and Satan's temporary victory."

"Are you sure it's temporary, Uncle George?"

"I'm positive. Evil thinks it's winning, but it's just an illusion. Goodness will prevail in the end. We just have to be patient, Heather, and that is sometimes difficult."

Heather had a lot more questions, but she had heard as

much as she could handle for now. Images of private ceme-
teries, cat-ghosts, and demons ran through her head. She was
sure Uncle George thought the cat-ghosts were demons. Yet
he didn't want to worry her, so he kept the conversation general. If it were demons who attacked her mother, than it must
be demons who lurked in the shadows of her bedroom. But
the same old question kept returning: "Why? Why my mother?
Why are they coming for me?"

If her grandfather made a deal with the Devil, could there
be a curse on the whole family? How did Grandfather get
involved with such dealings? How black was sin? How wicked
could evil be? Then something odd hit her. Since Grandfather
had moved to England, eight years before, her mother had
visited him every year. But Uncle George had never visited
him. He hadn't even written him—not once. Vaguely, she
recalled a falling out between father and son. Grandfather had
not approved of Uncle George going into the priesthood. They
had argued and never again had spoken a kind word to each
other.

Chapter 9

Several days later Heather received a brief note from her Uncle George:

Dear Heather,

Enclosed are some copies of pages from your grandfather's diaries. Please do not share these with others. This material is dangerous and someone might misuse it with wicked intent. In fact, after reading it, wisdom might dictate you to destroy it.

I'm not sending this merely to satisfy your curiosity, but to demonstrate the reality and seriousness of your grandfather's dabblings with the demonic.

God Bless.

Heather set down the letter. Did she really want to read about her grandfather's dealings with evil? It might simply increase her fear and paranoia. But if she didn't, she might be left ignorant of the danger to which she and Jennifer were exposed. Heather's hands shook as she picked up the pages. The words in the diary were written in cursive with a creative flair.

November 1, 1929

Last night I went to a celebration of the Vigil of Samhain. Thirteen members of Aliester Crowley's Silver Star met me at Stonehenge. The site was perfect, for it conjured mystical images of ancient Druids. At twilight we gathered in a field one hundred feet north of the monument. Each of us had fasted for twenty-four hours and had drank a special potion of magical drugs. The thirteen wore white robes, like the Druids and the Templars. I was told I would receive my robe after the ceremony.

The first order of business was to teach me how to prepare the sacred site. A circle was drawn with charcoal and sulphur, exactly nine feet in diameter. The leader, who held the level of Magister Templi, lit the circle on fire and sprinkled the perimeter with sea salt.

He turned to me and said, "Do not break the circle until you are called forth." He then drew a large triangle around the circle in a configuration commonly referred to as "Solomon's Triangle."

A group of sorcerers placed two bronze dishes in the center of the circle and kindled a small fire in each. I was exiled to the monoliths of Stonehenge while the thirteen finished their preparations. I paced the modern replica, caught between anxiety and excitement. In the distance I heard a train.

A white robe came from behind, grabbed my shoulder, and handed me an opium pipe. I inhaled the smoke as he said, "The time is near." I looked up and the Magister Templi stood between the two bronze dishes. His face was painted black except for a silver star on his forehead. His eyes glowed red in the reflection of the fire as he howled above the wind.

"Tonight there exists a crack in time. Tonight the gates of the underworld will be opened. Tonight a pact will be sealed with the great horned god." The twelve repeated the sacred triad.

The Magister Templi lifted both hands above his head. His palms were painted black with a silver star and baphomet. "Let us call forth the ancient serpent. Let us awaken the eternal black cat. Let us worship the almighty baphomet." The leader raised his voice and spoke the mighty words that opened the gates of hell. "Zazas, Zazas, Nasatanada, Zazas."

The twelve knelt and spoke in unison, "Oh, come to us Rex Mundi."

I stood in the shadows of Stonehenge, listening to the incantations and memorizing each line. I was mesmerized by the ritual.

A serpent rattled its tail and coiled at the foot of the leader. Someone threw sand at the snake. Its tail shook with fury and it raised its head to attack. The twelve magicians danced around the snake, making strange and eerie noises. The leader grabbed the snake behind the head and slipped it into a pocket of his cultic robe. The magicians' dances escalated to a frenzy. The leader sprinkled witchcraft onto the fire and orange smoke billowed from the bronze dishes. A pungent smell mingled with the dancers, leading them in wild and primitive steps. A black cat walked between the twin flames, tiptoeing through the orange mist. Green eyes looked beyond the white robes and met my nervous stare. Foam drooled from the corners of the feline's black mouth and the cat roared. Everything stopped. Silence echoed down the gorge to the river below. The cat disappeared.

The leader raised his hands and called, "Will the initiate come forward and prove his willingness to deal with the ultimate magick and ultimate power?"

The white robes parted, and I stepped into the flickering circle. The leader forced a cat-knife into my hand and said, "Before the full moon falls, an evil sorcerer will be initiated and his heart will be darkened forever and ever."

The twelve pointed at me and asked in unison, "What will you give as a token of your secrecy?"

I tried to speak, but nothing came. Finally I cleared my throat and whispered, "My blood."

I fingered the handle of the sacrificial knife, staring at the ornate carvings of a cat with its mouth wide open. Sharp teeth pointed toward the blade and blended into its cutting edge. Thirteen sets of wicked eyes watched and waited. I gripped the cat's neck and took a deep breath. The blade sparkled in the midnight air as I ran its sharpness across the circular print of my right thumb. A thin red line contrasted with the white flesh. The observers drew closer to smell the blood.

I gritted my teeth and repeated the cutting procedure on my pointing finger. The observers came a step or two closer. I closed my eyes. Did I really want to do this? I pushed the thought out of my mind. My hand trembled as I slashed the next finger, driving the blade deeper than I intended. The wound stung as blood dripped down the digit into a pool in the palm of my upturned hand. The crowd jumped forward in ecstasy, thirsting for more of the red liquid.

I wiped my brow with the back of my left hand. I swayed with claustrophobia and gasped for more air. Was this worth it? The price was awfully high.

Somebody threw a log on the fires and a thousand tiny stars jumped skyward. The heat burned my face as I cut the next finger. Time was running out. If I wanted to change my mind, I had to stop now. I swallowed hard and jabbed the baby finger.

The twelve smothered me. The leader took the knife, pushed back the crowd and said, "The red waters of life flow into the rivers of death. In the ancient tradition of the shedding of blood, this initiate calls for the Luciferian scroll."

The twelve spoke in unison, "What will you give to

gain the infinite knowledge from the tree of good and evil?"

"My life," was the reply.

Two of the twelve stepped forward. One handed me a deep red apple. I bit into it and gagged. It had been drugged. The leader demanded firmly, "Swallow." I obeyed and a sorcerer took the apple. The second handed the leader a scroll of rough parchment. It was unrolled and the leader grabbed my right hand. He squeezed the tips of each digit until the hand was sweating blood. He pressed the fingers of my right hand to the fingers of my left hand and forced the prints to the calligraphied parchment. My hands were red.

"So mote it be," the thirteen magicians replied.

"The scroll is sealed. The pact is signed. The deal is done. The Gnostic riddles shall be proclaimed: Good is evil, evil is good. Light is dark, dark is light. Life is death, death is life."

The twelve stared at me, "What will you give to gain the everlasting power?"

"My future progeny."

The leader set a golden cross between the two fires. I spat on the cross three times and repeated the Lord's Prayer backward.

"You and three generations," the leader spoke. "One, two, three generations are given to Satan. You, your son, your son's son, and your son's son's son are the property of hell. You, your daughter, your daughter's daughter, and your daughter's daughter's daughter are Beelzebub's harlots."

"So mote it be. So mote it be." The twelve slashed their fingers and sucked the blood. Dancing began and orange smoke enveloped the secret ceremony. The magicians ripped away my clothing, leaving me naked to the night wind.

Above the wild celebration the Magister Templi yelled, "Blessed is he who reaches deep into the earth, who draws down the moon, who bequeaths his seed to the evil baphomet. Dear Vincent, this is a night you will never forget."

All in all, it was a fascinating evening.

Disgusted and frightened, Heather dropped the diary pages. How could her own grandfather become involved in such evil? What right did he have to pledge Jennifer and Heather to the Devil? She grabbed the pages and tore them to shreds.

Chapter 10

Heather watched Jennifer through the screen door as she sat on the front porch steps, a kitten in her arms. Jennifer had wrapped the little animal in her doll's blanket and it was doing everything it could to struggle free. Jennifer held it tightly, rocking it and singing:

"The owl and the pussycat went to sea
In a beautiful pea-green boat.
They took some money and plenty of honey
All wrapped in a five pound note.
The owl looked up to the stars above
And sang to a small guitar:
'Oh lovely Pussy, oh Pussy my love.
what a beautiful Pussy you are.' "

The kitten hissed and squirmed around in the blanket.

"Now kitty you must be still." Jennifer kissed its head and pushed a baby's bottle into its mouth. "You must drink your milk or I'll have to put you in time out." The kitten meowed its protest and almost wiggled out of Jennifer's hands.

Jennifer turned slightly and saw Heather through the screen door.

"I'm feeding my new kitty," she said.

Heather opened the screen and let it slam shut. The startled kitten screamed, twisted out of Jennifer's arms, and darted across the yard toward the neighbor's house. Jennifer jumped up and chased after it, but the cat was too quick.

"Oh, it got away and look what it did to me." She pointed to a scratch on her leg.

"Honey, kitties don't like to be wrapped up. It just went home to look for its real mother."

"Can I please have a kitty of my very own? I want one so bad. They are so fluffy and fun to play with."

Heather stumbled for an answer. She couldn't handle the thought of owning a cat. Shivers went down her back. "Maybe when you're older, but not now. It's not a good time."

"Please . . ."

"Jennifer, I said no and . . ."

A local florist's delivery truck stopped in front of the house and a man climbed out, his hands full of flowers. He strode up the walk. "Is this the Davis residence?"

"Yes."

"I have flowers for Heather Davis." He handed her a bouquet of snapdragons, mums, carnations, and daisies. She stood speechless as he walked back to the van. Heather lowered her nose to the blooms and inhaled deeply the fresh scent. Who would send her flowers? She found a card tucked under a yellow mum.

Dear Heather,

Carolyn told me that this past year was rough for you. I hope these brighten your day.

Kent Thomas

Jennifer stared at the spots of color with her mouth open wide. "How pretty! Can I keep them in my room?"

"We can put some of them in your room and some in the living room."

They went into the house to look for another vase.

Later that evening Heather relaxed on the sofa and flipped through a fashion magazine.

The phone rang.

"Hello, this is Kent. I hope I'm not calling too late."

"No, this is a perfect time. I just tucked Jennifer into bed. We both enjoyed the flowers you sent. Thank you. That was very sweet."

"It was my pleasure. How was your week?"

"Interesting, but it's a long story."

"I love long stories."

"You'd think I was crazy if I told you everything that has happened in the past two weeks."

"Try me."

Swallowing hard, Heather told Kent bits and pieces about her grandfather's wicked deal. She was scared to tell him too much. But she did mention her fears about Jennifer's safety. Kent listened closely and asked a lot of questions. They had talked for twenty minutes when Heather said, "That's just the beginning. I don't want to bore you."

"You certainly aren't boring me, but it is getting late. How about dinner Friday night? We can finish our conversation then."

"That sounds like fun." What a fantastic guy! Heather tried to stay calm as she hung up the phone, but her heart was moving faster than her brain. Kent seemed so perfect that she wondered what he saw in her. This was her first date since Chuck's death and she wasn't sure if she was ready. Heather felt like a teenager again—full of excitement and apprehension. She knew Chuck would encourage her to stretch her wings and date, but it seemed so awkward. Maybe she shouldn't have said so much to Kent, especially about Jennifer's safety. Yet she was sure the threat was real.

Heather yawned and looked at the clock. It was almost 11:00. Curling up on the sofa, she pulled a quilt around her shoulders. She thought about going up to bed, but the room began to fade. Sinking deeper into the sofa, her eyelids dropped. Her thoughts grew fuzzy and she was transported to an open field under a gray and ominous sky. Twelve white-robed men stood in a perfect circle, each looking inward. Two men faced each other in the center of the circle. One wore a white robe and was a spokesman for the coven. The other wore a black robe. He emanated power and demanded respect. He was the Ipsissimus.

"The pact must be completed regardless of the cost," said the man in black.

"But the white cub doesn't understand her role," said the spokesman.

"Why?"

"The lioness is double minded. She didn't train her offspring in the rites of the Silver Star."

"What must be done to correct this situation?" demanded the black robe.

"We have already eliminated her mate. He wasn't one of us and he was becoming suspicious. Currently, the Evil One is pressuring the cub with night terrors and demonic presences."

"How long until her spirit breaks?"

"Soon, very soon."

Heather moved closer as the discussion continued. She looked through the circle to the two in the center. The black robe was wild and frightening. The white robe was familiar and comforting.

"You are supposedly a mighty lion seeking someone to devour and yet you can't even manage your own family," the black robe sneered.

"I promise the situation will be corrected." His brown shining eyes shot in Heather's direction and pierced her heart. Heather wanted to run, but the lion's eyes drew her forward as he spoke. "Today the albino has returned to the coven . . ." The white robes parted and Heather stepped into the circle. ". . . and her young one will be known from this day on as the second cub."

Heather tore her eyes from her father and stared at the ground. She was standing in the middle of a black pentagram and at her feet were blood-red letters spelling out the name "JENNIFER."

"Nooooo!" Heather screamed as she sat up and oriented herself to the living room. Over and over again she repeated, "It was just a dream. It was just a dream." Flashbacks and premonitions also appear dreamlike, but Heather was afraid to consider those options. Heather got up from the sofa and made sure all the doors and windows were locked.

The clock said 12:30 as Heather climbed the stairs and checked on Jennifer. Sitting on the edge of the canopy bed, Heather watched her daughter sleep—so young and innocent. She whispered to herself, "If anything happens to her, I'll die." Jennifer was curled up on her side, her arms wrapped around a large stuffed animal. She stretched and rolled over to her stomach, kicking the blankets to the end of the bed and getting her legs twisted in her cotton nightgown. Heather smoothed back Jennifer's tangled hair and gently rubbed her back. Then she kissed her baby goodnight, tucked her back into bed, and turned out the light.

Small bubbles glistened in the sun as they floated above the porch and burst. Jennifer giggled and blew more. She tried to pop the fragile circles, but a few escaped into the front yard. Heather stood at the window and watched Jennifer chase the rainbow colors, jumping and clapping her little hands. Suddenly Kent appeared out of nowhere.

"My, my Jennifer, you sure make pretty bubbles."

"Hi, Mr. Thomas. I like to break them, too."

"How many have you broken?"

"Millions and millions," Jennifer said. "Do you want to see my mommy?"

"Yes, I do."

"She's inside getting all fixed up for you. She wants to look beautiful."

Heather moved to the side of the window so no one would catch her eavesdropping.

"I think she'll look beautiful no matter what she wears."

"I think so too. Do you love my mommy?"

"That's a hard question. I try to love everybody I meet, especially little girls who blow bubbles."

"Where are you taking my mommy?"

"It's a secret, but I'll tell you if you promise not to tell anybody."

"I promise. Cross my heart and hope to die, stick a needle in my eye."

Kent bent down and whispered something in Jennifer's ear.

"Can I come too? I've never . . ."

"Hi, Kent," said Heather as she stepped out onto the porch. "I hope you haven't been waiting long."

"No, not at all. But if I had, it would have been worth it. You look lovely."

Heather blushed. "Thank you." She turned to Jennifer. "It's time to go to Brittany's house. I'll pick you up later tonight. I love you." She kissed her daughter on the cheek and reminded her to obey Brittany's mother.

Kent walked Heather to his red Celica and they sped through the early evening with the top down. They ate an intimate dinner in a colorful Italian bistro. The two laughed and shared their childhood dreams over a spicy pasta dish. The conversation was light, at least it started out that way.

"Kent, this is the most wonderful evening I've had since I don't know when. It helps me forget how crazy life has been lately."

"Speaking of craziness, that reminds me, we didn't get a chance to finish our conversation the other night."

"If I tell you much more, I'm afraid it might scare you away."

"I'm not easily scared," said Kent.

"Maybe you should be." Heather looked away.

"What's wrong?"

"I'm also afraid that if I tell you too much, something will happen to you."

Kent laughed. "Nothing's going to happen to me. I promise."

"Promises are difficult to keep when you're face to face with evil."

"That's probably true, but I believe that good is more powerful than evil and, no matter what happens, good will prevail."

"That's what I'd like to believe."

The two finished their conversation with a rich chocolate desert between them. Kent then hailed an old-fashioned horse-drawn carriage.

"Oh, how romantic," Heather said as she climbed in. Then she froze with her mouth open. Parked across the street was a black Cadillac. A sick feeling hit her in the stomach, but she quickly pushed it away. After all, there were probably thousands of black Cadillacs in the city. Heather settled into the carriage and tried to focus on Kent. But as they rode down the cobblestone streets, Heather had an uneasy feeling that something or somebody was following them. Out of the corner of her eye she watched behind them. Several times she saw black cars and tensed up. Then, when she realized they weren't Cadillacs, she relaxed.

"Heather, why are you so jumpy?"

"I feel like somebody is following us."

Kent looked behind them. "I don't see anything."

"I don't either, but somebody's out there." Heather looked over her shoulder and gazed into the dark. "You know the other night after our conversation I had a horrible dream. My father was in a coven, and he was trying to force me to join it. He said they had killed Chuck and they wanted Jennifer."

"That sounds terrible, but nightmares can't hurt you."

"This was more than a nightmare. I think it really happened and that's what scares me. What if Chuck's death wasn't accidental? In the dream my father said Chuck was killed because he was too suspicious."

"Suspicious of what?"

"I don't know, but I want to find out. Chuck was curious. If he thought something wasn't right, he'd try to discover what was wrong."

"Heather, are you sure you aren't making too much of a simple nightmare?"

"Maybe I am."

The clip-clop of the horse's hooves stopped and the two climbed out of the carriage. Heather looked up and down the street for a black Cadillac. There was none in sight. She sighed, leaned onto Kent's shoulder, and the two walked along the waterfront in silence. But the quiet didn't last. Ten minutes later they sat on the grass as the sun set and talked the stars out of hiding. With the city to their backs, the two tossed pebbles into the river, making wishes as the ripples glimmered with the reflections of the lighted bridges. They tried to make the evening bright and playful, but they kept returning to the subject of evil.

"Kent, do you remember what I told you about Halloween night, 1929?"

"Yes."

"That was all real. My grandfather is evil and my parents worship him. My father is meeting with him right now down in Mexico and they're planning something—something bad—and I think it involves Jennifer. I know it sounds paranoid, but these people are capable of anything. Even my Uncle George thinks Jennifer and I are in danger. He's a priest and one of the most rational people I know."

"Heather, I don't mean to doubt you. If you say this may be happening, I believe you."

"Thank you for humoring me, even if I do sound like a lunatic."

"If you're a lunatic, you're the most beautiful one I've ever met." Kent slipped his arms around her and gave her a gentle hug. Heather held on to him and rested her head on his shoulder.

"Kent, I'm not crazy. I promise you I'm not."

"I know you're not and that's what makes me nervous. I think we need to take all this seriously." He squeezed her tighter and she wished the embrace would never end.

An hour later the two walked hand in hand back to his car. Driving home, the warm night air seemed magical and thoughts of danger temporarily faded. Kent and Heather laughed again. As Kent stood on Heather's front porch and said goodnight, she couldn't help thinking that if she let herself get close to him, they would do to him what they did to Chuck. She trembled as she watched his car drive away. She raced through the front door, slammed it shut, locked it, and placed her back firmly against it. Sweat dripped down her forehead. She was absolutely sure a black Cadillac had been following them.

Chapter 11

"How was your date last night with Kent?" Carolyn asked as she sat in the kitchen drinking coffee with Heather.

"Wonderful, absolutely wonderful. It reminded me of the great times Chuck and I used to have together. It's hard to believe Chuck's been gone for over a year. He was the kindest person I ever met."

"I wish I'd had the privilege of meeting him. How did the two of you get together?"

"We went to the same college," Heather said. "He was a senior and I was a junior. We met in a psychology class about six months after my grandfather moved to England. Chuck asked me out for coffee after class and life was never the same. A year and a half later we were married. We were so happy, even though my parents hated him."

"Why did they hate him?"

"My mother felt like he wasn't someone Grandfather would approve of. The first time she met him, she gave me a nasty look and said, 'Look what the cat's drug in.' I was so embarrassed. Later she refused to come to the wedding. I was devastated. I think it bugged them that they couldn't control him like they could my other boyfriends. Chuck was his own person and that made everybody nervous."

"Why did they need to control him?" Carolyn asked.

"I didn't know why back then, but now I think it has to do with keeping family secrets. The other night I had a dream in which my father said Chuck was suspicious. And now that I think about it, Chuck acted strangely the day before his death. He was worried and distracted. When I asked him what was wrong, he just said, 'You wouldn't believe me if I told you.' I pressured him and he promised to tell me as soon as he gathered more evidence. He stayed in his den late that night, studying some old books and taking notes. When he came to bed he tossed and turned. At one point he even talked in his sleep, but he didn't make any sense. He said something about finding the key."

"So whatever he found was disturbing." Carolyn seemed deep in thought. "What sort of books was he studying and what did his notes say?"

"I don't know. His books and notes are missing. They weren't in his den or car and I can't find them anywhere."

"What do you think happened to them? He must have hid them."

"Or they were stolen," Heather broke in.

"Who would have done that?"

"I'm not sure, but Chuck always left his notes on his desk. Why would he hide them without telling me?"

"I guess it would depend on what he found."

"When Chuck talked about a key, I thought he was speaking metaphorically until I packed up the den. Take a look at this." Heather pulled a silver key from her purse and handed it to Carolyn. "I found this hidden behind a picture over Chuck's desk."

Carolyn turned the key over in her hands. It was an old-fashioned skeleton key attached by a small chain to a silver coin. On one side was written:

"Ye shall not surely die . . .
your eyes shall be opened,
and ye shall be as gods,
knowing good and evil."

"This is from the Bible," Carolyn said. "It's what the serpent said to Eve in the Garden of Eden." She turned over the coin and found a snake forming a circle by swallowing its own tail. In the center was the Greek motto *en to pan.* "What does this mean?"

"I don't know, but the words translate as 'all is one.' "

"Where did Chuck get this?"

"I don't think I want to know. If Chuck was killed for snooping around where he wasn't welcome, I don't want to make the same mistake."

"But he was your husband. You loved him."

"I still love him, but what good will it be to Jennifer if both her parents are dead?" Tears welled in Heather's eyes. "I don't know what to do. My life is like a nightmare and every day it gets more bizarre. I ought to be keeping a journal because this would make a pretty good book, except nobody would believe it was true."

Carolyn put her arms around Heather. "I'm sorry for pushing. I was just trying to help."

"I know, and I appreciate it. If it weren't for you, I'd crack up." Heather wiped the tears from her eyes.

Was that ever the truth, Heather thought as she walked home. How she needed Carolyn and Kent just to keep her sanity.

About an hour later Heather heard a knock at the front door. She looked out the window to see a silver Mercedes parked at the curb. Heather took a deep breath and opened the door.

"Mother, what are you doing here?"

"I was in the neighborhood, and I thought I'd stop and visit. Where's Jennifer?"

"She's upstairs sleeping."

"Can I peek in on her? I love to watch little ones. They're so innocent and peaceful."

"Sure. Come on in."

After looking in on Jennifer, they sat in the living room. Heather's mother was sleek and tan. She looked closer to forty than fifty-five. She adjusted her skirt as she sat back on the sofa. "Kitty, your new house has such charm."

"Thank you. Has Father come back?"

"Yes, we ended up meeting at Stonehenge during summer solstice and he's been back home ever since."

"Did he meet with Grandfather?"

"I was right," her mother gloated. "They met at Chichén Itzá and now Grandfather's going to travel this continent for a month or two before returning to his castle."

"Where's he going? Is he coming to Portland?"

"Heather, why all these questions? You know Grandfather goes wherever he wishes. How would I know where he's going? All I know is that later this month your father wants to go gold mining in Southern Oregon. Would you mind if we took Jennifer with us?"

Heather didn't answer. She stared at the silver bracelet on her mother's wrist: A realistically carved snake, with two small rubies as eyes, formed a circle by swallowing its own tail. It looked exactly like the snake on the coin attached to the key she had found. Panic pushed the breath from her lungs and she gasped for air.

"Excuse me." Heather ran to the bathroom, splashed water on her face, and breathed deeply.

"Are you okay?" her mother called.

"Yes, yes," Heather said as she returned to the living room. "I just . . . sometimes I get . . . it's hot in here. Would you like a glass of lemonade?"

"That sounds delicious."

Heather returned from the kitchen a few minutes later with two glasses of iced lemonade. "Mother, is that a new bracelet?"

"No, it's actually an old family heirloom. Your grandfather gave it to me. He loved snakes and claimed they were the guardians of ultimate wisdom."

"That sounds like Grandfather."

"When he was in India he studied the music of the cobra charmers. In Mexico he went to Chichén Itzá and watched the snake slither up the castle pyramid during the spring equinox. He even searched Egypt for information about the Orphites."

"Who were the Orphites?"

"They were Gnostic snake worshippers," Heather's mother said, "who mixed Christianity with black magic. This cult started in the second or third century and later had a strong influence on the Templars. Your grandfather used to say, 'Seize the serpent and let its . . .' Excuse me. I shouldn't be talking about this rubbish. I don't know what got into me. Please forget everything I said."

"Mother, it's okay. I want to know about Grandfather. I wish you'd tell me more about who he is and how he lives. It helps me understand who I am."

A strange disoriented look came over her mother's face. "One shouldn't talk. One shouldn't remember. Certain things shouldn't happen. And if you say they didn't, then they're erased. Reality is only what you remember. Talking makes things real. Silence brings oblivion. It is only when you forget that you can look at yourself in the mirror."

Heather listened to each sentence carefully. "Mother, that doesn't make any sense." Her mother stared at the floor. Heather wanted to know so much more—about snakes and cat-ghosts and Templars and deals with the Devil, but she knew her mother wouldn't tell her. The room filled with silence. Mother's eyes darted back and forth, while Heather tried to figure out a way to bring up her inheritance. "Mother, Uncle George says Grandfather is leaving me something in his will and I was . . ."

"Why are you talking to Uncle George?"

"Because he's my uncle. Is there something wrong with that?"

"What did he say to you?" Mother's nostrils flared.

"He thinks Grandfather is leaving me an old trunk and a few pictures. He said one of them is a print by Goya. Isn't all that stuff up in your attic?"

"Your uncle is treading on dangerous ground. There is a high price for betrayal."

"What are you talking about?" Heather asked. "He hasn't betrayed anybody. He simply thought I knew about the will and was surprised I'd never heard of Grandfather's old trunk."

"There is nothing to know."

"Am I going to inherit a trunk and some pictures?"

"There are stipulations in the will."

"What kind of stipulations?"

"Stipulations that you and your uncle don't understand."

"Mother, why are you avoiding my questions?"

"Kitty, please don't ask any more. Your grandfather may be almost ninety, but he isn't dead yet. When the time is right, you'll get your trunk and pictures. But if you push, something bad might happen to you and Jennifer." Shaking her head, cold and detached, Heather's mother stood and glared at Heather.

"Mother, what are you talking about?"

Without saying a word, the lioness walked out the front door. "Mother, wait a minute," Heather pleaded, but her mother was already in the Mercedes, starting the engine. Heather ran to the car and cried, "What's going on?"

Her mother's jaw was tight and her eyes looked through Heather. "Tonight," she said. "You will learn tonight."

"Learn what?" Heather begged.

Her mother turned away and the car drove slowly down the street as Heather stood alone in pain and confusion.

Chapter 12

Heather sat on the sofa, shocked and perplexed by her mother's visit. Why had the trunk and pictures been kept such a secret? Why was Mother so upset about her talking to Uncle George? What would happen to her and Jennifer if she kept up her detective work? The questions turned and twisted in her mind, but she came up with no conclusive answers. Tomorrow she'd call Uncle George; she just wouldn't let Mother know about it.

A few minutes before midnight Heather climbed the stairs to bed, but she couldn't sleep. One question really disturbed her: What was in the trunk? Awful images appeared in her mind, and as she nodded off to sleep they coagulated into a dream.

An old brown trunk with a large silver padlock rested half-buried in the sand of a solitary beach. The sky was gloomy, and ocean waves crashed upon the rocks. A tall woman in a white robe stood before the trunk. She took a silver skeleton key from a hidden pocket and unlocked the trunk. The lid raised and a horrible odor spread. Heather coughed and rolled over in her sleep.

A large rattlesnake slithered from the trunk and coiled in the sand. A black cat jumped onto the coils and roared. The snake hissed and swallowed its own tail. Heather's grandfather sat up in the trunk; laughingly he said, "All is one."

Heather's eyes flashed open and she pushed the pictures from her thoughts. Something in the hallway creaked and she nearly jumped out of bed. An odd smell of dirt, sulphur, and something bitter made her uneasy. She glanced about the dark room and saw nothing. When she closed her eyes, the dream continued.

Every frightening and evil image possible emerged from the old trunk: sinister men in black robes, striking rattlesnakes, possessed cats with glowing eyes, ugly beasts with giant horns. Each picture lingered and grew more grotesque as the dream stretched into hours. Heather coughed and sputtered as the wicked smell choked her. A terrifying beast flew at her. She screamed and sat up. The beast retreated. Somebody or some-thing was in the room. It was pitch-black, but Heather sensed a presence by the door. She stared into the darkness but saw nothing. The room suddenly grew cold. She pulled her blankets tightly around her shoulders.

Heather tried to convince herself that she just had an over-active imagination, but she knew differently. It was here and it was waiting. She squeezed her eyes shut and prayed, "God help me. I don't want to die. I'll do anything you want, if I live through this."

Minutes passed and she began to slip toward sleep. Suddenly it was on her. She fought and pushed and clawed as invisible hands wrapped around her neck. Coughing, she gasped for air. Her heart pounded hard and fast. She rolled off the bed and clutched her neck. "Leave me alone," she begged.

Heather tried to stand up but was knocked to the floor. Her head spun. She felt pressure on her chest, and she shoved the force away from her. The hand around her neck relaxed for a split-second and she breathed deeply. "Dear God, help me."

The demon withdrew to the other side of the room. Heather stood up and braced herself. It returned with a violence and fury. She fell to the floor, kicking and scratching. She refused to give up. If only she could distract it. She rushed to the door, slamming it closed behind her. "God, keep it away," she cried. The force hit the door just as it closed, banging and rattling the wood with a fearful strength. Would it hold? Heather braced herself, her back against the door and her legs pushing with all her might. "Go away!" she screamed, "I'm no threat. In God's name, go attack somebody with real faith, somebody like Carolyn."

Immediately the pushing stopped and everything was silent. Then "whoosh!" She heard a breeze rush through the bedroom rattling the pictures on the walls and knocking something to the floor. Suddenly all was quiet again. Heather slowly, cautiously opened the door and peeked into the room. Was this a trick? She stepped into the room and glanced around. Whatever it was, it was gone. The smell, the feeling, the evil presence—all gone. Why did it go? Heather didn't care, she was just thankful the force had disappeared. But what if it returned? She refused to even think about that.

She checked on Jennifer, who was sleeping peacefully, and then collapsed on her own bed. Exhausted and still shaking, she glanced at the red numbers of her digital clock-radio: 2:55. She buried her head in her pillow, tears flowing and sobs shaking her body until she was so drained she could do nothing but sleep.

The next morning at 7:30 sharp, Kent picked up Heather and Jennifer and took them to a local doughnut shop for breakfast. Jennifer sipped hot chocolate, while the adults made small talk over coffee. Kent was bright and attentive; Heather was cautious. Last night had left its mark. Opportunities to talk about it came and went, but Heather hoped if she ignored it, the memory would go away or, at least, be less real.

Pastor Freedman greeted them at the church door, and in the foyer Heather ran into Carolyn.

"It's so good to see you," Heather grabbed Carolyn's hand. "I had a terrible night and a terrible dream."

"So did I," Carolyn looked pale and shaken.

"You did?"

"It was horrible. I woke up screaming in the middle of the night and scared Dale half to death. I know it sounds crazy, but something evil was in my room."

Heather fidgeted with her purse. "What time did this happen?"

"Just before 3:00 A.M."

Heather turned white. "Tell me what happened."

"Let's step outside so we can have some privacy."

The two went out into the sunlight and sat on a nearby bench. Carolyn pulled a tissue from her purse and blew her nose. Heather sat quietly waiting to hear the story. When Carolyn began, it was in a soft, uneasy voice.

"I went to bed early last night and dreamed of a family picnic in a gentle meadow of yellow wildflowers. It was perfect. Dale gave Brittany a piggyback ride and Brittany laughed until she fell to the ground. I sat in an old wooden swing, watching them.

"But something happened. Suddenly this shadow entered my dream, a breeze pushed against my back and sent clouds of dust flying through the meadow. The breeze grew stronger and forced my swing into the air, higher and higher. I held on tightly with both hands. It climbed into the sky and I started to scream, but a pungent smell forced a cough instead—a deep, painful cough. Above me the shadow grew, absorbing the sun and turning the day into night. Then these huge wings carried an ugly black goat with human arms toward me. I knew it was about to attack.

"I grabbed my pillow with one arm and tried to push it away with the other. I knew it was a nightmare, but it seemed so real. I shook myself and tried to wake myself up. But before I could come to my senses, these demonic hands reached out of my dream and clutched my throat. I felt adrenaline rushing through me and I sat upright in bed yelling nonsense words. The gust continued blowing, knocking a fan off the windowsill. I screamed and cried and wildly waved my arms, pushing the dream creature away. Dale tried to wake me, but I only screamed and cried louder. He kept telling me it was just a dream, but my dream and real life had somehow gotten all mixed up.

"Suddenly it was over. I shook myself and let out a long sigh. Sweat streamed down my forehead. Dale let go of me and asked what had happened.

"I didn't know what to tell him. It was so bizarre and hard to explain. It was also so real. I said something evil had me and I couldn't get free." Carolyn took a deep breath and continued. "The creature was goat-like with large horns. I heard myself screaming, but it wasn't me. At least it didn't feel like me, it was as if this creature controlled me.

"Dale was so understanding, he just held me. He put his arms around me and I rested my head on his chest. I was still shaking. It was the strangest experience I've ever had. I felt so embarrassed, yelling my lungs out in the middle of the night. But Dale didn't say anything, he just kept on holding me until I fell asleep in his arms."

Heather was silent during Carolyn's story. Now she wasn't sure what to say. "I need to tell you something and I'm very sorry. I wasn't thinking straight. I didn't mean to use your name." Heather breathed deeply and gave a detailed description of last night's events.

When she finished, Carolyn said, "That's terrible! How could you do such a thing? I thought you were my friend. That thing tried to kill me," Carolyn sobbed. "I can still feel it around my neck. If this is all Satanic warfare, I don't want to have anything to do with it."

"I don't blame you. I'm so sorry. I didn't want to hurt you, it just happened."

"It didn't just happen, you did it—you and your family vow. I feel sorry for your spiritual battle, but I don't want any part of it."

"You're absolutely right. It's my battle and I have no business dragging anybody else into it. I'm having a hard enough time dealing with what I've learned the last few weeks, but it's my problem. I'm scared too and I want to forget it all. But I don't think I can. I'm afraid it's gone too far to back out now."

Chapter 13

Riding home with Kent from church, Heather stared out the side window of the car. She bit her lip and clung to her purse.

"Heather, what's wrong?"

Silence.

"Heather, what's going on?"

"I'm sorry, Kent. Carolyn was right. I have no business pulling other people into my problems."

"What do you mean?"

Heather checked the backseat to make sure Jennifer wasn't listening. The child was amusing herself by singing songs and looking through her Sunday school papers. Turning to Kent, she told him the whole story about the night before and her demonic visitation. When she finished he said, "No wonder Carolyn's upset. There's a difference between volunteering to help and getting forced into battle."

"I know. I can't believe I was so stupid. I told her this was my battle and I'll deal with it myself."

"Heather, I've thought about this a lot and I'm willing to help."

"Do you really want to get involved with me and my problems?"

"Yes, I think so. As long as you don't send demons over to kill me."

"That's not funny."

"I know, but I just hope you learned something from this. This is serious business. Satan doesn't take hostages. What's the next step?"

"I think I'll call Uncle George as soon as I get home and try to find out if there's something I'm doing wrong or need to be doing differently."

"Is there anything I can do?"

"You can pray that nothing like last night ever happens again."

"I'll do that, and if there's anything else I can do, call me. This stuff is way beyond me, but I want to be there if you need me."

"Thanks, Kent. Your concern means a lot."

"Would you like to get together tomorrow for the Fourth of July? Maybe we could have a picnic with Jennifer and watch fireworks."

Kent pulled his car into Heather's driveway. "That sounds like fun."

"Okay, I'll pick you up about 11:30."

Heather and Jennifer climbed out of the car. Waving good-bye, they walked to the house. Heather went straight to the phone and called her uncle. She told him all about last night's conversation with her mother. "I hope I didn't get you into any trouble."

"That explains this morning's mysterious phone call. About 4:00 somebody called and said, 'If you say anything to anyone about what you know, we will destroy you.' Then they hung up."

"Who do you think it was?"

"Probably someone your mother told about our telephone talks. But I'm not afraid of your mother, your grandfather, or any of his followers. I used to be, but not anymore. I believe God is in control and I've placed my life in His hands."

"Uncle George, let me tell you the rest. Last night, while I was trying to sleep, a demon attacked me in my bedroom."

"How do you know it was a demon? What happened?"

Heather described the events that took place in her bedroom. "You're right," Uncle George said. "It sounds demonic to me, especially because of what happened to Carolyn."

"Why is this happening?" Heather asked frantically.

"Your grandfather's deal with the Devil involved the whole family."

"Uncle George, I have a feeling there's a lot you haven't told me. Don't you think I deserve to know what's going on here?"

"There are some things it's better not to know."

"But I'm involved!" Heather insisted. "A demon attacked me in my bedroom! For God's sake, don't you think I need to know?" She was near tears, but she had to have more information, especially after last night.

"I wanted to protect you from this, but I guess it's time you heard the whole story." Uncle George gave a deep sigh.

"Sometime in the early 1920s your grandfather went to Paris and met Aliester Crowley. During this time he dabbled a lot with black magic. In 1929 he made his deal with the Devil and the next year he met my mother, your grandmother. They fell in love and for a little while he abandoned his evil ways. When she died, your grandfather was heartbroken. He was lost. He loved her dearly and always called her his little angel. She was beautiful with long, wavy black hair, a perfect complexion, and large brown eyes. She died when she was twenty-eight from influenza. I think she caught it while volunteering at the local hospital.

"After the funeral, he became a hermit and started writing to his old friend Aliester Crowley again. He stopped shaving and rarely bathed. He quit his job and refused to let me and your mother leave the house, not even for school or church. He cursed, yelled, and swore at God. He sat in his overstuffed chair in the living room, with his face in his hands, repeating, 'How could God take such a saint?' and 'If the reward for good deeds is an early grave, then I don't want anything to do with God!'

"Late one night, I heard him pacing the floor and praying to Lucifer. The next morning he gathered your mother and me together in the living room. He'd recently shaved and smelled of cologne. In fact he looked like his old self, except for a strange gleam in his eye. 'Children,' he told us, 'today we begin a new life. God has betrayed us. So I've sought help from another source, a source that will give us all we ever need. In return, I must keep a vow I made a long time ago.' Then he told us we'd been dedicated to Satan.

"I was shocked. How could he have made such a vow? From then on there was a wall between my father and me; nothing was ever the same. I refused to accept his devil worship. I went to the cathedral every day to light a candle for my mother and confess my father's sins. I loved the sights and sounds and smells of the holy place. I felt safe there and I hated going home. I told myself that my father was dead; God was my father now and the church was my mother.

"Your grandfather was evil; I avoided him. He became fascinated with Satan's symbols, especially the black cat, the snake, and the Templar's baphomet. He held seances and called demons into the house. He threw wild parties where people drank too much, said wicked things, and had group sex. He said God was for sissies and real men were driven by sex. He was obsessed with pornography: magazines, erotic books, and prostitutes. Secret societies were another fascination—The Scottish Rite, The Order of the Silver Star, The Church of Satan, The Order of the Templars of the Orient, The . . ."

"Wait a minute," said Heather. "You just mentioned the Templars again. Who are these people?"

"The Templars of the Orient, or OTO, is a German occult group. Aliester Crowley was the head of this organization in the 1920s, but the real Templars were religious knights set up to protect the crusaders back in the twelfth century. If you'd like to know more, I could send you a short paper on them."

"That would be great. What were you doing while Grandfather was into his dabblings?"

"By the time I was fifteen or sixteen I knew I wanted to be a priest. I felt I had no other choice. If I wasn't totally committed to God, I was afraid Satan would pull me into his kingdom. I prayed constantly for God's protection and wore a St. Christopher's medal wherever I went. But I believed my only hope was the priesthood. It was my refuge. Satan would never touch a priest. Your grandfather was furious when I told him my plans. He knew he'd lost all control over me and he disinherited me on the spot. I was relieved and that night was the first peaceful sleep I'd had in years."

"But what about Mother?" Heather asked. "She was so religious and she made sure I was in church every Sunday. How did she deal with her father's vow?"

"Your mother loved her father," Uncle George said. "She only saw the best in him. When I confronted her with the truth, she wouldn't believe it. He was her hero. Whatever he asked, she'd do. She was also afraid of him.

"Years later she realized I was right, but by then it was too late. He'd influenced her too deeply. She loved seances and the occult. She had an insatiable sex drive and a fascination with pornography. She tried to fight these negative forces by going back to church and reading her Bible, but it was a difficult battle. She was confused, but I know she was determined not to pass the curse down to you. She tried to raise you in a godly way and protect you from evil."

"She deceived me," Heather sobbed. "If she really wanted to protect me, why didn't she warn me? Maybe if I had known, I could have been more careful."

"I wish that were all," Uncle George said, "but the issue your mother is most afraid we'll talk about involves Chuck's death."

"I knew it. Tell me."

"As you've probably suspected, it wasn't an accident. Your parents had Chuck killed because he'd stumbled onto cult secrets and they were afraid he was going to tell."

"I knew it. I knew it." Heather burst into tears.

"I know this is hard," Uncle George said.

Heather kept crying with great sobs that shook her body. It took her a few minutes to control them. With a shaky voice she continued, "I'm sorry, Uncle George, but please tell me more. The more I know, the better equipped I am to fight this enemy." Heather caught her breath and asked, "How do you know about this?"

"A priest can't always disclose his sources."

"What if your source isn't reliable?"

"It's reliable."

"This is a serious accusation. My parents wouldn't have done anything like that."

"They would to protect cult secrets."

"What secrets?"

"To start with, Chuck found the Silver Key of Solomon."

"You mean the key with the snake coin?"

"Yes."

"How did you know he had that key?"

"My source has information from the cult."

"How do they know?"

"Heather, the cult knows everything. Besides that key is important and that coin is an old alchemy symbol."

"Alchemy? Isn't that where people believe they can turn common metals into gold?"

"Your grandfather called it an ancient science and he took it very seriously."

"What does this key and alchemy stuff have to do with Chuck's death."

"I don't know how Chuck found it, but it's the only way to open your grandfather's trunk."

"You mean the one I'm supposed to inherit?"

"That trunk supposedly holds the secret of alchemy."

"Uncle George, are you telling me my trunk holds a formula that can turn scrap iron into gold?"

"That's what your grandfather said."

"If that's the case, why don't my parents break the lock, take the formula, and make themselves filthy rich?"

"It's not that simple. If anybody opens the trunk without the silver key, they're cursed. They'll go crazy and die within a year."

"Do you really believe that?"

"No, but your grandfather's followers do," Uncle George said. "If you have the key, I don't want to know. But remember, certain people will kill for it."

They were both silent. "Thank you," she said, "for telling me the truth. It must . . ." The phone suddenly sounded hollow, like dead air. "Uncle George, can you hear me?" There was no answer. Heather turned the phone off and on again, but there was still no dial tone. She tried Uncle George's number anyway. Nothing. The phone was dead.

Running next door, Heather said to Carolyn, "I hate to bother you, but may I use your phone? Something's wrong with mine and I was cut off while talking to my Uncle George. I'm afraid something might have happened to him."

Heather dialed his number, it rang and he answered.

"I'm so glad you're there," she said. "What happened?"

"Everything's okay here. After we got cut off, I called your number and got a recorded message saying the service to your number had been temporarily interrupted."

"That's strange. My phone is dead. I wonder what's wrong."

"Why don't you check where the phone line comes into

the house and see if there's any problem with the connection?"

Heather hung up and returned to her house. She looked for the phone line and found it running along the side of the garage. She followed it until she saw the copper wires gleaming in the sun. There was a break in the line. How did it happen? Heather examined the damage more closely. The wires weren't just exposed—they'd been cut.

Chapter 14

Dreams came to Heather that night. Before her stood a medieval castle with gleaming turrets and a dark moat. The drawbridge was down and the castle gate beckoned her to enter. The courtyard was silent and deserted except for a few stray cats. Heather walked toward the largest building in the center of the courtyard. The door opened and she was drawn down a long candlelit hallway. The passage led past hidden rooms and secret stairways. Shadows reflected off trick mirrors, and false walls became trap doors.

She fell through the darkness into a labyrinth of dungeons. Hands grabbed her, held her, choked her. She tried to scream, but red hands tightened around her neck. She tried to run, but they wrapped around her ankles. They coiled and twisted and slithered. They were no longer hands, they were snakes. Long, black snakes surrounded her, first two or three, then hundreds. They closed in on her, crawling on her face and arms. She was terrified and a cry caught in her throat. Somewhere she'd heard if you don't move, snakes won't hurt you—maybe they don't notice you or they think you're already dead. Heather closed her eyes and kept perfectly still. More snakes crawled on her. She prayed for God to protect her. Snakes encircled her neck and slowly squeezed. "Oh, God, where are you? Why don't you answer? Save me!"

Heather awoke. Her body was drenched in sweat. Her bed

sheets were twisted around her arms and neck, but she was alive. Her first thought was: *Thank you, God, for saving me.* Her next thought was: *I'm not sure whether that was a dream or a memory.* Her clock radio read 3:00 A.M., yet she was wide awake. Slowly over the next few hours the details of a forgotten childhood trip emerged.

When Heather was thirteen she'd gone to England with her grandfather. It was a strange and hazy trip. Three men picked them up at the airport in a black limousine and drove them deep into the countryside—past stone fences and lush green fields spotted with grazing sheep. They were headed to Templestowe. The name was magical to Heather's grandfather and he was elated when he finally saw the silhouetted castle seated on a small hill, surrounded by fair meadows and pastures. It was early morning and the mists that shrouded their destination gave it a medieval aura. Templestowe seemed mystical, but it was also strong and well-fortified with its moss-covered battlements. The limousine sped past the outer walls and gatehouse. Two granite lions stood guard over the entrance, quietly watching. Heather stared into their empty eyes, amazed at the ferociousness carved into these stone beasts. Their muscles were taunt and she was convinced they could spring to the attack at a moment's notice. The castle itself was a large dark fortress which seemed impregnable. Its thick stone walls were some forty feet high and pitted with age. Three tall six-sided turrets were decorated with cat-like gargoyles. They snarled as Heather studied the walls; she shivered and quickly followed her grandfather through the front door.

Heather and her grandfather stayed at Templestowe for over a week. Vincent spent much of his time in the library browsing and studying. Here the oak bookcases with silver inlays held thousands of volumes on witchcraft, alchemy, sorcery, numerology, and all the occult sciences. On the third day, a group of international leaders from the Silver Star arrived. During the rest of the week Heather saw little of her grandfather. While he was busy, Heather explored the castle.

One afternoon she discovered a secret stairway behind a large marble fireplace in the great hall. Its narrow, spiral steps took her high above the rest of the castle. When she reached the top of the stairs she was exhausted. Before her stood a rough-hewn oak door. She pushed it open and walked into a small turret chamber. It was round with tall windows that looked every direction. Heather could see forever; she sat in this high tower for hours gazing at the enchanted country-side, pretending to be a princess in distress.

On another day Heather found a trap door under a thick oriental rug in the dining hall. When no one was looking, she opened the door and climbed into the darkness. The door fell shut and she peered down an earthy-smelling tunnel with her small flashlight. Pulling together all her courage, she stepped forward into the cold gloom of this underground pas-sageway. Deeper and deeper she went, exploring the black mazes beneath the castle until she stumbled into a dungeon. Rusty chains and shackles hung empty from the stone walls. Human bones were scattered at her feet. Horrified, she jumped back and her light flashed upon an image etched into the wall. Her attention was diverted by the primitive drawing of a snake forming a circle by swallowing its own tail. Beneath the picture were the words *en to pan.*

Why hadn't Heather recognized these words when she'd seen them before on the silver coin? She'd forgotten every-thing about the England trip until this morning's dream. Now the memory was returning in fuzzy pictures and distorted scenes. She closed her eyes and tried to recall the rest of the trip.

Heather began to choke. Clutching at something around her neck, she was transported back to England. Large hands grabbed her from behind, covering her mouth and nose. She tried to scream, but then she heard a familiar voice.

"What are you doing here, Kitty?"

The hands let go and Heather spun around. Before her stood Grandfather in a white hooded robe. With him were a group of others holding torches and staring at her.

"I was exploring," she stuttered.

"Exploration has its risks," Grandfather said as he reached into a hidden pocket of his robe and pulled out a large black snake. Heather looked at the snake and then at her grandfather. He smiled. "Embrace the serpent."

Heather panicked. She turned and ran, retracing her steps to the trap door. That evening at dinner neither Heather nor her grandfather said anything of their underground encounter.

Several days later Heather's grandfather shipped an old wooden trunk back to Portland, Oregon. When Heather asked him about the trunk he said, "It holds the secrets of the Templars."

"What sort of secrets?" she asked.

"The golden baphomet."

Heather was about to ask another question when Grandfather changed the subject. He had said as much as he was willing to say about the trunk. To ask more would've risked his wrath, and nobody could handle Grandfather's wrath. So Heather remained silent.

The next morning Grandfather, Heather, and a small entourage traveled south to Stonehenge. They reached Salisbury Plain during the summer solstice. A full moon rose over the moors, casting giant shadows through the stone circles. Grandfather said it was a sacred place of special rites and vows, of incantations and dark deeds.

Heather was left in the car, while the rest of the group disappeared into the ancient cathedral. Flames turned the rocks red; smoke enveloped Grandfather and his mysterious friends. Heather waited and waited. The longer the shadows danced, the wilder they became. Shortly after dawn Grandfather returned with three of the group. They all wore white robes and Grandfather's companions each had red hands.

Heather stiffened and the red hands disappeared. Why had she remembered this? She hated vacations. She hated red hands. Her body shook and she tried to forget. But images of red hands pursued her. What did they mean? There was more—she was sure of it. Something about Mexico . . . Grandfather . . . red hands. Slowly another memory surfaced.

When Heather was eight, her family went to Mexico. Grandfather Vincent and some of his traveling companions joined them. They flew deep into the Yucatan Peninsula and rented cars to caravan to the ancient Mayan ruins.

They visited the walled city of Tulum, perched on the cliffs above the blue Caribbean. Climbing the grand staircase of the Castillo, Heather saw for the first time the mysterious print of the red hand pressed into the ancient ruins. Then they drove north along the coast and chartered a boat to the island of Cozumel. There they touched the temple of fertility. Back on the mainland, they drove inland to the incredible ruins of Chichén Itzá, with its pyramids and observatory and ball court. Heather was terrified by the colossal stone serpents with mouths wide open and tongues protruding. There Grandfather told them about the cult of the rattlesnake and the human sacrifices performed to appease their blood-thirsty god, Choc Mool.

They visited other ruins on the trip and everywhere they stopped, Grandfather had them look for the red hands. He said the Mayans often marked their buildings with red hand prints which symbolized the vow. Heather asked, "What kind of vow?" Her grandfather said that someday, maybe before their journey was over, he'd show Heather how the vow worked.

Deep in the jungles of the Yucatan, the caravan left the main highway. They followed a narrow dirt road, bumpy and overgrown. When the cars could go no further, people continued on foot. It was hot and muggy, but they didn't stop. Several hours later they reached a high mound covered with bushes and trees. Halfway up, between the rocks, was a small irregular entrance to a cave. The hole was about two feet in diameter and partially hidden by vegetation. Grandfather squeezed through the opening and helped the other eight into a natural cavern. It was round, about twelve feet deep, with a high ceiling.

Grandfather lit an oil lantern and shadows flickered across the room. On the far end of the chamber was an ornate wrought-iron door: unlocked. Beside the door was the print of a red hand with thumb and fingers extended. It wasn't drawn or painted but stamped by a living hand. In the shifting light it almost appeared alive—so realistic that Heather could see every line and crease in the large palm.

Placing his hand on the red print, Grandfather opened the door and led the group into the dark passageway. The tunnel was narrow with smooth walls and a triangular arched ceiling. Heather held tightly to her mother's hand and followed Grandfather's light as it gradually moved downward. The path was smooth; the air stuffy. Turning and winding, the group moved silently through the hand-carved limestone. Deeper and deeper they descended into the earth. Grandfather stopped without warning and Heather bumped into the person in front of her. Listening carefully, Heather heard a strange humming. Someone yelled, "GET DOWN!" Everyone dropped to the ground, covered their heads, and waited. In the shadows of Grandfather's lantern, Heather saw the wild flapping of wings and the mad rushing of hundreds of bats. She closed her eyes and clung to her mother.

Somewhere up ahead Heather saw a spark of light; as she moved forward, it grew brighter. Suddenly the tunnel enlarged and before her stood a large, ornately-engraved archway. On each column of the arch were two intertwined snakes. Above the arch, etched deeply in the stone, was the open mouth of a giant serpent with sharp fangs biting down on a human head. Through the gate was a vaulted chamber with a high roof supported by massive rock pillars. The room was brightly lit and the dazzling light forced Heather to squint. The scene before her was surreal: a multitude of white knights standing at attention with silver swords drawn, gleaming in the brilliance of a thousand candles. Heather stood and stared. Her feet wouldn't move. Her brain couldn't accept the reality of what her eyes saw. Grandfather greeted the Templars and his voice echoed with such clarity that each word fought with the next. The knights cheered and dropped their swords. The noise was deafening.

In the middle of the cave was an altar of limestone engraved with Mayan hieroglyphics. Two intertwining snakes weaved in and out of the ancient writings. In the center of these images was a large cat with terrifying eyes performing a human sacrifice. The carvings were wicked and hypnotic, but it wasn't the altar that drew the Templar's attention. Resting on the limestone was a simple wooden trunk. Grandfather approached it with an air of formality and awe. Each knight picked up his sword and raised it toward the ceiling. The room was silent.

Grandfather knelt before the trunk and spoke exotic and frightening words. From his pocket he pulled an old skeleton key and the lock released. The chanting became wild. He dropped his hands into the trunk and it overflowed with water—thick, red water. The crowd waved its swords and yelled. Grandfather pulled a golden idol from the trunk. It was dripping red, but it still sparkled in the candlelight. The crowd went hysterical. Heather covered her ears and tried to hide. Yet she couldn't pull her eyes from the glittering statue; it was a morbid, dangerous fascination. Grandfather set the baphomet on the ground before the altar and raised his hands to the crowd. They were red—blood red. Heather closed her eyes. It was hot and smoky. A strange odor permeated the room.

Someone screamed and Heather opened her eyes. The room was chaotic with blurred images twisting and swirling. She had to find something to focus on—something clear. Behind the crowd, on the far wall, was a clear image. She directed all her attention on it and tried to decipher its form. Then it hit her. It was the print of a red hand. Her vision broadened and she saw it was not one or even two hands, but a whole wall covered with hundreds of them: bright and distinct and evil. Heather screamed and the cave faded.

Heather snapped out of her early morning reverie. Why had she forgotten these trips? Were there others? If she had forgotten these two, what else had she forgotten? All of this made her more curious about the trunk. Could it be the same trunk her grandfather sent from Templestowe? And the same trunk she saw deep in the caves of Mexico? Maybe tomorrow she could convince Kent to go with her to look for it.

Chapter 15

Jennifer sat alone on the sunny porch with a scowl on her face. Heather watched her daughter in silence from inside the house. Tears ran down Jennifer's cheeks as she pulled petals from a daisy. "Loves me, loves me not, . . ."

Kent pulled into the driveway and called, "Hi, Jennifer!"

"Loves me, loves me not, . . ."

Kent sat down beside her. "You don't look very happy today."

"Loves me, loves me not, . . ."

"What are you doing to that poor daisy?"

"I'm finding out if Mommy loves me," Jennifer said with a pout.

"Of course she loves you."

"Then why won't she let me go on the picnic with you?"

"I don't know, but I'm sure she must have a good reason."

Kent knocked on the front door.

"Hello," Heather said as she welcomed him into the living room. "I heard you talking to the unhappy little girl on the porch."

"She said there might be a change of plans."

"I have an idea, if it's okay with you. First let me tell you about my conversation with Uncle George." Heather gave Kent the details of yesterday's phone call. After she finished, she added, "Then we were cut off. Somebody sliced the telephone line."

"Who would do that?"

"I'm afraid to even think about it. I couldn't sleep last night."

"You could have called me."

"I didn't want to worry you. Especially since there is one more thing." Heather pulled the silver skeleton key from her purse and turned it over in her hands. "I don't know where Chuck found this, but Uncle George is sure the cult would kill to get their hands on it. But I figure even if my parents did kill Chuck, they won't hurt their own daughter."

"Heather, are you sure your uncle's okay? Nobody believes in alchemy anymore. And a secret trunk with an evil curse sounds like an old fairy tale. I don't mean to be disrespectful, but this is hard to believe."

"I know. I don't think the trunk holds the mystery of alchemy or a deadly curse. It's probably just a silly hoax. My grandfather used to make up incredible stories. Most people said you couldn't believe a word he said. They called him a charlatan and an impostor. But what's confusing is that some of his more preposterous tales are actually true. He loves to mix a lie with truth and vice versa."

"So why would he create a superstition about an old trunk?"

"I'm not sure, but he has a reason for everything he does. There's something in that trunk he doesn't want anyone to find and it has to do with me. I have to find out what's in there. Will you help me?"

"Do you know where the trunk is?"

"I'm sure it's at my parents' house. They're out of town for the day, so it's a good time to go over there and explore. Carolyn has agreed to watch Jennifer, if we want to look for it."

"I thought Carolyn was upset with you."

"She was, but she apologized and told me she was just scared."

"Well, I don't blame her." Kent looked at the living room floor. "I'm a little scared, too, especially when you talk about snooping around your parents' house. Are you sure it's safe?"

"They won't be back until late tonight. It's perfectly safe."

"If you say so, but this sort of thing makes me nervous."

"If you'd rather not go . . ."

"Heather, I'm with you."

Half an hour later Heather and Kent were driving up McLoughlin Boulevard toward Portland. Heather thought she saw a black Cadillac two cars behind them, but she wasn't sure. Kent drove through the city and into a fashionable upper-middle class neighborhood. The closer they got to the house, the more nervous they became. Heather wrung her hands and stared down the empty street. "It might be best to stop here. We don't want the neighbors to notice a strange car parked in front of my parents' house."

The two sat in the car and stared at each other. "Do you really think this is a good idea?" Kent asked.

"I have to find out what's in that trunk. I have to protect Jennifer."

"But what if we're caught? What will happen to Jennifer then?"

"Kent, if you don't want to do this, I understand. But I have to." Heather hid her purse under the seat, opened the door, and climbed out of the car. Kent followed.

When the doors of the car slammed shut, an elderly man looked out his living room window. Kent froze for a second, then casually swung his arms, to look innocent. Heather walked on ahead of him as if she were taking an afternoon stroll. Kent chased after her, nervously looking up and down the sidewalk before approaching the large English Tudor dwelling.

"Are you sure nobody's home?" Kent asked.

"They're supposed to be gone."

"Let's ring the doorbell just to be sure."

Heather rang the doorbell. Nobody came. She rang it again. Nothing.

"Maybe it's broken," Kent said.

Heather knocked loudly. "I'm sure nobody's home." Slowly and quietly she unlocked the door.

"Do you want me to go first?" Kent whispered.

"No, I know the place."

Heather gripped the door handle and pushed it open. Cautiously she tip-toed over the threshold with Kent close behind her. Suddenly she stopped cold. The familiar four glowing cat eyes forbid her to go further. Heather spun around, bumping into Kent. She clung to him while catching her breath.

"It's just a picture," he said.

"I know, but it still gives me the creeps."

They both listened carefully for noises—it was quiet. Heather let go of Kent and the two walked step by step down the shadowed hall, followed by four shining points of light. "Let's start upstairs in the attic," she whispered. Kent followed her up the creaky stairs.

The attic was cluttered with antiques, old books, and cardboard boxes in every possible size. It was dark and dusty and claustrophobic. It was also wonderful. As a child Heather had spent hours up here browsing through boxes and dressing up in old-fashioned clothing. It was an enchanted world of mystery and nostalgia. This room was a time capsule holding the family treasures of nearly two centuries—carefully packed mementos of past generations—postcards, report cards, a cigar box of marbles, magazines, a violin, an old ring, letters, maps, a leopard skin, dolls, photographs, a tarnished pocket watch, a collection of pressed flowers, silver stars, stamps, a mortar and pestle, a goat's skull, and a million other fascinating items.

Heather stood at the entrance of this family museum while Kent looked over her shoulder. Both were silent. Rays of light filtered through a small dirty window at the end of the room, casting a ghostly spell over its contents. Heather scanned the room for the trunk. Things had been rearranged and additions made since she was there last. Three large pictures in heavy wooden frames leaned against a book shelf. Something drew Heather toward them. They were tied together with twine and a note was attached. She bent down to read the faded words.

To Kitty,
For reflection and assimilation.
From Grandfather Vincent.

Curiosity and fear battled within Heather. Her heart pounded as she called to Kent.

He cut the twine with a pocket knife and pulled the top picture into the light. The dark and eerie painting was done in rough irregular strokes. A small gold plate on the frame read: "The Incantation" by Goya (c.1798). The scene included five grotesque witches huddling together late at night. One held a basket of tiny children, one read from an evil book by candle-light, one jabbed a long needle into an infant, one listened intently, and the one in the middle muttered the incantation over a terrified woman in a nightgown.

"This is sick," Kent said.

"Knowing my grandfather, the next two are probably not any better."

Kent pulled the second picture into the light. It also had a small gold plate on the frame. This one read: "Witches' Sabbath" by Goya (c.1798). The painting was a grisly scene of necromancy. A giant he-goat stood in the center with a wreath of oak leaves over his curved horns. This satanic figure was encircled by old hags holding the bodies of babies, some dead, some alive. The sky was dark, a crescent moon and huge black bats hovered above.

"This is horrible. I don't understand what's happening," said Heather.

"It's a ritual of child sacrifice," said Kent. "Satan is pointing to his next victim, this small child over here."

"What a ghastly picture. How could anybody paint such a horrid thing?"

"Why would anyone want to own such a horrid thing?"

Kent pulled the last picture out of the shadows. Its gold plate read: "The Goat of the Witches' Sabbath" or "The Baphomet of Mendes" by Eliphas Levi. An evil-looking creature sat on a sphere. It had the head of a goat with menacing eyes, large horns, and a pentagram on its forehead. Its upper body was human; its right hand pointed up toward a white crescent moon and its left hand pointed down toward a black crescent moon. The scales of a reptile covered its stomach. It had dark wings and the feet of a goat. In its lap were two intertwined snakes, one white and one black.

Heather felt sick. "That's the most wicked creature I've ever seen. Let's find that trunk and get out of here."

"Are you sure you don't want to just forget about the trunk and get out of here right now?"

"It has to be here somewhere. You look over there and I'll look here."

A few minutes later Heather moved a heavy wool blanket and found the old wooden trunk underneath. The two stood awe-struck before this mysterious box, fearful of opening its lid, yet determined to explore its secrets. They both whispered silent prayers and held their breath. Heather's skeleton key fit perfectly into the large silver padlock. She turned the key and they both jumped as the lock clicked. Kent held the lid and asked, "Are you ready?"

Heather nodded. Kent lifted the lid and the hinges creaked. Heather shuddered. They both sighed and Heather giggled. Stale air rose from the trunk as they stared at its contents. The top layer consisted of a white hooded robe, two bronze dishes, a silver sword, and thirteen black candles. Heather removed each item, studied it, set it on the floor, and dug deeper. An aura of evil surrounded the trunk and a putrid odor rose from the next layer. Carefully packed in small strips of cloth were twenty or thirty glass containers of various sizes with small handwritten labels. Each of these jars contained various herbs, spices, poisons, and potions: mint, marjoram, rosemary, sea salt, myrrh, musk, mandrake, sulphur, vinegar, wormwood, mercury, arsenic, laurel juice, cobra venom, and nightshade. There was also a small wooden box of five vials with instructions that the contents would provide special powers when burned. The vials were labeled hemlock, henbane, opium, hellebore, and powdered brains of a black cat.

The bottom layer was more occult paraphernalia: a set of tarot cards, an Ouija board, a book on numerology, a magic circle, a triangle of Solomon, and a silver chalice with the inscription, "To drink like a Templar." That was it. Heather stood up and scratched her head. "I don't know what I expected to find, but it's not here. Of course, this proves that everything Uncle George said was true, but I don't see what any of it has to do with me."

"Wait a minute. What's this?" Kent reached into the bottom of the trunk and pulled out a handful of talismans, pentagrams, hexagrams, and incantations. Stuck to the trunk's bottom was a black envelope addressed "To Kitty (my little cub)."

"We've found it." Kent pried the envelope free and gave it to Heather. Her hands trembled as she studied her name written in Grandfather Vincent's elegant silver script. She turned over the envelope, running her fingers along a seal of silver wax with the ancient serpent swallowing its own tail.

Heather froze and her ears perked. Somebody was on the front porch rattling the door. She grabbed Kent's arm, silently motioning downstairs. A door creaked open.

"We have to get out of here," Kent said.

"First, let's put this stuff away. If they find the trunk open, they'll know it was me." Heather shoved the letter into her pocket, quickly set everything back in the trunk, and locked the silver padlock. Voices echoed in the entryway.

"What should we do?" Kent whispered.

Heather pulled him to the other side of the room and moved a few cardboard boxes to reveal a wooden grating in the floor. "This will get us to the basement," she said as she pulled up the grating. "You first."

"You have to be kidding."

"It's the only way out and we don't have a lot of time for discussion," Heather whispered. Footsteps started up the stairs.

Kent took a deep breath and squeezed into the old ventilation shaft feet first. He slid through the darkness, falling downward from the attic, through the main floor, to the basement where he landed in a pile of laundry. A second later Heather landed on top of him. It was pitch black. Heather felt dizzy and disoriented.

"What now?" Kent said.

"There's a window around here somewhere."

The two crawled on their hands and knees until they found a wall. Feeling their way along, hand over hand, they frantically tried to find the window.

Footsteps pounded the floor above them. Two, maybe three people were searching the house—searching for them. Doors slammed, voices called, and it sounded like they were tearing the place apart.

"The window . . . where is it? It has to be close," Heather said. She tried hard to stay in control, but she felt herself starting to panic.

"Heather we know you can hear us!" someone suddenly yelled high above them. The strangely familiar voice sent terror through Heather's body. "We know you're here and we're going to find you." The words were fuzzy, but they were coming closer. "We'll search every nook and cranny. You're trapped! If you give up, we'll be easier on you . . ."

Heather was frozen. How did they know it was her? Kent shook her. "Heather, we have to find the window. Ignore them.

We're going to get out of here." Heather just stood there. Kent grabbed her arm, pulling her along with him as he continued groping for the window.

"Yes!" Kent hissed and pulled back a heavy fabric curtain about five feet above the floor. Light from the window flooded the room. The two squinted at the brightness as Kent fumbled with the old and rusty latch. He tried to force it, but the window was stuck. He pulled and pulled, but it still wouldn't budge. The footsteps above them seemed louder. He pounded on the window and the glass rattled. He looked around the room and finally grabbed a small wooden chair. "Stand back!" he yelled as he picked it up and smashed it through the window. Glass shattered everywhere.

"Get on my shoulders and you can climb out," Kent said. Heather obeyed, carefully pulling herself through the broken glass.

Kent had pulled another chair to the window and started to climb out when the basement door flew open. Someone flipped the lights on and footsteps raced down the stairs.

"Heather, help me!" Kent cried. She grabbed one of his hands and started pulling him through the window.

Voices filled the basement and someone raced toward Kent's feet, still dangling through the window. But Heather pulled him up just in time. Kent climbed into the backyard, minus one boot.

"Run!" he cried.

Kent kicked off his other boot and without looking back, they sprinted to the car. Exhausted and breathless, they quickly unlocked the door and climbed inside. Gunning the engine, they sped from the neighborhood.

"That was too close for comfort," Kent said. "You can never say I didn't bring any excitement into your life." Heather laughed nervously. She leaned over and gave him a hug. "Thank you."

"I just want you to promise that our next date will be peaceful and relaxing."

"I promise."

Kent pulled over to the shoulder, stopped the car, put his arms around her, and softly kissed her lips.

Later that evening, loud explosions pierced a thousand holes in the black sky. The colorful lights glowed and twinkled before the darkness reclaimed its territory. Jennifer plugged her ears and snuggled closer to Kent. "I think fireworks are too loud." Another rocket exploded and Jennifer buried her fingers deeper into her ears. Heather leaned on Kent's shoulder, thinking about the old trunk. Suddenly she remembered the letter. She pulled it from her pocket and broke the wicked seal.

Welcome Albino Cub,

You and your children belong to us. We will take care of your every need—giving you knowledge, wealth, and power. To follow your destiny means life, but to stray means ultimate destruction. Your mission is:

14 1 22 3 4 12 20 18 4 25

20 16 11 4 4 20 25 2 22 20

9 2 11 26 5 3 25 10 5 20

4 2 11 24 3 2 25 4 4 22

13 4 26 4 20 5 22 16 2 25

10 22 4 4 25 20 2 24 26 20

May the demons guide you and the serpent encircle your heart. In all you do remember the magician's creed:

To Know

To Dare

To Will

To Keep Silent.

With eternal bonds that transcend death and distance, I walk in your shadow—watching, waiting, winning.

So mote it be,

Grandfather Vincent.

An explosion burst above Heather's head. She jumped and grabbed Kent's arm, clinging as closely to him as she could. "Please hold me."

He did.

Chapter 16

The next day Federal Express delivered a thick letter to Heather's house. She eagerly ripped the envelope open. She had hoped for a personal note from Uncle George, but the only thing inside was the promised report.

A Brief History of the Templars

On Easter Sunday, in the year A.D. 1119 a group of Christian pilgrims on the road from Jerusalem to Jordan were attacked by Moslems—three hundred pilgrims were killed and sixty were taken as prisoners. This news shook Europe. In response, Hugh de Payens and eight crusader knights dedicated themselves to monastic service and the military protection of Christians. Baldwin II, king of Jerusalem, welcomed these nine soldier-monks, giving them a residence near Solomon's Temple. Thereafter, they were known as "The Order of the Poor Knights of the Temple of Solomon" or more commonly, the Knights Templar.

During the next twenty years, the Templars grew at an amazing rate. Soon they had substantial holdings in France, England, Scotland, Flanders, Spain, Portugal, Austria, Germany, Hungry, and the Holy Land. With their wealth came great power. In March 1139 Pope

Innocent II issued *Omne Datum Optimum* which gave the Templars total freedom in their defense of the church from all enemies of the cross. It also allowed them to keep all booty taken from the Moslems and the right to construct their own churches.

As the Knights of the Temple grew wealthy and powerful, strange alliances were made. One of these was with a heretical group called the Cathars. This sect believed that God and Satan were equal; God created and ruled the spiritual universe, while Satan created and ruled the material universe. Satan was thus deified and called "Rex Mundi," king of the world. Another strange alliance was that made between the Templars and the Assassins, an Ishmaelite sect of Moslems whose purpose was political espionage and intrigue. The Assassins were well-known for their use of hashish, their expertise in poisons, and their suicidal attacks on crusaders. They were masters of terror and murder, but as the Templars established themselves as an economic force, secret deals were made, information was exchanged, and goods were purchased. In time the Templars adopted certain mystic hierarchies and occult practices from the Assassins.

By 1150 rumors of corruption and heresy within the Temple had spread throughout Europe. Young maidens were warned, "Beware of the Templars' kiss!" The carouser was said to "drink like a Templar." People whispered of something evil about these white knights and everyone knew of men who, caught spying on their secret proceedings, were never heard of again. The Templars were obsessive about their privacy. They stopped up every crack and keyhole before their chapter meetings and carefully guarded the temple from the curious.

The inner structure of the Knights of the Temple was complex and enigmatic. Aspirant Templars were carefully examined and sworn to secrecy. They were taken in the dead of night down hidden stairways and through vaulted passages dimly lit by candles. Two guards unbolted heavy doors and ushered the hopefuls into a shadowy meeting room with hundreds of knights in white mantles, standing with swords drawn. In the center was an altar, on each side small fires provided the only light in the room. Each future Templar was asked three times if he wished to enter the order and three times he had to affirm this as his greatest wish. At the end of the ceremony all proclaimed, "Behold how good and pleasant it is for brothers to dwell together in unity." Once a Templar always a Templar.

As the Templars grew in power, they became more bold and arrogant. On September 13, 1207 a letter from Pope Innocent III formally condemned the pride of the Templars. Twenty-two years later Frederick II was crowned King of Jerusalem, but he wouldn't stay in his own city for fear the Templars would kill him. He condemned them as traitors and heretics. Between 1265 and 1268 Pope Clement IV reprimanded the white knights for their immense fortune and fierce pride. In 1271 Pope Gregory X accused Grand Master Thomas Berand of nameless scandals and unspecified depravations. Thirteen years later King Hugh III of Cyprus, his son, and others of the royal household were poisoned by the Templars. The Knights of the Temple were out of control. Everybody knew it, but no one had the courage to do anything about it.

The phone rang, startling Heather from the paper.

"Hi, Heather," Kent greeted her. "Are you okay? Have your parents tried to find you?"

"I'm fine. I haven't heard anything from them. Maybe they'll just leave me alone. Anyway I've been reading a paper on the Templars. It's a little dry, but it pulls together a few of the pieces in this bizarre puzzle."

"That's great," Kent said. "Do you mind if I distract you from your reading for a while?"

"That depends on what you have in mind."

"I know this is short notice, but my mother called a few minutes ago and invited us over to their house for a barbecue this evening. Don't worry about Jennifer. I want her to come with us so Mom and Dad can meet her."

"Oh, it sounds like fun."

"What if I pick you up at 4:00?"

"We'll be ready and waiting. Is there anything I can bring?"

"Nothing at all. I'm sure my mom has everything under control."

Heather hung up the phone and went up to her bedroom closet. She glanced through her wardrobe, looking for the perfect outfit. Finally she chose a light blue sundress and white sandals. A gold necklace and earrings finished the ensemble.

Kent picked up the two Davis girls at exactly 4:00 and they drove across town to a large white colonial house in Portland's west hills. Mr. Thomas opened the door and greeted his son with a warm hug. He was a tall, thin man with gray hair in need of a trim. His blue eyes sparkled and he seemed to have an easy-going disposition. "So this must be Heather. My, my what a beautiful lady." Heather blushed. "And this must be little Jennifer." He bent down and shook her hand.

"I'm not little," Jennifer protested. "I'm almost five."

Mr. Thomas squatted down and said, "So you're almost five. What a delightful age. There are days I wish I was still five."

"Now Bill," Mrs. Thomas walked into the entryway, "why don't you take them all out to the back patio?"

"Mom, let me introduce you to Heather," Kent said.

Mrs. Thomas took Heather's hands and gave them a gentle

squeeze. "It's so nice to meet you, my dear. I hope Kent didn't put you on the spot by inviting you over to meet us. But after he told us what a wonderful person you are, we just had to see you with our own eyes." Now it was Kent's turn to blush.

The Thomas's were a close-knit Christian family. Kent was the first born of three, with two younger sisters. Mr. Thomas taught English at a small liberal arts college in town, and it was his love for literature that lured Kent into teaching English at the high school level. Mrs. Thomas was a talkative, over-protective mother. She was also a tasty cook, an energetic gardener, and an overly compassionate social worker.

Mrs. Thomas led her husband and guests to the backyard patio where the smell of barbecued chicken mingled with fragrant roses. The scent was heavenly. The yard was set up like a formal English garden with a small pond in the center. English ivy, honeysuckle, and deep red rambling roses climbed a rustic-looking brick wall that encircled the property. Beyond the brick wall, facing away from the house, was a beautiful view of downtown Portland. Inside the walls a stone walkway, bordered with boxwood hedges, cut through carefully laid beds of lavender, baby's breath, azaleas, daylilies, sweet alyssum, hollyhock, impatiens, and petunias. Yet what was most impressive in this sea of color were the reds, pinks, whites, and yellows of the roses. Chrysler Imperial, Mister Lincoln, First Prize, Tiffany, Iceberg, and Peace were just a few of the well-tended roses.

The five sat down at a wrought-iron patio table to eat barbecued chicken, green salad, corn on the cob, and watermelon. After dinner Mr. Thomas and Jennifer walked through the garden picking a bouquet for Heather. Jennifer presented the flowers to her mother with a big hug. Then the adults talked while the little girl skipped off to see the giant goldfish in the central pond.

"Kent told me earlier that you've been reading a paper on the Templars," Mr. Thomas said to Heather. "They're a fascinating group, but nobody could figure out whether they were priests, soldiers, bankers, murderers, spies, or Satanists."

"How do you know about the Templars?"

"Legend and literature periodically make reference to the Templars," Mr. Thomas explained. "In *Ivanhoe,* by Sir Walter Scott, one of the main characters is a Templar who lives in a mythical castle called Templestowe."

Heather choked. Templestowe wasn't mythical—she'd been there. But she kept quiet and listened intently.

"More recently Umberto Eco, the Italian philosopher, wrote *Foucault's Pendulum* about the Templars' secret plan to control the world. This international plot . . . "

"Now Bill," said Mrs. Thomas, "you aren't going to bore us with another one of your lectures, are you? I think we should all have some ice cream and watch the city lights turn on."

They all enjoyed the evening. Heather loved Kent's parents and so did Jennifer. The only thing that bothered Heather was that her parents were so different from Kent's.

The next morning Heather picked up Uncle George's paper on the Templars and finished reading it.

Phillip the Fair, king of France, felt so threatened by the Templars that he decided he had to do something. During the fall of 1306 he ordered twelve spies to infiltrate the Templars to gather information about their secret activities. Early the next year Phillip pressured Pope Clement V to open an official inquiry into the rumors about the Templars. In June of 1307 the master of the temple of France circulated a command that no Templar under any circumstance was to give information about the customs or rituals of the order, no matter who asked.

On September 14, 1307 an arrest order for all Templars in France was secretly drafted. Somehow Jacques de Molay discovered what was in the wind and immediately had many of the Templar's books and records burned. The rest were packed into wagons late at night, along with a large cache of valuables, and transported to the order's naval base at LaRochelle where it was loaded into eighteen galleys which were never heard of again.

At dawn on Friday the 13th, October 1307, all Templars in France were arrested and their property seized. On November 22, 1307 Pope Clement V issued *Pastoralis Praminentiae*, which commanded Christian rulers throughout Europe to arrest all Templars and confiscate their property for the pope. Between 1309 and 1311 there was an official papal investigation of 127 charges against the Templars. Some of these charges were: Worshipping the Devil in the form of a black cat; denying Christ during secret ceremonies; being addicted to sexual immorality; dabbling with witchcraft and sorcery; sacrificing children during black masses; participating in idolatry, especially with a wicked creature called a baphomet; making magical powders from the bodies of the dead; and murdering those who attempted to expose the secrets of the order.

During this investigation, many Templars confessed to all the charges, some died in jail, some killed themselves, and some were burned at the stake.

In 1312 the pope officially abolished "The Order of the Poor Knights of the Temple of Solomon." On March 18, 1314 Jacques de Molay, now in his seventies, was ordered by Phillip to be burned to death on a small island in the Seine River. As the flames encircled the last grand master, he cursed his persecutors and predicted their deaths within a year. One month later Pope Clement died of dysentery. That fall, Phillip the Fair died of mysterious causes. During the next fourteen years, each of Phillip's three sons took the throne and each died. Speculation and rumor has long attributed the deaths to underground Templars who were masters in the art of poison. Almost five hundred years later, when the guillotine cut off the head of Louis XVI, a man leapt to the platform, plunged his hand into the blood, flicked it over the crowd, and yelled, "Jacques de Molay, thou art avenged!"

Thousands of Templars survived the purge and escaped to Scotland, where the papal bulls dissolving the order were never proclaimed. Here a sizable contingent of fugitive Templars fought alongside Robert Bruce in 1314 at the Battle of Bannockburn. After that, the Knights kept themselves together as a secret society for the next four centuries. In the first half of the eighteenth century, Charles Radclyffe promulgated the Scottish Rite of Freemasonry, which structured itself after the Templars' secret degrees of revelation. In the 1750s Karl Gottlieb Von Hund introduced a further extension to the Scottish Rite called the "Strict Observance," which claimed to come directly from the Knights Templar. Some claim that freemasonry and its higher degrees are merely a cheap exploitation of the Templars, but others claim it is heir to the Templars' legacy.

In 1906 the Order of the Templars of the Orient, OTO, was founded in Germany. It believed the original Templars were magicians and sorcerers. In 1912 Aliester Crowley became head of the British chapter and ten years later he became head of the whole OTO. Crowley believed he was a reincarnated Templar and held within his subconscious all the secrets of the original knights. He used the OTO to promote his satanic dabblings and sexual magick. This group exists today as a conventicle of the remaining self-styled followers of Aliester Crowley.

The Knights of the Temple began with a divine calling. But they broke their vows. They lost their focus and strayed from the faith. The Templars dabbled with the Devil and their hearts were darkened. They survive today as secret societies, dedicated to rituals of occultism and black magic. Their evil grows and every year the danger increases. This is not an age for passivity or weakness. Heaven will ultimately prevail, but hell is currently celebrating.

Chapter 17

Heather's face twitched and a low, soft growl rumbled in the back of her throat. The sun was setting and the living room was golden. Heather's eyes opened wide. She listened closely with every muscle in her body—a dog barked several blocks away and a couple argued in the distance. She analyzed the shadowy room, looking for an escape. Moving to the window, she stared at the darkening neighborhood. Her heart grew wild and she crouched at the glass, ready to pounce to freedom. She had to run and roam and prowl and hunt. She swatted the window, snarled, and swung around. Trapped! Caged! Her eyes darted about the room as she began pacing—back and forth—over and over again with hypnotic precision.

A cry broke the spell. "Mommy, Mommy, help!"

Heather shook her head and went upstairs to check on Jennifer. "What's wrong, Sweetheart?"

"I had a nightmare. This thing was chasing me."

"Mommy's here now and you have nothing to worry about. I'd never let anything get you."

"But there's a monster under my bed."

"What kind of monster?"

"A yucky monster in a black robe," Jennifer explained.

"But he can't get you. It was just a dream."

"He's under my bed and he has long arms and he reaches up and . . ."

"Hold on for just a minute," Heather said. "Let me check under your bed and chase away all the long-armed monsters." She bent down and looked under the bed. "No monsters," she announced, "but I do see two books, a necklace, a doll's dress, and a star." She reached under the bed and grabbed the star. It was black and made of metal. "What's this?" she asked Jennifer.

"I don't know, but look . . . it has my name on it."

Heather looked closer and there in the center in blood red letters was Jennifer's name. It was a pentagram, just like in her dream.

Heather ran out of the room clutching the evil talisman. Hysterical questions pursued her: What did this mean? How did it get into her house? What kind of danger were they really in? Heather rushed downstairs to the garbage can outside her back door and violently threw the wicked star into the trash. The garbage truck was coming tomorrow and the pentagram would soon be buried at the bottom of some sanitary landfill.

Heather sat down on the sofa to try to calm down and catch her breath. Her mind processed everyone who might have had access to the house. Of course. Her mother. Her mother placed the pentagram under the bed when she unpacked Jennifer's room. Heather rubbed her forehead. No, she was over-reacting. Mother would never do anything to hurt her own grandchild. Things were just getting crazy lately with dreams and vows, Templars and demons, trances and . . .

Heather heard little feet making their way down the stairs and a tiny voice ask, "Why did you run away from me?"

"Oh, Sweetheart, I'm so sorry. I had to throw something away and I got distracted. I would never run away from you. I promise. I love you very much."

Jennifer hung her arms around her mother's neck. "I love you lots and lots, too."

Heather smiled. "I love you tons and tons."

Jennifer thought a few seconds. "I love you oceans and oceans."

"Well, I love you billions and billions."

Jennifer burst out laughing. "That's a funny word."

Heather carried Jennifer back up the stairs, tucked her into bed, and kissed her cheek. "Lay down your head and go back to sleep."

"Will you stay with me?"

"For a little while, but no more talking."

The two cuddled until Jennifer fell asleep. Heather slipped out of the bedroom and down the stairs. She pushed the star out of her mind and reflected on her earlier trance.

What's wrong with me? This hadn't happened in several weeks and she'd hoped she was over it. She knew she wasn't crazy, but this certainly wasn't normal behavior. What triggered it? And why Heather? Was it because the cat was their family totem? Was it because of Grandfather's deal with the Devil?

The what's and why's raced through her head, creating confusion and tears. She had to talk to someone. She called Carolyn, but nobody was home. Next, she called Kent.

"Hi, it's me. Can I ask you a strange question?"

"Sure."

"Do you think I'm crazy? I'm serious. Do you?"

"No, not at all. A little stressed—but not crazy. Why are you asking?"

"Just all this stuff that's been happening. Sometimes I wonder if it's all in my head. What's happening in your world?"

"Coincidentally, I was just getting ready to call you. I have a craving for Rocky Road ice cream and brownies. If I brought some over, would you join me?"

"I'd love some company and I'd never turn down chocolate."

"Then I'll be over in fifteen minutes with desert and a surprise."

"What kind of surprise?"

"If I told you it wouldn't be a surprise."

"You're right. I have something for you, too."

"I can't wait."

Half an hour later, Kent and Heather were sitting on the sofa enjoying ice cream. With a mischievous smile, Heather jumped up and pulled a package from behind the sofa. It was wrapped in burgundy and navy blue paper with a large gold bow.

"I figured I owed you something for creeping through my parents' attic with me," Heather said. "You're a real trooper."

"You didn't need to do this."

"Why do people always say that? I did it because I wanted to. Open it."

Kent snapped the bow off and tore away the paper. On his lap sat a pair of expensive cowhide Tony Lamas boots. "I hope the size is right. I guessed you wore about a ten and a half.

The store manager said you could return them if they didn't fit."

"They're great. I don't know what . . ."

"You don't need to say anything. I felt badly that you lost your boots at my parents' house, so I thought this was the least I could do."

Kent wrapped his arms around Heather and she leaned into his chest. It was a short hug, but she felt an intimacy that lingered beyond the embrace.

"Now I hope my surprise isn't too much of a let down," Kent said. "I've been working on that secret message all week and I've finally decoded it."

"How did you do it?"

"It was fun. I started by counting the numbers and found a total of sixty. Tabulating their occurrence I came up with this chart." He handed it to Heather.

4 exists 11 times
20 exists 8 times
2 exists 6 times
25 exists 5 times
22 exists 5 times
26 exists 3 times
3 exists 3 times
5 exists 3 times
11 exists 3 times

24 exists 3 times
10 exists 2 times
16 exists 2 times
1 exists 1 time
9 exists 1 time
13 exists 1 time
14 exists 1 time
18 exists 1 time

"How does this help break the code?" Heather asked.

"In the English language the most common letter is E. The frequency of the rest of the alphabet is: A, O, I, D, H, N, R, S, T, U, Y, C, F, G, L, M, W, B, K, P, Q, X, Z."

"I'm impressed. Where did you pick up that piece of trivia?"

"I read it in an old Edgar Allan Poe story. As a kid, it was helpful in playing hangman. Anyway, I assumed 4 was an E. Since E is frequently doubled, I checked for couplets of number 4. I figured three doubles, so I knew I was on the right track. Since 11, 20, 22, and 25 surrounded the double E's, I knew they were consonants. With 20, 22, and 25 being toward the top of my previous list, I figured they must be either D, H, N, R, S, or T. That meant 2 was probably an A, O, or I. After a few hours of trial and error, I came up with another chart:

E = 4   R = 22
T = 20   N = 25
O = 2

Plugging these into the puzzle, it was over halfway solved." Kent handed Heather the following:

```
_ _ R _ E _ T _ E N
T _ _ E E T N O R T
_ O _ _ _ _ N _ _ T
E O _ _ _ O N E E R
_ E _ E T _ R _ O N
_ R E E N T O _ _ T
```

"You've done an excellent job." Heather looked over the paper. "It's so close, but there's still a lot of blanks."

"Figuring out the rest simply involved recognizing the pattern between N, R, and T."

"They're all consonants in the last half of the alphabet."

"Yes, and a reversed numbering of consonants would fit with the previously assigned digits, so, N=25, P=24, Q=23, R=22, S=21, T=20. With some extrapolation and guesswork I figured the sequence started with L=6 and proceeded backward to M=26.

"I don't have a clue as to what you're talking about." Heather scratched her head.

"What if I just say that 1, 3, and 5 are the missing vowels? Once you have the letters all you need to do is separate the words. I guess it does sound complicated, doesn't it?"

"Way over my head."

"Anyway, this is what all these numbers are trying to say in plain English." Kent handed her a sheet of white notebook paper on which were printed the following words.

BURIED TWENTY FEET NORTH OF MAIN GATE

OF PIONEER CEMETERY ON GREENTOP MT.

Greentop Mountain! She hadn't thought of that place in years. Pleasant memories of hiking its wooded trails and playing in a sunny meadow drifted through Heather's mind. Greentop Mountain was a half mile from Grandfather Vincent's farm. As a child, Heather and her parents picnicked in a clearing on the south side of the mountain. It was a beautiful site with giant trees, soft grass, and a noisy brook. On the edge of the clearing was a small cemetery with fifteen to twenty tombstones surrounded by a wrought-iron fence. After lunch, her mother would pick wildflowers, and carefully set them on each grave while Heather's father sat in the shade of an old oak and told her stories of the pioneer families buried in this resting place. Life was wonderful on Greentop Mountain.

Heather shook herself out of her reverie. "I have to go

there. I have to find out what's buried by the cemetery. I know this is asking a lot, but would you please go with me? I have to get to the bottom of all this Grandfather Vincent stuff."

"I'm not sure, Heather. Last time we almost got caught."

"But I have to do this! It's so important to me."

"Okay, okay. I'll go exploring with you tomorrow under one condition."

"What's that?"

"That you go out to dinner with me tomorrow evening."

Heather burst into a smile and flung her arms around Kent. "It's a deal!"

Kent gently picked her up and the two stared into each other's eyes. Heather felt like a schoolgirl with a stomach full of butterflies. Kent's eyes were strong and she felt she could easily lose herself in them. Their faces moved closer and Heather felt flushed with excitement. The tender kiss came slowly, with a carefully restrained passion. Heather wished it would never end. When they parted, her lips still felt his love.

Late that night Heather was called into a nightmare. A familiar voice whispered through the black, waking her from a quiet sleep. She got out of bed and, with bare feet, followed the voice past the foggy images of unformed dreams. The voice called Heather down a narrow path into a dark, foreboding forest. The deeper she went, the more anxious she felt. Her nightgown, damp from the early morning mist, clung to her legs. Heather wished she were back in the safety of her warm bed.

The voice grew louder as she stepped into a grassy meadow. Before her was a rusty wrought-iron fence surrounding a small cemetery with broken tombstones. The voice pulled her forward. The simple gate was open, creaking in the wind. Heather inched through the entrance and looked around for the source of the powerful whisper. The moon threw shadows across the ground. Trembling, she tiptoed to the center of this resting place to peek behind the markers. Suddenly a black cat yowled; Heather spun around and tripped. A flash struck her right temple as she hit the ground. She rubbed her head as she lifted herself to her knees. Then she saw it— a new granite headstone among the old ones. Heather stared at the names and shook her head. "No, no, it can't be."

Before her sat a beautifully carved stone with the words:

Chuck Davis	Heather Davis
(1958-1993)	(1961-1994)

She jumped to her feet and ran through the rusty gate. Blocking her way stood a line of thirteen white knights, their gleaming swords drawn. One of the Templars stepped forward. "He attempted to expose the secrets of the order. If you do the same thing, we will also have to bury you."

Heather screamed with a terror that broke out of her dream and echoed through the bedroom. She sat up, rubbing her eyes and catching her breath. The morning sunshine chased away nocturnal dread, but the memories lingered. She pondered her night journey, recognizing the pioneer cemetery on Greentop Mountain as the one in her dreams and wondering what secrets might lie buried inside or outside its gates.

The next day Carolyn watched Jennifer while Heather and Kent drove an hour and a half southwest to Greentop Mountain. Nobody was in a hurry on this lazy afternoon. The two spoke of jobs, old friends, and favorite songs. They avoided talking about anything related to Grandfather Vincent, but the closer the car got to its destination, the quieter they became. Finally, Heather broke the silence. "I sure appreciate you. You haven't even known me for two weeks, yet you search my parents' attic for a mysterious trunk and now you drive to an old run-down cemetery to dig up something from my demented grandfather. Why are you helping me?"

"Maybe I'm bored and you're the most exciting person I've met in a long time."

"If this is excitement, you can have it. I'd trade this in a minute for a nice quiet evening at home."

"Heather, I like you. You're honest and caring and brave."

"Right now I don't feel very brave."

"Brave or not, I think you're terrific."

Heather leaned over and kissed his cheek. Resting her head on his shoulder she said, "I hope I'm not getting you into any trouble. I'm afraid to like you too much because something might happen to you."

"You mean like it did to Chuck?"

Heather stared out the window and felt tears form in the corners of her eyes.

Kent took her hand and squeezed it. "Heather, don't you think I've considered that? Sometimes I get worried and scared. I don't know why God allows evil to grow . . ."

"Sometimes it makes me mad, but I know I'm not supposed to be mad at God."

"Why not? He's a big God. He can handle it."

"But it doesn't seem right."

"Well right or wrong, God is always near and He'll watch over us."

Heather brushed a tear from her eye. "I hope you're right, because there's Greentop Mountain." She pointed to a heavily wooded hill on their right.

Kent pulled the car to the side of the road. "How do we get to the cemetery?"

"There's a trail over by that oak tree. We follow it about a quarter of a mile up the hill and we're there."

Kent took a shovel, pick, compass, and pair of work gloves from the backseat. Heather led the way to the trail. It was an easy walk, and the trees sheltered them from the heat. She would have enjoyed the stroll under any other circumstance. The two stepped quietly and jumped every time a squirrel fled or a bird called. Before long they stood in a meadow, facing the wrought-iron gate of an overgrown cemetery. Ivy tangled itself around the rusty fence and several small ferns flourished among the weather-worn markers.

"This place is creepy," said Kent. "I'm sure glad it isn't dark."

"Let's find whatever Grandfather buried and get out of here," Heather replied.

"I agree." Kent checked his compass and paced off twenty feet due north. "It ought to be right about here." He swung the pick deep into the earth and loosened the soil. Shoveling out the dirt, Kent dug a small hole. One foot . . . two feet . . . three feet . . . four feet deep and nothing but rich, black soil. The hole was empty.

Kent leaned on his shovel. "What if this is all a hoax and there's nothing buried in this meadow?"

"Let's not give up, yet. We can try digging over here." Kent dug another hole, and it too was empty. Then he dug a third, fourth, and fifth hole. Finally on the sixth hole, the shovel struck something hard—something flat and metallic.

"I think we've found it!" Kent yelled. He rapidly dug around the smooth surface and Heather helped him pull a green box out of the hole. The box was two feet square and one foot deep with handles on two opposite sides. Heather and Kent sat on the soft grass, staring at the box.

"I guess we should open it, huh?" Heather said.

"Are you sure you're ready?"

Heather nodded.

Kent used the pick to pry off the lid. Inside were a number of coarse cotton bags. One was stenciled with the following: "Three ancient invocations for demons." The bag was heavy for its size. Kent reached into it and pulled out three gold bars. The two gasped.

"Are these real gold?" Heather asked.

"I think so. These must be worth a lot." Kent ran his hands over the precious bars. On the face of each, a different invocation was inscribed deep into the metal: *Palas Aron Azinomas, Bagahi Iaca Bachabe,* and *Xilka, Xilka, Besa, Besa.*

Heather turned away for fear she might unconsciously utter the lines and therefore provoke the forces of hell. "Please put them down," she pleaded. "What else is in the box?"

From another bag, Kent pulled out a sacrificial knife. Aghast, Heather stared at the handle—a black cat with sharp teeth biting into the knife's blade.

"What?"

"The knife—it's the one Grandfather Vincent described in his diary when he made his deal with the Devil."

Kent slipped the knife back into its bag and picked up another smaller bag. Kent shook its contents into his palm. A dazzling ring tumbled out. It shone in the afternoon sun. On its metal band two snakes were intertwined in a circle—one white and one black. The white snake swallowed the black snake's tail, while the black snake swallowed the white tail.

Heather was hypnotized by the snakes; they seemed to move and call to her. She fought a strong impulse to slip the ring on. She tried to ignore the impulse, but it wouldn't go away. Suddenly the snakes coiled around her finger. The ring fit perfectly—too perfectly. Heather shuddered. Dark, cat-like feelings rose from deep inside her. Yanking the ring off, she shoved it back into its bag. The spell was broken.

"That ring . . . I hate it . . . I hate it . . ."

Kent's arm was around her, strong and comforting.

"I've seen it before," Heather said, "and it's incredibly evil."

"It looks evil to me, too. Where have you seen it?"

"I'm not sure. It's a Gnostic symbol in the Orphic style used in a ceremony called 'The Marriage of the Beast.' What else is in the box?"

Kent picked up the last cotton sack; it was larger than the previous two bags, but not as big as the first. He uncovered a gold image and they both stared at it in total silence. The idol was twelve inches tall and embedded with precious stones—diamonds, emeralds, and sapphires. The body was human, but the head was that of a goat with long, twisting horns. Large wings, like those of an eagle, sprang from its back as this creature perched on a perfect sphere. Heather knew the eyes—menacing, psychotic, satanic—they saw her terror and laughed. The golden devil was an exact three-dimensional replica of the picture by Eliphas Levi they had found in the attic. It was a baphomet.

Heather was pale and shaken. Turning away she whispered,

"Three things we can't forget—
the black cat,
the poison snake,
the unholy baphomet."

The two carried the box and the digging equipment back to the car. What did the contents of this box have to do with Heather's mission? All it contained was occult paraphernalia—albeit expensive occult paraphernalia. The question wouldn't die.

Kent and Heather were both lost in thought on the way home. Finally Kent broke the silence. "Okay, we've found the buried treasure. Now what?"

"Nothing. I don't think we should do anything."

"What do you mean?"

"I feel as if someone is watching us and the next twenty-four hours are dangerous. I'm not sure whether it's women's intuition or my own paranoia. Or maybe it's even God himself warning us before it's too late."

"Too late for what?"

"I wish I knew. I just think we'd better be careful."

Chapter 18

An old Beach Boys' song drifted through the open-air cafe as Kent and Heather ate a light dinner. The place was crowded and the people boisterous. It was a sultry evening—Heather's sleeveless blouse clung to her shoulders and Kent kept wiping his brow. Four hours earlier they were digging up occult artifacts; now they were trying to forget the events of the afternoon.

"You know so much about my family," Heather said, "tell me more about yours."

"They're really great people. You met my parents, what did you think?"

"They seemed the opposite of mine. Are they really that nice?"

"Yes."

"Do you have a grandfather?"

"Both of my grandfathers were devout Christians, but I was especially close to my dad's father. He was strong and rugged. He was a cowboy in his younger days, but when I knew him he was a farmer. Each summer I spent a month or two on his farm. We'd plant fields, milk cows, and feed chickens. I loved it."

"Keep going."

"Well, Grandpa was the sort of person I always wanted to be. I admired almost everything about him but especially his faith. It wasn't superficial or fake; it was deep and he lived it. He didn't care what anybody thought, he just wanted to do the right thing and walk with God. Every morning he got up before sunrise to read the Bible and pray. He was a quiet man, but when he spoke, I remembered his words. One time I asked him why he woke up so early. He smiled and said, 'Some things are worth waking up for.' Another time I asked him what he did while the rest of us slept. 'Kent,' he said, 'I try to focus on what is important and turn away from that which is not. Then I pray that my grandchildren will love God.' I bent my head, not knowing how to respond. Grandpa noticed my guilt, laughed, and gave me a hug. Life was okay when Grandpa laughed."

"I wish my grandfather was like yours."

"My grandpa didn't just pray for me every once in a while; my grandmother said he prayed for me every day."

"That's incredible," Heather said. "Your grandfather sounds like quite a man. Tell me more about him."

"Let me think," Kent said. "He taught me about life and God. He taught me how to ride a bike and drive a tractor. He taught me how to swim and dive. He even saved me from drowning once."

"Oh, what happened?"

"I was about ten and was spending the summer at the farm. Every afternoon Grandpa took my two cousins and I down to the river. We'd fill his 1947 Chevy truck with old inner tubes and fishing poles. Then we'd jump into the bed, bouncing on the rubber tubes all the way to the old swimming hole. When we got there my cousins would let out wild screams, race to the river, and recklessly dive into the chilly water. I was more cautious. I would inch my way into the river. Grandpa would sit on the bank reading the newspaper while we played in the water.

"One day my cousins, Mark and Jeff, climbed the cliffs on

the east side of the river—twenty, maybe thirty feet above the water. Mark, yelled, 'Geronimooo!' and jumped feet first. He hit the water with a giant splash and disappeared below the surface. Suddenly a head popped out of the water and shouted, 'Awesome!' Then Jeff took his jump. When he bobbed to the surface he said it was my turn. I told him I didn't want to do it, but they both laughed and called me a chicken. I was scared to death of heights, but nobody was going to call me a chicken. So I climbed the cliff and stood on the ledge. My whole body shook and, when I looked down, my head spun. I was sure I was going to die, but I jumped. When I hit the surface, my breath was knocked out of me. The next thing I remember is hitting the bottom. Dizzy and disoriented, I tried to make my way to the surface. My air was gone and it was hard to focus. I begged God to help me. The water grew darker and I knew I was dying—it was all over. I asked God to forgive me for all my sins. I prayed he would take me to heaven. My body drifted with the currents and everything went black. Then a bright light shone down from above and the water sparkled. Large hands reached down and pulled me upward, out of the water. I choked and opened my eyes. Grandpa was bent over me, pushing on my chest while praying and crying.

"Years later when I asked him about the incident, he smiled and said, 'It was nothing. God told me what to do and I simply did it.' "

"Someday I'd like to meet your grandpa."

"I wish you could, but he died years ago. I was fourteen."

"How did he die?"

"Cancer," Kent said. "He went quickly. It was a shock to everyone. Grandpa was as strong as an ox and never sick. One morning my grandmother took him to the doctor; the next thing we knew they cut him open and found incurable cancer all through his body. I couldn't believe it was true. When I went to the hospital, Grandpa seemed small, propped up in bed reading his Bible. He'd lost weight and his wrinkled skin hung loosely around his face. He looked old and sick. I wanted to run and hide; I wanted to cry and scream and shake my fist at God: 'What have you done? This isn't fair.' But I couldn't do anything, so I just stood and stared across the room with my feet stuck to the floor and my voice caught in my throat. Five or ten minutes passed. Then he saw me.

"A twinkle came to his cloudy eyes and a smile stretched across his face. Grandpa set down his Bible and I came forward. He took my hand and his voice trembled. He told me to love God and follow His word. I promised I would. I told Grandpa I loved him and then he choked. He grabbed my hand and squeezed. His grip was weak and his hand shook. With his free hand, he pointed to his Bible and said it was for me. 'Read it and hide its words deep in your heart. It's . . .' Grandpa's voice faded and his grip loosened. Those were his last words. I wrapped my arms around him and he died."

With their meal finished, the couple paid their bill and left the cafe. The night was clear and the city lights sparkled about them as they walked through town. They stopped at Pioneer Square for a moment, and Heather began to cry.

"Kent, you were so lucky to have a Christian grandfather. I wish I had a godly heritage."

"Godly heritage or not, God still loves you."

"That's easy for you to say. You're good and so were your parents and grandparents. Look at my family! They pray to Satan and worship everything that's detestable to God. How could He love me?"

"He just does," Kent insisted. "His love is unconditional. It doesn't depend on your family. The Bible says that if you draw close to God, He will draw close to you."

"If only I could believe that," Heather paused. "When I was a little girl, my grandfather said sickening things about God. He said I had to curse God, but I didn't want to. He told me I had to choose Satan and if I didn't, I would die. So I said what Grandfather told me to say. God must hate me for that."

"God knows you didn't mean it. Your grandfather forced you to say those words."

"But Kent, I'm still scared. I want to choose God, but I'm afraid the cult will kill me. They used to tell me terrible stories about what happened to those who followed God rather than Satan."

"On the flyleaf of the Bible my grandpa gave me, he wrote: 'Faith paralyzes fear, fear paralyzes faith.' I've thought about those words a lot. It seems to me if you focus on what you're afraid of, it swallows up your faith. But if you hold tightly to your faith in God and who He is, your fears will disappear."

"I wish I had that sort of faith."

"Ask God and He'll help you believe."

Heather took Kent's hand. "Right now?"

"Why not?"

"It just seems awkward to stand here in the middle of the big city praying. Should I bow my head or kneel or what?"

"I just close my eyes and talk, but there's no special method. Just do it any way that feels comfortable to you. God's more concerned with attitude than technique."

The couple sat down on a park bench. Heather closed her eyes, leaned on Kent, and prayed quietly to herself. After a few minutes, she lifted her head and gave him a hug. "Thanks for being so patient. I know it sounds amazing, but I don't feel afraid anymore. There really is hope."

The two laughed and decided to only speak of positive things the rest of the evening. Again Heather wondered if a black Cadillac was following them. The couple walked hand in hand down Broadway, sat beside the downtown fountains, and kissed at midnight under a lamp post.

As Heather watched Kent drive away at the end of the evening, a strange shadow seemed to follow him as his car faded into a menacing fog. Heather sighed and walked cautiously into her home. An ominous feeling came over her as she thought of Kent. Then a tragic and painful premonition overwhelmed her. She began to cry as she walked up the stairs to bed. She slipped out of her clothes and tried to shake the sense of foreboding that besieged her. No matter what she did, the thought would not leave. Deep inside she was haunted by the disturbing rumblings of five simple words: *You'll never see Kent again.*

Chapter 19

Heather gazed at the textured ceiling of her bedroom and smiled. She dismissed last night's strange foreboding as fragile emotions at the end of a long, exhausting day. A light breeze moved through the window and tried to push her out of bed. She ignored it and stretched a long stretch. Heather loved Sunday mornings.

The phone startled her.

"Hello, I hope you were awake."

"Yes, I was just lying here thinking about how wonderful our date was last night."

"I enjoyed it, too." Kent paused. "Something unexpected came up this morning and I can't make it to church. I was looking forward to taking you and Jennifer, but I can't. I'm sorry."

"I understand. I hope it's nothing bad."

"No. It's a previous commitment that slipped my mind. I'm so embarrassed."

"Don't worry about it."

"Thank you, Heather. I'd better run."

That was it. Heather's gaze returned to the ceiling, but the smile was gone. She wanted to call Kent back and ask what was wrong. Why was his voice so strained? Why didn't his words ring true? Heather rolled out of bed, telling herself not to worry. If there was a problem, Kent would have told her.

Two hours later Heather and Jennifer drove into the parking lot of Riverside Community Church. Pastor Freedman welcomed them at the front door with a handshake. Heather felt safe in this building. It was her refuge and hiding place.

"There's Brittany," Jennifer cried as she moved through the crowd.

"I'll see you after church," said Heather. The two children walked hand in hand to their Sunday school class.

Heather searched the entry hall for Carolyn and Dale. After finding them, the three made their way into the sanctuary. Heather sank into a pew and a peace washed over her. Fragments of colored light drew her eyes to the four stained-glass windows, especially the one with Daniel standing in the lions' den. His hands were folded as he looked skyward. The lions surrounded him with their glowing eyes and sharp teeth. They stared at Daniel and snarled, but they couldn't hurt him—their mouths were held shut by the power of heaven.

In the distance, Pastor Freedman stood behind the pulpit and read the scripture for the day. His words floated above the congregation and Heather heard Daniel praying. Her vision grew fuzzy and the light through the painted windows shifted. The colors muted, the face changed, the clothing reshaped. For a brief moment it wasn't Daniel with the lions, but her own pleading face looking heavenward and the prayer was hers.

"Oh, God,
Please listen to me
And come quickly to my rescue;
Be my refuge,
A stronghold to save me . . .
For your name's sake lead and guide me.
Pull me from the snare they carefully set for me.
I place myself totally into Your hands
For you are my strength."

A lion growled at Heather's back, but she kept her eyes focused upward. Quietly repeating the prayer, she felt the power of each word. Oh, she longed to be in God's hands— protected by his strength. The pastor closed his Bible and the service moved forward. Heather lingered in her thoughts a moment before joining the rest of the congregation. They sang several old-fashioned hymns before Pastor Freedman began his sermon on God's loving protection. Heather enjoyed this traditional little church, even if Kent wasn't there. The people were sincere and friendly, but she couldn't help wondering if they even knew they needed protection. The Enemy was out there somewhere, waiting for one false move.

When the service was over, Carolyn turned to Heather and asked about Kent.

"We had a wonderful time last night. At least, I thought we did."

"You don't sound sure."

"Well this morning he called to tell me he couldn't pick me up for church. Maybe he's avoiding me."

"Heather, it's nothing. Kent is very honest and if something is wrong, he'd tell you. I know him well, and he doesn't play games."

"I hope you're right."

She visited with Carolyn for a few more minutes, picked up Jennifer, and drove home. But the closer Heather got to her house, the more nervous she became. Something wasn't right. Her grip tightened on the steering wheel and she considered not going home. But where else could she go?

"Oh, no," Heather sighed as she saw the silver Mercedes parked in front of her house.

"What's wrong, Mommy?" Jennifer asked.

"Oh, I just feel a sudden headache coming on."

Heather's mother met them in the driveway and gave Jennifer a long hug. Then she turned to Heather. "Where were you, Kitty?"

"We went to church."

Her mother frowned.

"Would you like to stay for lunch?"

"No, I just dropped by to let you know I'm setting up a little rendezvous."

"What? What do you mean?"

"James misses you."

"Thanks, but I'm not interested. Besides, I'm dating someone."

"I know, but you never gave James a chance."

"Why are you forcing him on me now? I've been single for over a year."

"Yes, and James is so kind. He wanted you to have at least one year to mourn your loss."

"I don't want to see him."

"I'm sorry, but it's too late."

"You can't control my life," Heather insisted. "James isn't the sort of person I want to spend time with. I don't care if I ever see him again."

"You'll see him again. He's dropping by your house at 3:00 this afternoon. I gave him your address."

"I can't believe you did that." Heather's face was red with anger. "What right do you have to invite him here without my permission?"

"Mothers always have that right," she stated with cold precision. Turning around, she walked toward her Mercedes.

"How can you do this to me?" Heather yelled at her back. But her mother slammed the door to her car and drove leisurely down the street.

During the next few hours Heather's chest tightened and a dull throb formed at the back of her head. She knew James would come and there was nothing she could do to stop it. At ten minutes before 3:00 Heather watched a black Cadillac pull into her driveway. A tall, thin man with raven black hair pulled back into a ponytail climbed out of the freshly waxed car and approached the front door. James looked exactly as she remembered him. He had bushy eyebrows and a dark complexion made even darker by fast-growing whiskers which he had to shave twice a day to look presentable—and looking presentable was important to him. He played with his mustache and adjusted his loose-fitting silk shirt into neatly pressed canvas pants before ringing the doorbell. Heather didn't answer the door immediately. She studied him anxiously from the front window as he quickly polished several specks of dust from his expensive Italian shoes on the back of his pants leg and rang the bell again.

"Hello, Heather. Your mother encouraged me to visit you."

"I know," said Heather, "and I'm afraid you're wasting your time."

"I thought it might be fun to reminisce about old times."

The two stood at the door with the screen between them. Heather felt disgusted. She knew she should invite him in, but she didn't want him in her house. "I apologize for my rudeness, but I have nothing to say to you. In fact, I'd appreciate it if you'd go home and pretend we never met."

"I can't do that," said James. "We've been through a lot together, and we have important things to discuss."

She couldn't believe her ears. What could she possibly have to discuss **with** James? She looked away. "Like what?"

"Your grandfather's wishes."

"He's an evil man and I don't care about his wishes."

"You'd better care. Or you'll soon regret it."

"Is that a threat?" She hated James.

"You need to take your grandfather more seriously."

"He's almost ninety."

"That won't stop him," James said.

"Grandfather is just a man—finite, mortal, fallible, crazy. In a month he'll be back in England and he can't touch me from there."

"Heather, you're being naive. Ipsissimus has followers all over the world."

"I'm not afraid of his followers," Heather winced. "They can't hurt me."

"But he has power beyond what you could ever imagine."

"God is stronger!" Heather sounded more confident than she felt.

"Listen to me," James insisted, "he can call forth real demons. I'm not risking his anger. If he tells me to do something, I have to do it. When you and I were children he determined that we would be mates. You know that. We were chosen for each other. A year before he left for England he made me promise I'd do whatever I could to marry you."

"What happened to love and free will? If you're trying to ask me out, you've blown it. I don't date to please my family. In fact, the opposite is true. If my family wants me to date someone, that's good enough reason for me to stay as far away from that person as possible."

"I guess I hit a nerve," said James. "Let's go for a drive and relax. I just want to talk. What's wrong with that? And for the record, I've thought the world of you ever since we first met. I'd want to date you whether your grandfather suggested it or not."

"I'm sorry, James, but you aren't listening to me. I don't want to go on a drive or anything else with you. What we had was over a long time ago. Now please leave me alone."

"I can't do that," James insisted. "I have orders to spend time with you. And you know what will happen if I disobey. I have to follow you until you, at least, talk to me. I'm stuck, just like you are. They're trying to force us together. You can't get rid of me, so you might as well cooperate."

"Do you promise to leave me alone if I take this one drive with you?"

"You never have to see me again."

Heather didn't believe him, but she knew he wouldn't take

no for an answer. So she settled on a compromise. "Okay. I'll spend one hour with you. No more. If it's one minute longer, I'll call the police."

"Relax, you can trust me."

"We'll see," Heather said. "Let me call someone to watch Jennifer. Why don't you wait in the parlor while I call my neighbor and get ready? It should just take a few minutes."

Heather let James into her house. He sat on the sofa and she went upstairs. She called Carolyn, who said Brittany would love to have Jennifer over for the rest of the afternoon. Then she went into the bathroom to freshen her make-up. Heather stared into the mirror and pounded her fist on the bathroom vanity. "How could Mother do this to me?" She buried her face in her hands and her mind drifted back a year and a half.

The music was too loud and the room was too crowded. Heather could hardly move without bumping into someone. She hated these parties, but her mother had talked her into coming. Chuck was out of town on another business trip and she was bored. Mother grabbed her hand and pulled her from guest to guest, introducing her as "my lonely little daughter."

In front of Heather stood a tall man with a deep tan—the image of suave and sophistication: the proverbial ladies man. "This is James, the master of the Ouija board," her mother said as she wrapped her arms around his waist. "He's also a great dancer."

"Hello, James," Heather said. She couldn't stop staring into his eyes. There was something familiar and hypnotic in his quiet gaze.

"Hi, Kitty," James said.

"How did you know that name?"

"Don't you remember?"

Heather stared at his face. She had seen it before, but she couldn't put it with a time and place. "I'm not sure."

"Years ago my family came to your house every summer

solstice. Your parents always called you Kitty."

"Oh, Jimmy, I'm sorry. It's been a long time. I didn't expect to see you here. How are you doing?"

"I'm keeping busy. You look great. How long has it been?"

"It feels like a hundred years."

"Remember, our parents sent us down to the basement and we played the Ouija board. You were the albino cub."

The two talked and talked. People left, but Heather and James didn't notice. She laughed and he slipped his arm around her waist. They danced and drank champagne and danced some more. He was polite and charming.

During the next few months they grew closer. Every time Chuck was out of town, Heather called James and they'd go dancing or to a movie.

One day an elderly lady, who lived next door, confronted her. "What's going on, Heather?"

Heather blushed. "What are you talking about?"

"Whenever Chuck is gone, you disappear and don't show up until late at night. It looks suspicious."

"What I do with my time is none of your business."

"But how is it affecting Jennifer?"

"My mother watches her when I'm busy. Jennifer is in good hands. I don't see what the problem is."

"Heather, I'm just a snoopy old lady. Why are you so defensive?"

"I'm sorry. I'm feeling overwhelmed lately."

"What has you overwhelmed?"

"I'm not sure we can talk about it."

"If you want to talk, I'll listen."

Heather took a deep breath and told her about James.

"Does Chuck know about him?"

"I don't think so, but he knows something is wrong."

"Heather, is this worth it? You're risking your marriage and everything."

"There's something that draws me to him. It's almost as if it were out of my control. I can't stop thinking about him. James is at the same time both wonderful and frightening."

"What makes him frightening?" the lady asked.

"It's hard to pinpoint. Sometimes when I look at him, I get cold shivers down my spine. It's irrational, but I think there's an evil side to him. Yet, he's so kind and gentle. He's never said a mean word to me."

"There must be something you're picking up."

"Maybe it's because he's into seances and the occult."

The next day James and Heather met at her parents' house.

"James, we've had a lot of fun together, but I don't feel right about this relationship. Thank you for being a gentleman and not pushing me sexually. Yet we've been more physical than we should. It's just not fair to Chuck." She took a deep breath. "What I'm really trying to say is that I don't think we should see each other anymore."

"You can't break us up. We're soulmates. Our relationship is destined for eternity."

"I'm happily married and I'm not about to let anything destroy my relationship with Chuck."

"You don't love Chuck and you never have."

"That's a lie!" Heather yelled.

"If you're so in love with him, why are you spending time with me?"

"I was restless, that's all, but no more. It's over and I never want to see you again."

"Heather, you'll pay for this! Certain arrangements aren't easily broken. I swear you'll pay for this." James marched out of the house, slamming the door behind him.

Heather was relieved. How could she have been so stupid?

Now she was more in love with Chuck than ever before. Their relationship became more romantic—long walks and deep conversations. They even planned a second honeymoon. Life was perfect for three incredible months before the accident. Now it was mixed with grief and guilt: If she hadn't gone out with James, maybe Chuck would still be alive. It was all her fault. Certainly this was her punishment.

Heather felt a combination of shock and devastation. On the evening after Chuck disappeared, she couldn't sleep. Lying in a bed too big for one, her mind raced and her heart ached. Life didn't seem worthwhile anymore. If it hadn't been for Jennifer, she might have rummaged through her medicine cabinet for the perfect mixture of pills to make sleep permanent. The house seemed empty without Chuck and every sound made her jump. Jennifer woke up in the middle of the night, crying for Daddy. Heather held her closely and the two cried together. Heather's tears were hot and uncontrolled. Her sobs reverberated through her whole body. Jennifer cuddled into her mother's arms and slept soundly, but Heather felt alone and abandoned. She longed for someone to hold her . . . comfort her . . . protect her. She felt lost and vulnerable. Her head spun recklessly and she felt she was going crazy. That's when the night pacing began.

Heather refocused on the bathroom mirror and finished her make-up. Her hands trembled. She took two aspirin with a tall glass of water. She shouldn't be doing this. She slipped out of her red sundress. She told James before that she never wanted to see him again and here she was going on a Sunday drive with him. She changed into a casual blouse and jeans. Why didn't she just go downstairs and tell James to forget it? She couldn't answer that question. She laced up a pair of canvas sneakers and went down to meet him.

Ten minutes later Heather and James climbed into his late-model black Cadillac. They drove the freeway up the Columbia Gorge, past Multnomah Falls and the Bridge of the Gods. Heather knew where they were going. A steady wind blew down the gorge and the wind surfers packed the beaches.

East of The Dalles, the black Cadillac crossed the river and continued eastbound on a two-lane highway past outcroppings of lava and wildflowers. Barbed wire separated fields of golden grass and sage brush. Turning off the main road, a sign read: Notice: Closed 10:00 P.M. to 7:00 A.M.

Beyond the sign, perched on a cliff overlooking the Columbia River, stood Stonehenge.

James parked the car and the two walked toward the sacred site. Wind whistled through the giant stones as they entered the outer circle. Something drew Heather toward the altar at the center of this primitive temple. A soft purring began deep in her throat and pictures flashed before her: thirteen Templars in white robes, snakes swallowing each other's tails, four glowing cat eyes, Grandfather looking right through her. Strange chants and incantations lulled her into a trance.

Heather stood before the altar, a silver knife clutched in her hand. Her purring grew louder. Suddenly the altar burst into flames and a hypnotic voice called her name from the center of the fire.

"Heather . . ."

She stared into the heat and was drawn closer. Something moved among the flames, leaping and dancing.

"Kitty . . ."

The trance deepened and she leaned forward. Beads of sweat dripped from her red forehead.

"White cub . . ."

Her lips cracked. The baphomet beckoned her to join the dance.

"Chosen one . . ."

She refused to move. The baphomet hissed.

"You possess the tools. Embrace the cat. Perform the ancient rite. The vigil of Lammas is in twenty-one days. Then you'll be reborn."

The fire surrounded her and she let out a blood-curdling screech. Everything faded.

Early the next morning Heather awoke with a start. Her head throbbed and her throat was raw. Memories of yesterday's trip were foggy and distorted. She remembered nothing after her screech. Jumping out of bed, she checked on Jennifer—everything seemed okay. Heather returned to her bedroom. Sitting on the bed, she placed both hands on her temples and pressed. She didn't feel like herself. What was wrong with her? What had happened last night? When did she get home? Where was she supposed to meet James?

The last question surprised her, but it was the only one she could answer. Her head felt numb. She could hear James say, "Meet me at your parents' house around 10:00 tomorrow morning, and be sure to bring Jennifer."

Heather looked at her clock radio. It read 5:45. During the next three hours she acted without thinking. As the hours passed she fell deeper into a trance. A trance induced by James. A trance Heather was powerless to resist. At 8:45 mother and daughter headed for the car. Taped to the outside of their front door was an envelope addressed to Heather Davis. She opened it.

Dear Heather,

I've become fond of you over the past few weeks, but things are moving too fast. Our time together has been great and you're an incredible woman. However, our backgrounds are so different. I'm not sure how compatible we are. I'm confused and I need some space to sort out my feelings. I'll miss you, but in time you'll see this is best. Hopefully we can be friends. I wish I could explain more.

Sincerely,

Kent

Heather wanted to cry, but her eyes were dry and something inside was dead. She looked at the words again and the letters ran together. Her fingers went limp and the paper fell from her hands. She didn't care. The world turned dark as she took Jennifer's hand and moved slowly, methodically to the car. The letter rustled on the front porch, Heather hesitated and turned around. This didn't sound like Kent. She needed to call him, talk to him, ask him what was wrong. But she couldn't. The program was set: Meet James. There was no other choice, she had to obey.

"What's wrong, Mommy?"

Heather looked at her daughter with vacant eyes. "Nothing," she said. "Nothing at all."

Chapter 20

All the shades were pulled, and a darkness hung over the house. Cars were parked in the driveway and crowded onto both sides of the street.

"Are Grandma and Grandpa having a party?" Jennifer asked.

Heather was silent.

The two walked to the front door and James welcomed them. The inside of the house was black: the lights were off and heavy drapes covered the windows. Jennifer clung to her mother's hand. James locked the door behind them. A single candle burned on the entryway table.

"Did you bring the sorcerer's tools?"

"Yes," Heather said in a monotone. "I brought everything from the buried box. I left them in the car—it's unlocked."

"How about the skeleton key?"

"Here it is." She handed James the key and he disappeared into the shadows for a moment, passing the precious object to an unsavory man in a dark suit. Heather and Jennifer stood in the entryway as the four glowing eyes from the haunted picture watched them. When James returned he slipped her the Gnostic coin, but the key had been removed.

"You still might have need of this."

Heather pocketed the silver piece. "Where are my parents?"

"They're downstairs making final preparations."

"Preparations for what?"

"You'll find out," said James.

"Who else is here?"

"All thirteen and the Ipsissimus. We were waiting for you and Jennifer."

"I'm not feeling well, James." Shaking her head, the trance weakened. Her eyes focused, her mind cleared, and she gripped her daughter's hand tightly. "This wasn't a good idea. We should be getting home." Heather reached for the doorknob.

Stepping between her and the door, James pushed her back. "It's too late," he said. "You're here and the ceremony is about to begin."

"Let us out," Heather demanded and forced her way back to the door.

"Please don't make me be rough with you," James said. He took her arm and pulled her back. She slapped him hard across the face. He slapped her in return and she fell backward to the hardwood floor. Scrambling to her feet, Heather grabbed Jennifer's hand and ran for the door. James took her by the waist, twirled her around, and slammed her into the wall. Her head struck the corner of a bookcase and she collapsed to the ground. Jennifer's cried out and dropped beside her mother's limp body. Heather's eyes opened, but she couldn't move. A white-robed figure put a hand over Jennifer's mouth and carried her up the stairs.

Another of the thirteen dragged Heather to the basement and pushed her into a dark, shadowy room. The only light was from flickering candles. A large woman took off Heather's clothes, placed her in a deep washtub, and scrubbed her thoroughly. Then she pulled Heather's hair back and painted her face black, except for a silver star on her forehead.

Heather started to regain consciousness. "Where's

Jennifer?" She tried to push the woman away, but her movements were weak and in slow motion. The woman forced a bitter tasting potion to Heather's lips. Her head swirled and her body grew numb. The woman pulled Heather from the tub, toweled her off, and dressed her in a white hooded robe.

When all was ready, the woman ushered Heather into the main room. Thirteen people in white hooded robes stared at her. At the head of the room, in a black hooded robe with a silver star hanging around his neck stood Ipsissimus. He was old and gray, but his piercing eyes still held their power. The room was smoky and filled with incense. Each person held a black candle and the shadows from each flame distorted their faces.

"Where's Jennifer?" Heather mumbled. "I have to find her."

Grandfather Vincent held a silver sword and with it he formed a perfect, unbroken circle exactly nine feet in diameter. As he moved, he whispered secret words and spells which sanctified the magic circle. One of the thirteen sprinkled sea salt and sulphur around the perimeter. Another carefully drew three lines around the circle, thus creating Solomon's Triangle. The three gold bars from the buried box were set at the midpoint of each line. At two of the corners bronze dishes with burning oil blazed brightly. At the apex of the triangle was the golden baphomet—the one from the buried box. Heather gasped and shrank back. Its precious stones glittered in the firelight, making it look alive.

The one who had sprinkled the salt stood in front of Heather. Her face was painted black with a silver star on her forehead. She grabbed Heather's left hand and slipped a ring onto the third finger—it fit perfectly. Heather stared at the two intertwining snakes who now tried to strangle her finger. She pulled off the ring and was about to throw it at the baphomet, when a high voice stopped her.

"One false move and Jennifer is dead."

Heather froze. Not only because of the threat, but because she recognized the voice. How could it be? No one could be so evil as to kill her own grandchild. Heather's mother slipped the ring back onto its proper finger.

Someone threw a potion into the fire and flames burst high. The room filled with a horrid odor and Ipsissimus began his summoning.

"Awake, ye powers of hell, thy wandering servants call. Awake, Lucifer, welcome thy followers. Oh, maker of hatred and father of lies, listen to our words."

Two followers, her father on the right and James on the left, led Heather to the center of the circle, where a small altar rested. Neither would look her in the face. She stood before the sacrificial place while the thirteen moved to the perimeter of the circle. She was surrounded.

Grandfather raised his arms. "Monarch of the dead, master of all rebellious spirits, we beg thee to favor us in this conjugation. We make this sacrifice to three, O Prince Beelzebub. May the peace of Satan always be with us."

The followers said, "So mote it be!" three times.

Two white robes brought in a cage with a white kitten inside of it. One of them took the kitten from its cage and placed it on the altar. Heather reached out and petted its soft fur. The kitten purred. Then her mother forced the silver cat-knife into Heather's palm, placing her hand firmly over her daughter's so she couldn't let go. Mother raised Heather's hands over the kitten while Father held it still.

"Oh, dear God, I don't want to do this."

Mother forced her hand down. Heather screamed. It was too late.

Mother cut out the kitten's heart and squeezed the blood into the silver chalice. Father sliced up the heart and put a chunk of it into Heather's mouth. She gagged and tried to spit it out, but someone pushed her to the ground and forced her to swallow. Then Father placed the chalice to his daughter's mouth. She squeezed her lips together. Someone punched her in the stomach; when she cried out, the blood was poured into her mouth.

"This kitten represents you," Mother said as she dropped the animal's broken body into one of the bronze dishes. Its white fur burst into flames and the body burned. The rest of the heart and blood were circulated among the thirteen, each partaking of the unholy communion.

"O Lord of the flies, accept our humble sacrifice," Ipsissimus spoke. "We call thee to this circle by the sacred rites of magick. We invoke and conjure thee by the waters of the everlasting flame. O great dragon and ancient serpent, honor the pact we are about to seal."

The thirteen quoted in unison the incantations etched in the three golden bars: *Palas Aron Azinomas. Bagahi Iaca Bachabe. Xilka, Xilka, Besa, Besa.*

The smoke in the room grew thicker and the shadows on the wall came to life. The snakes around Heather's finger rattled and hissed. Somewhere in the background she heard a cat howl and the baphomet laugh. A putrid smell made her gag and she shivered. Demons swarmed through the crowd. A man near Heather yelled obscenities, another slashed his own arm with the cat-knife. Heather covered her face and whispered, "Jesus please save me."

Mother again forced the silver knife into Heather's hand. "It's time to cut yourself," she said, "and shed some human blood."

Heather stared at the intricate cat-carvings on the knife's handle.

"Now or the child dies!"

The blade drew blood from Heather's right thumb—not just a thin red line, but much more. It didn't hurt. "I'll do anything, just don't hurt my baby." Heather sliced each finger on her right hand and held them up to prove her obedience. The knife fell to the floor.

The circle began to chant.

"Now we shall complete the sacred vow," Mother said, "by dedicating the fourth generation."

Ipsissimus stepped forward, placing his gnarled hands on Heather's shoulders. "Congratulations, Kitty. I have something special for you."

He fumbled in the pocket of his black robe, pulling out a small piece of jewelry. His hand trembled as he forced it into her palm. Looking down, she saw the miniature black pentagram she had thrown into her garbage can. Her stomach tightened as she was mesmerized by the blood red letters in the center of the star. How did Grandfather get this?

"What's wrong, Kitty?" he cackled. "Cat got your tongue?" Turning around he called, "Get me the sacrifice!"

Father and James left the room for a minute, returning with Jennifer dressed in a white robe. A rush of adrenaline pumped through Heather's body and the trance was broken. She yelled, "No!" and started for her daughter. Three of the followers grabbed her, holding her back. She screamed and twisted and clawed, fighting with all her energy.

"Get away from her or I'll kill you!"

Heather bit one in the leg and pushed the others back, upsetting a dish of burning oil onto the carpet. The flames ignited the sulphur and raced around the circle. Mother screamed, "Hurry! Put it out before it hits the gas cans in the corner."

Several people pulled off their robes and beat the burning carpet with them. Others tried to stamp out the fire. In the confusion Heather grabbed the cat-knife and ran to her daughter. Father and James held the girl tightly. Heather flashed the knife and yelled, "Let go of her or I'll use this!"

James reached for the knife and Heather slashed his hand. He let go of Jennifer, but Father pulled her in front of him, using his granddaughter as a shield.

"Daddy, don't make me hurt you."

"Put the knife down," her father said. "We're all family. We love Jennifer just as much as you do. All we want is what's best for her."

"Liar!" Heather screamed as she charged her father, knocking him onto the burning carpet. Father's robe caught fire and Heather pulled her child from his grip.

Suddenly a huge explosion shook the room as the gasoline

cans ignited. Flames and debris flew across the room, leaving bodies strewn over the floor. People were screaming and crying. The circle was in chaos. White robes trampled each other to escape. They blocked the stairs, pushing and yelling at each other. Looking about the smoky room, Heather spotted the window she and Kent had used to escape a week ago. She carried Jennifer across the burning basement and tore the black drapes from the window. "Oh, no!" she cried. It had been boarded up with plywood.

Heather set Jennifer on the floor, pulled over a chair and picked up Grandfather's silver sword. She climbed on the chair and jammed the sword between the window casing and the plywood. She pulled hard; nothing moved. Leaning back, she put all her weight into the effort. The plywood groaned and broke free, as Heather tumbled to the floor. Air rushed in and Heather took a deep breath. She climbed back on the chair and pushed her daughter free from the inferno. Hands gripped Heather's shoulders as she tried to climb out the window and pulled her to the basement floor. She fell on top of a large man, and the two rolled across the burning carpet. He wrapped his hands around her neck and banged her head against the floor. She wrestled and screamed. Pushing, clawing, fighting—anything to escape. In her frantic battle, her hands came upon the silver sword. Swinging it around, she caught her foe on the shoulder. Stunned, he cried out and loosened his grip on her neck. She struggled free, scrambled to her feet, and swung the sword again, hitting him in the face with the dull side of the weapon. He fell back and stumbled to the floor. Heather turned around and ran. She jumped on the chair and squeezed through the window into her parents' backyard. She was free.

Heather rolled in the grass, snuffing out the sparks on her back. She soaked her white robe with the garden hose and washed paint off her face. Jennifer whimpered and Heather wrapped her arms around her.

"Sweetheart, I love you so much. I'd never let anybody hurt you."

Heather held her baby tightly and together they cried. She knew they should run and get as far away from the house as possible, but they were too exhausted. Smoke billowed from the broken window as the two sat on the ground, shaking and catching their breath. Something exploded in the house and a lady screamed. Heather grabbed Jennifer and ran around to the front yard.

"Help, somebody help!" Heather cried.

A man standing across the street yelled, "What's wrong?"

"There's a fire in the basement. Call 911."

The man disappeared into his house and Heather crumpled to the sidewalk. A crowd collected in the street while smoke rose from the burning house. An elderly lady wrapped Heather and Jennifer in a thin blanket.

People, yelling and screaming, banged on the inside of the locked front door. The fire was spreading rapidly. A young man in a blue denim shirt ran to the front door and tried to open it. He slammed his body into the wooden entrance. He pounded and shoved and pushed until the heat drove him back. By now the house was engulfed in flames.

Sirens sounded in the distance and then three fire engines screeched down the street. Firemen hooked hoses to hydrants, sprayed water on the house, and axed down the front door. Five bodies were carried out of the entryway and placed in the yard. Some choked, some didn't move. A fireman called for ambulances and the crowd grew larger. Cars drove by, the occupants peering intently at the excitement.

Heather was stunned and slightly disoriented. All that was important was that she and Jennifer were safe. Paramedics checked her, policemen interviewed her, neighbors stared at her, and the young man in the blue denim shirt offered her a ride home. None of this mattered, in fact she hardly noticed. Amidst the crowded hubbub, mother and daughter sat alone on the curb, a blanket half-covering their once white robes, now splattered with dirt, sweat, soot, and blood. Jennifer sat on her mother's lap and Heather put her arms around her.

"You were so brave, I'm proud of you."

"Mommy, why did they have that scary knife?"

"They aren't very nice people."

"Are Grandpa and Grandma bad?"

"They don't know God. They're sick and confused. Sometimes sick people do bad things."

"I thought they were going to kill you."

Heather pulled her closer. "Nobody's going to kill anybody. It's all over. They can't hurt us now, even if they wanted to."

"Are they all dead?"

"I don't know. I don't think so, but we don't need to worry about them anymore. Mommy will never let them do anything like that to us again."

"I don't like those people. I want them dead. I hope that ugly monster with all the diamonds is dead."

"Let's hope that it melted in the fire."

Leaning back, Jennifer rested on her mother's breast and fell asleep. As the hours passed, the crowd dispersed. Heather was exhausted. She could hardly believe the events of the day. They all seemed like a twisted nightmare. She stared at the house, or at least, where the house had once stood. Ashes, smoke, and a blackened fireplace were all that remained. Heather sat on the sidewalk in shock and clung tightly to Jennifer. She wasn't sure whether she should feel sad or relieved. Either way it was over. Her mother was dead, Grandfather had disappeared, the cult paraphernalia was destroyed and the circle was broken. She was free, but why did it have to end so violently? Why did her mother have to die?

Why?

Tears trickled down her soot-smudged face.

Chapter 21

"Heather, I'm so sorry," Kent said as she opened the front door. "Carolyn just told me about yesterday's fire and your mother's death. How are you doing?"

"I'm still numb. I don't know what I feel."

"How's your father?"

"He's in the hospital with second-degree burns and an irregular heart beat. The doctor says he's lucky. They'll release him sometime next week."

"Is there anything I can do to help?" Kent said. "Can I take you to the hospital to see him?"

"No, I'll be okay. I can handle it by myself. After all, you need your space."

"What are you talking about?"

"You said you needed some space to sort out your feelings."

"Heather, I've never said anything about needing space."

"You certainly did. It was in the letter you taped to my front door."

"What letter? I've never taped a letter to your door."

"It was signed by you."

"But it wasn't from me."

"If you didn't write it, who did?"

"Heather, strange things have been happening the last few days. Early yesterday morning somebody tampered with my car. They removed the spark plugs and cut my brake fluid line. And Saturday night, right after our date, I received a threatening phone call. This guy told me if I ever saw you again, I'd be eliminated. At first, it threw me for a loop. But after I thought about it, it made me angry. Nobody's going to tell me who I can or can't date."

"I bet this has something to do with my parents and James."

"Who's James?"

"An old friend of the family who my grandfather chose for me to marry. My mother was trying to get us back together when, . . ." Heather looked at the floor, tears forming in her eyes, ". . . when the fire . . ." Her body shook as she broke into sobs. Kent embraced her and she buried her face in his shoulder.

"Heather, it wasn't your fault. It was an accident."

"No it wasn't. If I hadn't agreed to meet James at my parents' house, Mother would still be alive. *It was my fault!* I panicked and knocked over the oil. Why didn't Jennifer and I just leave the house without creating a scene? I never meant to hurt anyone."

"What happened? How did you knock over the oil?"

"They were having a ceremony in the basement and there were fires in those bronze dishes we found in the trunk."

"Why were you at this ceremony?"

"I'm not sure. I was in a trance—nothing seemed real. They were trying to get me to give Jennifer to them. I don't remember how I got there or anything."

"It doesn't matter now, the important thing is that you and Jennifer are safe. I'm truly sorry about your mother, but she was trying to harm Jennifer."

"You don't understand. She didn't want to hurt Jennifer,

she was just obeying my grandfather. He made her do it, it wasn't her fault. She was my mother and I loved her. She may have had her problems, but she was the only mother I had."

"Heather, she was trying to hurt Jennifer."

"I know it doesn't make any sense, but I still love her and I always will. I hate what she did and what she believed, but I love her. And I love my father. In fact, I was just going to the hospital. If your offer to take me is still good, I think I'll take you up on it."

Heather's father looked ashen. His eyes were only half open as he stared out the window, whispering, "I tried my best. I hope Vincent isn't angry. Please tell him I'll do everything I can to keep his sacred vow. Kitty didn't mean to run. It's not too late. We still have until the Vigil of Lammas."

The nurse on duty had warned Heather that her father was delirious, but it still shook her. Kent stood beside her as she tried to get her father's attention. She studied his face, running her fingers along his unshaven chin. His eyes were dark and unfocused.

Heather's mind wandered as she gripped his quivering hand. She squeezed it tightly, hoping for some response, but there was none. As a child, Heather always thought he was so strong and powerful. Every summer they drove to Southern Oregon to pan for gold. They'd follow the Redwood Highway down the Illinois Valley to Rough and Ready Creek, then take a dirt road up into the mountains. Each year they'd camp somewhere different and have a wonderful time. Father and daughter were inseparable; both loved the outdoors. They'd hike up dry creek beds, Heather watching for deer and rattlesnakes, while her father looked for gold. They'd walk and talk until Heather said, "Daddy, my legs are tired." Then her father swung his little princess onto his back and the two returned to camp. Even as a teenager, Heather rode her father's back through the manzanita and poison oak. Her father was strong, her weight never slowed him down. Nothing slowed him down—until now. He shifted in his bed, letting out a low, painful groan.

The nurse came in and said, "Your father has had a difficult day. He needs his rest. It would be best if you'd come back this evening."

Heather and Kent left the room. She looked back at the fragile gray-haired man in the bed and wondered where her father had gone.

Two days later, Heather found herself at a Requiem mass for her mother who would've loved it. The music was powerful, and the words were eternal. The cathedral, however, was nearly empty.

"Where is everybody?" Heather asked Uncle George.

"I didn't expect many to come to the church. They'll be at the grave."

Uncle George was right. Hundreds packed the green slopes of Lincoln Memorial cemetery to say their goodbyes to Heather's mother. The afternoon was blue sky and sunshine. Uncle George, Heather, and Kent stood beside the large wooden casket. The crowd drew in closely and everyone's eyes rested on an elderly white-haired man. He moved slowly to the head of the casket. The crowd was silent, but Heather felt their disgust. The old man adjusted his tie and leaned forward on an ornately carved walking stick. Heather stared at the stick—it was Grandfather's stick. The cat's diamond eyes peeked from between the old man's wrinkled fingers. He cleared his throat.

"We have gathered here to pay our final respects to a beautiful woman. Unfortunately, her beloved mate is detained in the hospital. We pray for his recovery, while we mourn her passing. She was an outstanding woman in so many ways—a meticulous teacher, a great leader, a devoted wife, a caring mother . . ."

Heather's head bent and Kent put his arm around her shoulders. Yes, her mother was caring, some of the time. Flashbacks of her mother rocking her frightened little girl to sleep settled upon Heather. Her mother's gentle touch and tender song calmed her. All was safe when Mother tucked Heather into her cozy canopy bed.

Suddenly a contrasting image filled Heather's mind. When she was about seven she crashed her bicycle and skinned her knees. She ran into the house crying, blood dripping down both legs. Mother was mad. "Why can't you be more careful?" She pushed Heather into the bathroom and examined her knees, poking and prodding at them. "Stop the tears," she ordered. It hurt so badly. Heather just wanted her mother to hold her and let her sob. But instead, Mother made her stand straight, while she scrubbed her knees with an old toothbrush until they bled even more. Heather was hysterical. "Mommy, don't hurt me. Please don't hurt me!" She slapped the little girl across the mouth and poured hydrogen peroxide onto her wounds. Once the situation was under control, Mother grounded Heather for crashing her bike.

"She has added to many lives, enriching and challenging us all. She will not be easily forgotten by those who knew her. Dearest lioness, daughter of our grand master, we will always miss you."

In unison each member of the crowd raised a left hand and flashed a hundred silver stars toward the casket. "So mote it be," they repeated three times. Then each one passed before the grave and dropped a black rose on top of the wooden casket. Intently, Heather watched this group of old family friends who shared her parents' perverted beliefs. Then James stood before her in a smartly-tailored suit. He played with his mustache, looked her squarely in the eye, and winked. Heather shuddered. There was a cut over his right eye, a gauze bandage on his hand, and he walked with a limp. She grabbed Kent's arm and held it tightly.

"Let's go home," she whispered to Kent. Then turning to Uncle George, "Would you like to come to my house for dinner? I have so much I'd like to ask you."

"I'd enjoy that," said Uncle George. "Thank you for the invitation."

The three quietly left the graveside service as the coffin slowly lowered into the ground.

That night after dinner, Uncle George and Heather sat in her living room sipping coffee. Uncle George wore his priestly attire: black slacks, black shirt, clerical collar, and black coat. He wore a cheap watch and a simple gold cross. As far back as Heather could remember, this was the only clothing she had ever seen him wear. She stared at his furrowed brow and wondered what he was thinking. He was handsome, though he had a general disregard for his appearance that left him looking somewhat unkempt—tousled hair, a wrinkled jacket, a razor knick on his clean-shaven face, a button missing from his shirt, scuffed shoes.

Heather smiled. She loved her uncle despite his eccentricities. Setting down her coffee cup, she asked, "Who was the elderly gentleman who gave the eulogy for Mother?"

"Even Shakespeare thought the Devil was a gentleman." Uncle George laughed. "This so-called gentleman was a close friend of your grandfather's from Templestowe."

"I expected Grandfather to show up at the funeral or memorial service."

"Your grandfather would never be seen in broad daylight with that many people," Uncle George insisted. "But he might have been there, lurking in the shadows and watching every detail. He'll hang around town for a few more days and then he'll head back to his friends at Templestowe."

"Is that where he lives now?"

"Yes, ever since he moved to England."

"Last week I had a dream about Templestowe. I remembered a trip Grandfather and I took to the evil castle."

"It was evil all right," Uncle George said. "The Templars built it in the eleventh century, but in 1312 King Edward II confiscated it along with the rest of the Templars' properties. Deep in its dungeons all the evil secrets of the Templars were supposedly hidden. The OTO bought the castle in the early

190

1900s and Aliester Crowley was a frequent visitor."

"So this man was a what? A Templar?"

"Yes, and so were most of the people at the grave. They are your grandfather's followers, members of the Silver Star and the OTO. If we hadn't been there, they would've tried to turn the graveside service into a black mass."

"Maybe they just waited until after we left," Heather said. "What exactly is a black mass?"

"It's a ritual to promote evil and glorify Satan. It comes in many forms, even Aliester Crowley wrote one called the Mass of the Phoenix."

"Uncle George, it's so hard to believe that any of this is real."

"I know, but the Bible says we live in a world of spiritual warfare. The forces of good and evil are in constant conflict. There's no neutral ground—ultimately one belongs to either God or Satan."

"I used to think Mother belonged to God, but not anymore," Heather said. "How did Satan get control?"

"Through human invitation and demonic influence."

"I can understand the invitation part, but I still wonder about demons. What do you think?"

"Jesus cast out demons, so they must exist. The Jewish Talmud says there are 7,405,926 demons. Besides, look at everything you've experienced during the past month. Don't tell me you actually doubt their existence or their power?"

"No, I don't," Heather said. "I know they exist."

"Eliphas Levi said, 'When anyone invokes the Devil with intentional ceremonies, the Devil comes and is seen.' "

"Isn't that the artist who drew that horrible picture of the baphomet Grandfather left me?"

"Yes, but Levi was much more. He was a parish priest who became a master magician. He was called 'the last of the magi' and wrote a number of books on ritual magic. He died in 1875, the same year Aliester Crowley was born. In fact, Crowley believed he was the reincarnation of Eliphas Levi."

"Aliester Crowley sounds crazy. I don't understand how anyone could take him seriously. Where did he get all his terrible ideas?"

"In 1903, on his honeymoon in Egypt, Crowley was visited by a spirit named Aiwass. Crowley later claimed this spirit was in reality Satan and Satan had chosen him to usher in a new age—an age of ancient magick."

"So this stuff is ancient. For some reason I thought most of it came from the middle ages."

"No, even Moses warned people against it. He said that anyone who practices witchcraft or sorcery is detestable to God."

"Obviously Grandfather and Crowley ignored the Bible's warning. How did the black mass and pacts with the Devil actually get started?"

"Be careful! Curiosity about evil can quickly turn into an unhealthy obsession. And before you know it, it has you in its clutches."

"Don't worry about that, I'm committed to God now, thanks to Kent. I just want to understand how Grandfather got so wrapped up with a wicked man like Aliester Crowley."

"He wanted power and wealth. People throughout history have dabbled with evil to get what they wanted."

"When I think of black masses, I think of the middle ages. Is that when they became popular?"

"Yes, during the middle ages many dabbled with white and black magic. People had incantations and spells for everything. During the twelfth century there was a manuscript, I think it was called 'Liber Pedition', which gave the names, habitats, and special powers of major demons. Making pacts with devils was common practice at this time. But even today people still dabble. It's all around us; just go to your local library, book shop, or video store."

"I know. I saw something on TV the other day that looked satánic to me."

"Heather, it's everywhere. In 1966 Anton LaVey founded the Church of Satan and in 1969 he wrote the *Satanic Bible*. Six years later Michael Aquino founded the Temple of Set, another cult that worshiped the Devil. Currently there are hundreds of smaller satanic cults, such as the Worldwide Church of Satanic Liberation, the Brotherhood of the Ram, the Illuminati, and the Process Church of the Final Judgment."

"How do you know all this stuff?" said Heather. "You sound like an encyclopedia."

"When I finally realized how deeply your grandfather was into satanic activities, I researched the subject. I hoped to find something I could use to convince him of the dangers of his dabblings, but he wouldn't listen. Later I tried to talk to your mother, but she wouldn't listen either."

"Now she's dead and she'll have to face God with what she's done. And Grandfather won't live forever; sooner or later he's going to have to meet his maker."

"Heather, I hope you know how close you came to being under your family's control."

"I know and I'm thankful all their satanic paraphernalia was destroyed in the fire: the trunk, the entryway picture, the Goya prints, the gold bars, the baphomet, the cat-knife, and even Aliester Crowley's ashes. It's all gone! After I got home Monday night I even destroyed the robes they made us wear. Then we took hot showers, scrubbing away the soot and grime and smell of evil. I'm so glad it's over. Now I can finally have a peaceful night's sleep."

"I hate to tell you this," said Uncle George, "but it's not over yet. I saw James wink at you during the graveside service and your father will be released from the hospital next week. He's committed to fulfilling your grandfather's vow. Besides, as long as your grandfather is alive, this isn't over."

Chapter 22

"Daddy, why do you do the things you do?" Heather held her father's hand as he stared at the ceiling of his hospital room. "You say you love me, but you don't act like it. Do you even know what you're involved in? You don't have to follow in Grandfather's footsteps. You don't have to worry about pleasing Mother. It's all over."

"No," he groaned without moving his glazed stare from the ceiling.

"Mother is dead, the house is burnt, all your evil artifacts are gone. Why don't you give up?" She squeezed his hand, but he didn't respond. "If you really love me, you'll forget your past—the cats, the snakes, the baphomet. You'll start fresh with Jennifer and I. Oh, Daddy, the Bible says, 'Resist the Devil and he will flee from you.' "

Heather bent over him and kissed his forehead. She whispered, "Please, Daddy, I wish and pray you'd resist him. I'd forgive you of all the times you hurt me. Please, Daddy . . ."

Suddenly he swung his arm around Heather's neck. His eyes were wild and his body strong with a supernatural surge of energy. Caught off balance, Heather's arms gave way and she fell face-first onto the bed. Turning her head, she screamed in a piercing hysteria. Father cupped his hand firmly over her mouth and pushed until it hurt. Her cries were muffled.

Without moving his hand, he violently twisted her onto her back, sat on her chest, and held down her arms with the weight of his legs. She shifted and squirmed. He was trying to kill her; she sensed it in his crazed breathing and jagged movements. She swung her knee forcefully into his back, and something popped. She did it again with even more power, and the impact caused him to wince. The pressure on her mouth loosened. She lunged forward and bit into one of his fingers; her teeth sunk deeply into his flesh and locked in place with a singleness of mind. Father howled in pain and beat her face with his free hand until she released his finger. She screamed again a long savage wail. He stuffed the end of the bed sheet into her mouth and spit into her face. "Shut up, you dirty murderer!" From under the mattress he pulled the blackened cat-knife he had retrieved during the fire. He gripped the knife and went for Heather's throat. Forcing an arm free from beneath his leg, she blocked his thrust. The knife sliced across her hand, splattering blood on her face. He pulled back for another thrust just as two orderlies grabbed his arm and knocked the knife from his hand. But he wouldn't give up. He shoved both orderlies to the floor and yelled, "If she won't cooperate, she must die. It was ordained by the vow."

Heather's father lunged forward, clutching her neck and squeezing. He laughed a wicked laugh as he put all his strength into choking her. She coughed and fought to tear his hands from her neck. Both orderlies were back on their feet, trying to pull him away. But his strength was superhuman. She felt herself fading. Gasping for air, she begged him to let go.

"Only if you and Jennifer complete the vow."

"I can't," Heather sputtered. "I won't . . ."

At the far side of the room, she saw Grandfather Vincent standing in the shadows. His eyes twinkled as he folded his arms and smiled.

Her father tightened his grip around her neck and everything went black.

The world looked fuzzy and alien as Heather's eyes slowly opened. Someone stood over her—a shadow. It stroked her right hand with a gentle, worried touch. Her left hand was numb. She tried to move it but couldn't. Looking down, she saw it neatly wrapped in white cotton gauze. Shaking her head, she pulled herself to a sitting position. Dizziness overtook her and she fell back to the pillow of her hospital bed.

She groaned and Kent spoke softly, "It's okay. Take it easy."

Heather groaned again and tried to reorient herself to the room. She blinked several times and rubbed her eyes with her good hand. Looking up she saw Kent. "You look awfully tired."

He laughed. "So do you. How are you feeling?"

"Fine, except for when I try to sit up." She stared at her bandages. "What happened?"

"Your father went crazy," said Kent. "He cut your hand and you had to have twelve stitches. He also choked you until you were unconscious. The hospital placed him in restraints and heavily sedated him. The police were here earlier to ask if you want to press charges."

"No, he's my father. I couldn't do that."

"What got into him?"

"I don't know. It must have been Grandfather Vincent. It's not like Father. The only time he's ever been mean to me was when he was drunk."

"Did that happen very often?"

"More than it should have. Daddy was terrible when he was drinking. When I was little, I'd escape outside to the weeping willow tree. It was another world up there, far away from those who hurt you. I dreamt of knights in shining armor with gentle, loving ways. Then Daddy would call me and all the images would vanish. 'Heather, you stupid little brat. Where are you hiding?'

"His gruff voice scared me. I would hold tightly to the willow tree while my sobs shook its branches. Daddy would hear

197

me and look up. He'd make me come down and then he'd beat me. The more I'd cry, the more he'd beat me. I just wanted him to love me and hold me, but that never happened when he was drinking.

"There were other times when Daddy would drink too much and do things he didn't mean to do. One time he tossed all my clothes out the window and lit them on fire. Another time he locked me in the spare bedroom and forgot me for almost twenty-four hours."

"I'm so sorry," Kent said. "I knew your father was into wicked stuff, but I didn't know he had an abusive streak."

"At times he could be so kind. I was his princess until I was fifteen years old. Before that he'd apologize for hurting me, at least once he was sober. After that he didn't seem to care."

"What happened when you were fifteen?"

Heather bent her head and blushed. "It was my first kiss. I'd gone to school with Andrew since the first grade. We'd dated for almost six months, and he finally kissed me on the front steps of my house. When I went inside my father was standing beside the window staring at me. I could smell alcohol and I knew he was drunk. He called me a little slut and slapped me across the face. My lower lip was swollen and I was crying so hard I couldn't think straight. He told me to never call him Daddy again. He kicked me in the stomach, then walked out the front door. Things were never the . . ."

"Excuse me," interrupted a doctor, who had just stepped into the room. He examined Heather's neck and hand, asking the sort of questions doctors always ask. "Everything looks good," he said. "You can go home now, but I want you to relax during the weekend and I don't want you to drive for the next forty-eight hours." The doctor scribbled something on her chart and set an appointment to check her stitches. After he left, an orderly wheeled Heather to the front of the hospital where she was gingerly eased into Kent's car. The car top was down and the warm wind was refreshing as they sped down the freeway. The breeze pushed her head back and blew through her hair in a reckless sort of way. She closed her eyes and breathed deeply through her nose, blowing the air out with a long soothing sigh.

"This feels so good. Let's drive to the beach."

"What about Jennifer?"

"Oh, yes," Heather said, "she's at the baby-sitter's. I suppose we'd better be responsible and pick her up, but I wish we could escape this crazy city."

"Tonight you need to rest, maybe next week we can escape."

Jennifer was sitting on the sidewalk with a teenage baby-sitter drawing yellow, pink, and blue chalk pictures.

"Mommy, Mommy." The little girl ran to the car and looked at Heather's bandages. "Is that what Grandpa did?"

Heather nodded.

"He's bad. I hate him."

"Jennifer, Grandfather is sick. I don't like what he did, but I don't hate him. Maybe we should pray that God will change his heart."

"No, I hate him. I hate him."

"I know he's done some mean things, but we're both going to be okay."

"Do you promise?"

"I promise."

Jennifer picked up her chalk while Heather paid the baby-sitter. Then they drove home. Heather's hand throbbed and she grew quiet.

"How're you doing?" Kent asked.

"A little shaky, but I'll be fine."

Kent and Jennifer helped her into the house. Heather insisted she could do it herself, but she enjoyed the extra attention.

"Between your hand and the bump on your head, I think you could use some help." Kent eased her onto the sofa. "Now just sit here and relax, I'll take care of everything."

"Aren't you playing basketball with some friends tonight?"

"I was, but I called and canceled."

"You really don't have to."

"I know, but you're more important than basketball. Are you trying to get rid of me?"

Heather laughed. "Not in a million years."

For the rest of the evening Kent waited on her. He fixed a delicious dinner and even tucked Jennifer into bed. Then he sat on the sofa next to Heather, arm around her, and together they watched *An Affair to Remember,* starring Carey Grant and Deborah Kerr.

A couple of hours later, as the final credits rolled, Kent handed Heather a pink envelope. She slit it open with her fingernail and pulled out a card. "I didn't know you wrote poetry."

"Only on special occasions. Remember I was an English major in college. I'm not very good with talking about how I feel, but for some reason it's easier to put it down on paper."

Heather read the poem to herself slowly.

I love you quietly
between moon and morning
as you rest on my shoulder
catching your breath
watching your back
hoping nightmares
won't break into your wide-awake world.

"This is beautiful." Setting down the card, she started to cry—a soft, muffled cry. "I'm sorry . . . I don't know why I'm being this emotional . . . maybe I'm just overly tired."

"Did I do anything wrong?"

"No, just the opposite. Nobody has ever written me poetry, and it's so . . . so perfect."

Chapter 23

It started off as a normal morning, but by 10:00 Heather knew something was wrong. The feeling came slowly and without warning—a subtle, almost non-detectable, scent of danger. It grew stronger as each minute passed.

A dull headache settled over her and her neck muscles tightened. A strangely evil stench burned her nose. The house creaked and she jumped. Somewhere a cat screeched. Heather looked out the window and saw the black Cadillac parked in front of the house. Of course. James was somewhere close. She felt him watching her and waiting for the perfect moment to catch her, terrorize her, frighten her back to the cult. Heather walked Jennifer to Brittany's house so the two children could play together. Then, back in her kitchen, she waited. This was just like James. Eventually Heather grew tired of this cat and mouse game and went out in search of him.

In the backyard, beneath a giant oak tree, she found him. He'd sprouted at least two days' growth of beard and heavy bags drooped below his eyes. He wore the same smartly-tailored suit as at her mother's funeral, but now it was wrinkled and tired, the collar loosened, the diamond cuff-links discarded, the expensive shoes scuffed.

"What are you doing here?" Heather asked.

James didn't move, not even his eyes. It was as if she didn't exist and her question was never asked.

Finally he spoke. "Do you know the mystery of the oak tree?" He didn't pause for an answer, for none was expected. It was as if he spoke to the wind. The reply was his own. "It is sacred to the druids, the keepers of Stonehenge and magicians to the moon. They buried their dead in the hollowed-out trunk of a tree like this." His voice was detached. "They'd gather mistletoe from its branches and burn it in giant bonfires on moonlit nights, calling forth tricksters from the nether world to do their bidding. The ancient druids, like the Templars, consummated their vows and sacrifices at one of their quarter lunar holidays—the next is Lammas." Suddenly James moved and the monotone broke. He stared directly into Heather's eyes. "You've destroyed everything. If you would've only cooperated, the vow would be complete."

"I hate Grandfather's vow. I will never cooperate and neither will Jennifer."

"Heather, I would've done anything for you. Why do you have to be so stubborn? Why do you fight the ways of your family?"

"Because they're wrong!"

"Who are you to say they're wrong?" demanded James. "Life is relative. Maybe you're the one who's wrong."

"Certain things may be relative but not everything. There is a basic morality—a simple right and wrong."

"That's just your opinion."

"No, that's what it says in the Bible."

"So you go to church for a few weeks and think you have the corner on morality."

"I know there are two sides: God's and the Devil's. My family made their decision and I've made mine."

"God has no power," James said. "Just look around and tell me who has the power."

"Jesus came to earth and died to destroy the Devil's plans. By looking at my parents' house, it seems God's gotten a pretty good start."

"God didn't do that, your stupid act of disobedience did. We won't be destroyed. This world belongs to the Devil and he'll have his way."

"You are so deceived, James. No one is greater than God."

"What is this? You talk a little bit about God and that's supposed to shut me up. Well, I'm scared. You fool! You still don't understand what you're up against, do you? You were promised to Satan and he'll never let you go. Remember, Lammas is only fifteen days away."

James walked to the Cadillac, slammed the door, and screeched down the road.

That evening Heather and Jennifer played Candyland. They laughed and giggled, fixed pizza, and made cookies with colorful sprinkles on top. After all the seriousness of the last week, Heather enjoyed the time alone with her daughter. As the sun set, Heather tucked Jennifer into bed and told a story she had told many times before.

"Once upon a time there was a little princess named Hope who lived in a dark kingdom that was under an evil spell. In this kingdom the sun never shone—the world was in constant twilight. Without the sun's warmth, the land was always cold. The people there were bundled up and bitter. They were also cruel, for everybody was controlled by the dark king, even the little princess' parents. Hope was forced to live alone at the top of a tall tower. The dark king kept her captive because he planned to have her marry his wicked son when the moon turned blood red. Each night she prayed that God would save her from the dark kingdom and each night the pink hue of the moon grew darker.

"One morning Hope noticed a cloud of dust on the horizon. As she watched, she saw a shining knight galloping toward the tower on a powerful white stallion, but he was far away. That night Hope was excited until she saw that the moon was very red. Would the knight reach her before the moon turned to blood? She bowed her head and prayed hard for the shining knight.

"The next morning Hope's rescuer was closer, but he was still a full day's journey distant. Suddenly the evil king burst into the tower. 'The time has come,' he said, 'to marry my son. The royal astrologers have calculated that tomorrow night the moon will be blood red.'

"Hope broke into tears as the king slammed the door. As night fell, Hope saw the moon was indeed almost blood. She cried out to God to give the shining knight strength and speed.

"On the third morning, the dark king saw the shining knight headed toward Hope's tower. The king called forth a legion of foot soldiers and had them encircle the tower with swords pointed outward. Each soldier was ordered to lay down his life to keep the shining knight from freeing Hope. The soldiers looked fierce with hate in their eyes as they growled and swung their silver swords through the air.

"That evening the blood-red moon rose and the king's trumpeters sounded the beginning of the royal wedding. A large hall was full of dark people bundled in black robes, shivering. Candles flickered in the wind, casting ghastly shadows about the room. A giant pipe organ rang out the traditional march. Hope entered, gorgeous in a white satin dress with delicate lace and an impressive train. Tears ran down her cheeks. She was sure God had sent the sparkling knight to save her. But now it was too late. The crowd parted as Hope walked through the hall. The wicked son waited with a dirty grin on his twisted face.

"Suddenly the hall was ablaze with light. The crowd cried out and covered their eyes, for they were not used to such brightness. The shining knight on his magnificent stallion rode toward Hope, knocking down the foot soldiers and dispersing the crowd. When the wicked son saw this mighty intruder, he ran from the hall and hid in a nearby forest. The knight leaned down and lifted Hope onto his horse. She wrapped her arms around her champion as they rode toward the exit.

"*'Stop!'* boomed the dark king. 'Those who enter my kingdom shall never leave. Release my son's bride or you shall die!'

"'Hope doesn't belong to you or your son,' said the knight. 'She has prayed for deliverance and God has heard her prayers.'

"*'Surround him!'* commanded the dark king, and foot soldiers encircled the white stallion.

"'You can't stop God,' said the knight to the king. The stallion reared onto its hind legs and galloped through the frightened soldiers.

"*'Shoot them!'* called the king. The royal archers let their arrows fly, but none hit their mark.

"Hope and the shining knight rode out of the dark kingdom and into the light. Once safe, she kissed her hero and thanked him for saving her.

"The shining knight embraced her and said, 'My name is Christian. Will you marry me?' And they lived happily ever after."

Heather looked down at Jennifer who was fast asleep. Her face looked so innocent and angelic. "Oh, God, thank you for this little treasure. Help me to teach her right from wrong and protect her from the Evil One. Amen." Heather tucked a blanket around the sleeping child and kissed her goodnight.

But when Heather turned out her own light and tried to sleep, something wouldn't let her, even though her eyes were tired. The house creaked and groaned. Heather sat up and listened intently. She thought she heard purring in the hallway outside her bedroom. She tried to ignore it, but it wouldn't go away. Sighing, she slipped into her bathrobe and stepped into the dark hallway. Four glowing eyes watched her. Heather gasped and ran back into her room.

"I can't let myself get spooked like this," she whispered to herself. "God is with me. He'll protect me."

Heather pulled a flashlight from her nightstand and went in search of the cat eyes. They blinked in front of Jennifer's room. But when Heather flashed the light in that direction, there was nothing. Slowly, cautiously she stepped forward. Then she froze. The purring had moved to the bottom of the stairs. Heather looked toward the sound and there were the eyes. Again when she pointed the light at them they disappeared. She tiptoed down the stairs, listening and watching. Something creaked in the kitchen, but the room was empty. Then she caught a glimpse of light in the parlor. She followed it and the purring became louder. It was in the far corner. She stared into the dark and two sets of eyes stared back. When she flipped on the overhead light, though, the corner was vacant. She checked each room and found the same thing—nothing.

Finally she went back to her bedroom, degrading herself for an overly-active imagination. Again she tried to sleep, but her body was tight. Frightening images crept into her mind. First came scenes of two cats, a black one and a white one, batting at each other with razor sharp claws. Then snakes, hundreds of them, swallowing each other's tails. Heather squirmed and the pictures faded. But another image, more disturbing than the others, forced its way through—a giant baphomet, laughing and pointing at her. Its eyes were like fiery embers and they stared right through Heather into her soul. She felt naked and vulnerable. She opened her eyes—the satanic creature still hovered over her. The three pictures kaleidoscoped into a blur. As they spun so did her head. She tried to focus on each image, but they collapsed into a blazing fire, sending sparks throughout the room. Heather sat up in bed and rubbed her eyes. Then everything went dark. Lying down, she tried to distract herself by imagining she was basking on a beach in Hawaii, but the sun burned hot—too hot. She had to escape.

Heather's brain raced without direction. Thoughts, pictures, emotions, sensations, and memories whirled through her mind. When she tried to focus, all she could recall were James' last words. And that was the one thing she wished to forget, yet the words kept going through her head: "He'll never let you go. Lammas is only fifteen days away." The words wouldn't stop. They raced faster and faster, turning into a high-pitched whine. Yet, beneath the noise she heard: "*Palas Aron Azinomas. Bagahi Iaca Bachabe. Xilka, Xilka, Besa, Besa.*"

Heather sat up, plugged her ears, and screamed. The noise and words stopped, but before her, just beyond the foot of her bed, four glowing eyes met hers. She threw her pillow at them and they shattered into a thousand reddish-orange sparks. Jumping out of bed, she tried to stomp them out, but there were too many. They grew and burst into flames, catching the pillow and curtains on fire. Heather's mouth was dry; the heat stung her nose. The fire spread quickly, like a match in dry grass driven by a strong wind. She had to protect Jennifer. Running to the bathroom, she grabbed a wet towel and tried to beat the flames back. The blaze surrounded her—crackling, popping, screaming. Memories encircled her—the fire dream, Father's bonfires, her parents' house ablaze, Mother holding a white kitty over flames. Heather dropped the towel, coughing and choking. Smoke pushed her back. She rubbed her burning eyes and the fire disappeared—it had been a hallucination. She looked again in disbelief. It had seemed so real. How could she have made it all up? She must be crazy! Grabbing her pillows, she returned to bed. The smoke faded, but the heat remained hotter than ever.

Heather's body sweated and pressure increased in her temples. A foul-smelling odor filled the room; her skin prickled. Then tension built with a hard-pounding headache. Heather sat up, turned on a lamp beside the bed, and read a few paragraphs in a paperback novel. It was hard to concentrate; she read the same sentence over and over again. She finally tossed her book on the floor, turned off the lamp, and stared at the dark ceiling.

"This is ridiculous," she mumbled to herself as she jumped out of bed. She had to pace. The compulsive back and forth movements were out of her control. She needed more space. She slipped on her bathrobe and moved down to the living room. Her body ached; her muscles tightened. The pacing increased. She wanted to stop. She was exhausted and dreamt of sleep, but she was haunted by strange, unspeakable memories. Her body grew warm, her breathing became shallow, and her heart beat faster.

"God, help me! Oh, God, help me!" The pacing became wild with eyes darting. She wanted to scream. A low purr rumbled in her throat, growing louder until it sounded more like a growl. "Oh, God, help me! Anybody, please help me!" The vibration settled into her chest and surrounded her. A breath of foul air blew into her face. She inhaled and an evil taste filled her mouth. It was inside her. She prayed for it to stop, but it was too late. She was no longer alone.

Heather raced to her bedroom, slamming the door behind her. It was on her heels. The door creaked open and a rush of cold air slapped her face. Frightened and disoriented, she grabbed a pillow and held it before her like a shield. The force, the cat-ghost, the demon was in the corner by the door. Her eyes pierced the darkness and saw a vague shadow moving closer. Her body stiffened and the pillow dropped from her hands. She heard raspy breathing. She squinted to make out its outline but saw no shape. She felt its presence press against her. Shivering, she leaned back and at the same time tried to push away the shadow. Her hands passed through the air meeting no resistance. Heather gasped and fell backward onto the bed. The room swirled and the blackness of the night surrounded her.

She couldn't fight it this time. She screamed and yowled as she felt herself drop into the fire. Sweat beaded on her forehead and flames surrounded her body.

Chapter 24

The next morning Heather awoke feeling dirty. Her bed was disheveled, and her nightgown torn. An ashen face with swollen blood-shot eyes glared at her in the bathroom mirror. She splashed cold water on her face and ran a brush through her tangled hair. An ominous presence lingered in the bedroom. She had to get clean. She turned on the shower as hot as she could stand it, stepped in, and let the heavy steam make her invisible. Water pounded her head and ran down her body. She shampooed her hair three times and then thoroughly soaped every inch of her body. Tears mingled with streams of water as questions flooded her:

Why did Grandfather make his stupid vow?

Why was I born into this family?

Why don't they just leave us alone?

Why? Why? Why?

She stood under the water for half an hour scrubbing her skin raw, trying to remove every bit of the previous night's filth. Finally, she climbed out of the shower and pulled on an over-sized sweater and a pair of jeans. Jennifer was still sleeping. Heather fixed a cup of tea and bowed her head.

"Dear God," she prayed, "please forgive me. I don't want the wicked deeds of my grandfather or parents to influence me, but they already have. Please help me to stop it before it gets worse. I feel as if I'm losing the battle." Heather hesitated, brushing a tear from her eye. She cleared her throat and continued in a shaky voice. "And protect Jennifer from any evil that might come her way. Amen."

As Heather finished her tea, Kent called.

"Heather, you sound terrible."

"That's exactly how I feel."

"Are you sick? Did something happen? What is it?"

"It came back again last night."

"I hope you aren't talking about what I think you are."

"The demon, or whatever it was, that invaded my bedroom two weeks ago."

"Are you okay? I can be there in a minute."

"I'm fine, but I wouldn't mind some company." Heather longed for Kent to hold her.

"I'll be right there."

Jennifer stood in the kitchen with sleep in her eyes and a smile on her face. "Was that Kent?"

"How did you know?" her mother asked.

"'Cuz' it's Sunday and he's going to take us to church."

"Not this morning, Sweetheart. I'm not feeling well."

"So Kent's not coming?" Jennifer's face tightened into a pout.

"He's coming," Heather said, "but not to take us to church."

"If you're sick, you should go to church so God can make you well."

"Who told you that?"

"My Sunday school teacher, Mrs. Jones."

"She sounds like a pretty smart lady."

"Can we please go to church?" Jennifer begged.

"Maybe we should do that, after all. Let's ask Kent when he gets here."

The two sat down to a breakfast of oatmeal, toast, and orange juice. When Kent arrived, he agreed to take Jennifer to Sunday school. Heather was anxious to get away from the house—it felt dark and contaminated. After dropping Jennifer off, they parked the car across the street from the church and Heather told Kent everything about the evil force in her house. When finished, she asked, "What do you think?"

"I wish I'd been there. I don't know what I could have done, but at least you wouldn't have been alone. It sounds like you're in the middle of a spiritual battle."

"That's what it feels like. I hate the pressure and the pacing and the evil presence in the shadows. I'm afraid to spend another night in that house. I'm sure it'll come back." Heather shivered and took a deep breath. "Should I call Uncle George again?"

"What can he do?"

"I don't know. Maybe I'm possessed or my house is haunted. He's a priest. Maybe he could make a deal with God."

"Have you ever asked him if he thinks you're demon possessed?"

"He thinks evil forces are putting pressure on me and trying to get possession. He thinks I'm in danger."

"How far does your uncle live from here?"

"About an hour and a half away. Why?"

"Ask him to come up here. He knows all about your family and I bet he can do something to take care of this problem. Even if he can't help, you have nothing to lose."

"I'll give him a call right after church.

Heather stared at the stone sanctuary and the two giant stained-glass windows facing her. She was glad they were on the left side of the building so she could see her favorite picture: Daniel and the lions. The pipe organ started up, and the congregation burst into song. The ethereal melody tugged at her spirit.

"Let's go into the service," Heather said.

Pastor Freedman had just started his sermon as the two slipped in and sat toward the back of the church.

"Moses was 120 years old and he was about to die. He had lived a full life; he had experienced fear and courage. Now he stood before the children of Israel giving his farewell address and summarizing all he had learned during his long life. The children were about to enter into the Promised Land, but the people of the land—the Hittites, Amorites, Canaanites, Perizzites, Hivites, and Jebusites—were determined to destroy the children.

"Forty years earlier the children of Israel had stood ready to claim the Promised Land, but the people panicked. Their fear was greater than their faith.

"Now Moses wants to reassure them, for God is always stronger than His enemies. If God is on your side, who can stand against you? Moses' words to the Israelites are words for us. For we have things that frighten us and bring panic. At times our fear is greater than our faith. At times we feel little and lonely, and during those times we forget how powerful our God is.

"Moses put it simply. In Deuteronomy 31:6 he said, 'Be strong and courageous. Do not be afraid or terrified because of them, for the Lord your God goes with you; he will never leave you nor forsake you.' "

Heather took Kent's hand. These were the words she needed.

On their way home from church Kent suggested they go to the zoo.

"That sounds wonderful," said Heather, "but could you give us an hour, so I can talk to Uncle George?"

"I'll pick you up at 2:00."

"Perfect."

Heather was relieved to hear Uncle George answer the phone a few moments later. "Uncle George, the cat-ghost came again, but this time it attacked me." Heather went on to explain the events of the previous night. When she finished, she asked, "I'm a Christian, how could this happen?"

"If you belong to God, demons can't take you out of His hands, but they can deceive you. Remember, Satan is the great deceiver."

"How would they try to deceive me?"

"Satan has a deep bag of tricks. He might try to convince you that you have to follow in your grandfather's footsteps, that you have no other choice."

"But I've already chosen to follow God, instead of evil. So why is he still hanging around?"

"He wants to scare you back into the cult."

"Should I be scared of that happening?" Heather asked.

"You should be cautious, but you don't need to be scared. You belong to God and He protects His own."

"But what about last night? Where was God then?"

"He was there. He won't leave you." Uncle George paused. "You know, when you thought about the inscriptions from the three gold bars, fear might have overtaken you at that point and given Satan a foothold. The words themselves don't hold any special power, but if you believe a certain incantation can summon demons, that belief creates a self-fulfilling prophesy."

"Are you saying this is all in my mind, like a hallucination or delusion?"

"No, demons are real and they have power, but it's limited. They can't hurt you unless you take your eyes off God."

"Is that what you think happened last night?"

"I think demons were pressuring you and you panicked. One minute you asked for God's help, the next you asked for anybody's help. As soon as you said that, you opened the door to demons and they entered. Instead of pushing them away, you invited them in."

"How stupid. I didn't know. I didn't mean to open the door."

"You have to be more careful of what you ask. Don't ask help from just anybody. That opens you up to forces you don't want. God is your only true source of help."

"You're right, Uncle George. I can't believe I was so dumb, but what do I do now? How do I get rid of them?"

"Commit yourself to God and resist evil. The only power demons have over Christians is the power we give them. When you're frightened, focus on God. Don't let anything distract you. God, the Father, is our shelter from the storm. God, the Son, is our Good Shepherd. God, the Holy Spirit, is our Comforter. God loves us and once we're in His hands, nobody can steal us away from Him, not even Satan himself."

"That's reassuring. It almost sounds too easy. But I'd do anything to get rid of them. Then once they're gone, all I have to worry about is the cult."

"You won't have to worry about it much longer. Your grandfather is too old to keep the Silver Star going. He'll soon return to Templestowe and die. Without your parents, the cult group will fall apart. The members will probably find some other blasphemous group to join, but at least they won't be bothering you anymore."

"What about James? Grandfather was determined we should marry."

"He's dangerous when he's in a group, but he's just a follower. If he doesn't have somebody telling him what to do, he'll go away and leave you alone."

"I hope you're right. But I won't be able to get rid of my father that easily, and they can't keep him in the hospital forever."

"Your father is going crazy. What he did yesterday proves that. I told you before that ultimately pornography, drugs, and witchcraft lead to insanity. It happened to Goya, the Marque de Sade, Aliester Crowley, your grandfather, and now your father. Tomorrow they'll hold a competency hearing and he'll never be released."

"That's tragic."

"True, but the consequences of evil are tragic. Ultimately evil, in whatever form, leads to destruction. I just didn't think it would happen so quickly."

"Maybe God was trying to protect me."

"In what way?"

"Yesterday James threatened me by saying something bad would happen in fifteen days, on September 1st. He called it Lammas. Have you ever heard of it?"

"Yes, it's a holy day in the Catholic Church. The eve of Lammas has a full moon. It's also one of the four major cult holidays of the lunar calendar. The druids celebrated Lammas with animal and sometimes human sacrifices. They claimed the blood would produce fertility for the following year's crops."

"I'm glad nobody's left to pursue me this Lammas. I keep reminding myself that it's all over, and it feels so reassuring to have you confirm that. The coven is dispersed and all their paraphernalia was destroyed in the fire."

"Are you sure?"

"What do you mean?"

"Are you sure all the paraphernalia was destroyed in the fire?"

"Yes, I was there. The magic circles, the pentagrams, the potions, the gold bars, the baphomet—everything was burned and buried under the ashes. Everything except the cat knife, which the police have, and the Gnostic ring, which I want to give to you as soon as possible."

"Heather, you've forgotten one thing—gold doesn't burn. The gold bars and the baphomet are still out there. They weren't destroyed—maybe damaged a little, but definitely not destroyed. We have to get them before the cult does."

"That's why I called you. I need you to look over my house and make sure I'm safe. This call has been helpful, but if you could actually be here to bless my house or cast out demons or whatever priests do, I'd appreciate it so much."

"I understand," Uncle George said. "I'll drive up tomorrow afternoon after my classes. We can talk about the Gnostic ring, then bless your house and look at what's left of your parents' house."

Heather felt greatly relieved knowing her uncle would be coming the next day. Uncle George's calm academic attitude gave her confidence. She was determined to resist evil. With her uncle's help, what happened last night would never happen again.

Soon Kent arrived and the three headed for the zoo. The afternoon was sunny and most of the animals were relaxing in the shade. Heather coaxed the elephants out with a handful of peanuts. The monkeys swung about their cages, making faces at the spectators. Heather and Jennifer made faces back at them and everybody laughed until their sides ached. The three closed the day with a ride on the zoo train and an ice cream sundae. On the way home, Jennifer fell asleep in the car. Finally Kent and Heather got a chance to finish the morning's conversation.

"I had a great talk with Uncle George and he'll be here tomorrow. I wish I had more faith and courage, like Pastor Freedman talked about in this morning's sermon. But I get scared and sometimes I want to run away from this town. Sometimes I want to get as far away from my father and my house as possible."

"Where would you go?"

"That's what's frightening. My family is cursed and there's no place to hide—there's no escape. How do you run from the Devil?"

"Your uncle seems to have escaped."

"But he's a priest. God gives him special protection."

"Heather, you're a Christian. Don't you think God will give you the same special protection?"

"I hope so. Uncle George is concerned that some of the satanic paraphernalia might not have been totally destroyed in the fire. I told him I still have the Gnostic ring."

"Why do you still have it?"

"Mother slipped it on my finger at the beginning of the ceremony when the house burned. I forgot all about it until the next morning."

"Where is it now?" said Kent.

"In a jewelry box in my bedroom."

"Where in your bedroom is this jewelry box?"

"It's on my dresser by the door . . ." Heather began to shake, "over where the demon stood. Do you think there's a connection?"

"I don't know, but it's an interesting coincidence. I'd encourage you to get rid of it."

"I'll give it to Uncle George tomorrow, but I'm still scared to spend the night alone, ring or no ring."

"Don't worry about it. I can spend the night downstairs on the sofa, if that's okay."

"Thank you, Kent. I'd feel so much safer. My bedroom still makes me nervous, though. Maybe Jennifer and I will bring our sleeping bags down to the living room and we can have a slumber party."

"That sounds fun. Then tomorrow your uncle will hopefully put an end to all this demonic activity, so you can get on with your life—or maybe I should say, we can get on with our lives."

"That would be wonderful, but do you think it's that simple?"

"Tomorrow we'll see. In the meantime, pray like crazy. Make sure you're grounded in God so that Lucifer and all his demons don't even have a chance."

"I'll do it. I'll pray until my voice cracks and my knees hurt, if it will get rid of this terrible nightmare."

Chapter 25

"You horrid little traitor. I hate you. I hate you. I hate you!" The gray-haired man spit out his words. His wild eyes darted about the room, never seeing the sadness in his daughter's face. He squirmed and twisted with frantic jerks, but the four-point restraints, which tied him to his hospital bed, held tightly.

Heather wasn't sure what drew her back to visit her father. She felt sorry for him, but she was also angry. She knew he was just a puppet with Grandfather Vincent pulling the strings. Yet he was the attacker and Heather was the victim. She wanted to look her father in the face without flinching. People had always controlled her and she was tired of that role. Now she wanted to control her own life. No one was ever going to take that away from her again. Somehow facing her father felt like claiming her own power. She looked straight into his eyes.

"You stupid, stubborn brat. I tried so hard to bring you back into the family. You ignored your grandfather's wishes and married an outsider. I adjusted his car and forced him off the road. I killed Chuck and I tried to kill you. But I forgot that a cat has nine lives."

Father's words shocked Heather—not only because of their naked truth, but because she couldn't believe he'd admitted what he'd done. Hearing his confession caused intense pain. Her insides ached. She wanted to scream as her pain grew into anger and then hate. But then the sting melted and a peaceful feeling settled over her. She moved toward her father.

"Daddy, I forgive you. I love you. You didn't know what . . ."

"Shut up, you dirty, rotten gossip," he screamed. "Your mother told you not to talk. I threatened George and Kent. I even cut your phone line, but you still made your cat-calls." He yanked hard against the restraints. When they wouldn't give, he bit and chewed them with savage fury. After a few minutes he relaxed. Saliva foamed at the corners of his mouth and ran down his chin.

Noticing Heather was still there, he continued, "I paid James to follow you. I adjusted Kent's car and forged a note from him. Then I gave James a thousand dollar bonus to bring you and Jennifer to the house. Everything was set, just like Vincent planned. It was perfect, you ungrateful fool. We didn't know which way the cat would jump. We didn't know you'd kill your mother and destroy it all—the vow, the cult, the house, the unholy baphomet. How could you do it?"

"Daddy, I didn't mean to hurt Mother. I'm so sorry. I was trying to protect Jennifer. She was . . ."

"It's too late! I disown you, strike you from my will, cross you from my heart. You are no lion cub of mine!"

Heather walked out of the room, her head bent. He was crazy. Uncle George was right; Father would never pass his competency hearing. She walked up to Kent, who waited for her in the hall, and said, "Let's get out of here before I cry."

Two hours later Heather met with Uncle George and Kent. Uncle George wore his usual black suit with a clerical collar and carried a simple leather satchel. The three sat down in Heather's kitchen, for a cup of coffee. "Thanks for coming, Uncle George. This will help me feel so much safer."

Uncle George crossed himself and prayed, "In the name of the Father, of the Son, and of the Holy Spirit, I sanctify this place and ask protection of the most high God from the Evil One and all his dominions."

"Thank you, Uncle George. I may be paranoid, but I feel like something evil is always following me."

"It could be that you're more aware of the presence of supernatural forces than the rest of us," said Uncle George. Turning to Kent he asked, "What do you think of all this?"

"Heather believes demons are pursuing her. We know you're a servant of God and hope you can chase them away from her and provide protection from future attacks."

"The church has priests who specialize in exorcism and deliverance. I know one such man personally, but he's very busy and . . ."

"Uncle George," Heather interrupted, "Can't you do this?"

"Demonology is dangerous business. The forces of evil are deceptive and powerful. They're not to be taken lightly."

"I'm not treating this lightly. I'm terrified. I wish I'd never heard of demons. It's not my fault that Grandfather made a deal with the Devil."

"Of course it's not. And I'm with you. I wish I'd never heard of demons, either. Let me see what I can do." Uncle George's voice became a whisper. "Have you ever seen a demon?"

"The strange shadows in my bedroom this week had to be demons. I felt their evilness. I'm sure they were demons. How about you?"

"Yes, years ago I saw them surrounding your grandfather. He believed they gave him power, so he gathered them around him. He'd ask them questions and use an Ouija board to get the answers."

"How about my parents? Did you ever see demons around them?"

"I'm not sure. I've seen ominous shadows surrounding them at times. I wouldn't be surprised if your father was demon possessed. He probably sent the shadow in your bedroom."

"That's what I'm afraid of, but didn't want to admit."

"What we want to know," Kent spoke up, "is how to deal with these satanic attacks."

"We have to confront the demons," Uncle George said.

Heather wrung her hands. "I'm afraid. Is there any other way besides confronting them?"

"This is a spiritual battle. You can't run away from them, but you can defeat them."

"How?"

"By confronting them directly."

"But I can't do that. If I confront the demons, they'll get me for sure. The cult said the demons own me because of Grandfather's vow."

"What else did they tell you?"

"That God hates me because my family joined with the Devil."

"That's a lie, Heather. You're forgiven, you're free. Demons have no authority over you anymore."

"But what about the other night?"

"Who's stronger, God or Satan?"

"God, of course."

"Then why are you so afraid? We have the power of Jesus Christ to chase them away; all we have to do is appropriate it. Do you want to do this?"

"Yes." Heather grabbed her uncle's arm and stared into his eyes. "I believe God can do this, I really do. I just get nervous. But God is with me. I know he'll help me confront the demons."

Uncle George walked behind her chair. "Just relax and focus on something good and positive like a beautiful sunset or a special song. I've always thought you were a survivor. I knew sooner or later you'd be free." Uncle George crossed himself and placed his hands on her shoulders. "In the blessed name of the Father, of the Son, and of the Holy Spirit, I command all demons to leave. Now!"

Coldness ran up Heather's back. Terrible pictures of distorted, twisted faces with bulging eyes and flared nostrils flashed through her mind; she tried to push them away. She wanted to pace, but her uncle's hands held her down. She squeezed her eyes shut and bit her lower lip. A noise rumbled in her chest, but she couldn't determine whether it was a purr or a muffled scream.

The room darkened and filled with an overwhelming evil. Heather heard shrieks and gnashing of teeth. Giant black wings beat violently all around her. Suddenly a shadow touched her and its iron hands clasped around her neck, tightening and suffocating. Stale air filled her nostrils as darkness swallowed her. Down she fell—fast and reckless—through a vortex toward insanity . . . toward the black cat, the ancient serpent, the wicked baphomet . . . toward that place of hopeless weeping called Tartarus, Gehenna, Sheol, Hades. Heather gasped for breath. She coughed and sputtered. Her heart pounded so hard she was sure it would burst. For an instant she felt lost, but the voice of Uncle George reached out to her.

"In the blood of Jesus Christ," he boomed, "bind these demons and the one who sent them."

Everything went silent. The evil disappeared and she could see again. The demon was gone. Gentle hands caught her and cradled her, pulling her upward, freeing her from darkness, and carrying her to safety. They were God's hands—strong and tender. Heather breathed deeply and let out a long sigh. She sank into the chair exhausted. She'd made it. She was ecstatic. *She'd made it!*

She jumped out of the chair and hugged Kent. But then she froze. Shadows were returning. She tried to scream, but her voice was mute. Invisible hands tightened around her neck, and this time there wasn't just one pair. It felt like five or ten or maybe more. She choked and clawed at her throat. Suddenly her ears perked as someone laughed a wicked laugh. It was Grandfather Vincent. Heather stared at Uncle George. He hadn't heard it. She wanted to run. Somewhere in the distance, she heard Kent's voice.

"What's happening?"

"He's sending more," Heather said.

"Who is?"

"Help me, please help me!" she screamed as the Abyss began to swallow her once more.

"Almighty God . . ."

"You can't make us go. You can't," came an eerie voice from around Heather.

Uncle George ignored it. "Drive these demons from Heather so they never return. Protect her from her grand-father's wicked ways, in the name of the Father, of the Son, and of the Holy Spirit." He crossed himself again.

Heather's body shook and invisible fingers loosened from her neck. A long hollow shriek cut the air—loud and angry—but soon fading to an impotent whimper. She was free, and this time it was real.

Uncle George grabbed her hand and prayed, "Dear Father, fill this child with your eternal peace and power. Never allow evil to touch her. Keep her in the palm of your hand. Amen."

Heather was exhausted. Tears lined her cheek. "Uncle George . . . I don't know what to say . . . thank you . . . I'm sorry . . ."

Uncle George put his arms around her and she broke down, sobbing uncontrollably for several minutes. As her emotions ebbed, the priest wiped her tears and she kissed his cheek. Heather knew their bond was now greater than blood; it was rooted in a common belief that God can do all things.

Heather breathed deeply and sighed. "Uncle George, do you think they'll come back? If they do, I don't have to do what they say, right?"

"Right. You can command them to be quiet and leave by the power of Jesus."

"Are you positive they will?"

"Positive. The only way they'll come back is if you invite them."

"How would that happen?"

"By rejecting God or by dabbling in the occult or by having a cursed item."

"A cursed item? What do you mean?"

"A symbol of evil that the cult uses in their ceremonies."

"Like the Gnostic ring I mentioned to you yesterday?"

"Where is it?"

"Upstairs in my bedroom. How can I get rid of it without being attacked?"

"Remember who has ultimate authority."

"God does. But I'm still too scared to go into my bedroom."

"Maybe your uncle can get the ring and pray over your bedroom, while he's at it," Kent suggested.

"Good idea," Uncle George said. "Nothing would make me happier than to see this family curse end."

Uncle George slowly walked up the stairs, while Heather and Kent followed several feet behind. Cautiously entering Heather's bedroom, Uncle George crossed himself, and said, "In the name of the Father, of the Son, and of the Holy Spirit, I sanctify this place and ask protection of the Most High God from the Evil One and all his dominions."

Suddenly a rush of cold air pushed him back. Evil emanated from the room. Uncle George whispered a short prayer for courage. An ugly smell filled the room. Heather and Kent stood in the hallway and watched Uncle George place a handkerchief over his nose and glance about the room for Heather's jewelry box. It was small and made of teak; the box sat alone on her dresser—open. He reached for it and it slammed shut. Uncle George jumped back, white and breathing hard.

"Get behind me, Satan!" he said. Uncle George tried to open it, but it wouldn't budge. He gripped the box with both hands, trying to break the seal, but it was too strong. He pounded it on the dresser; it still wouldn't open. Reaching into his pocket, he pulled out a small knife and pried it open. With calm determination he fumbled through the box until he found the Gnostic ring. He dropped it into his pocket and turned to leave. The bedroom door slammed shut, blocking his way out. Heather and Kent jumped back almost tripping over each other. Heather heard Uncle George pounding on the other side of the door.

Kent grabbed the doorknob and pulled, but the door was stuck. "God help me." Placing both hands on the knob, Kent jerked hard several times until the door gave way.

Uncle George burst out, shaken and intense. "Let's get out of here." He raced down the stairs with Heather and Kent at his heels. "Come with me," he called. "we have work to finish."

"Where are we going?" Heather asked as they followed Uncle George out the front door.

"To your parents' house. We have to see if any of the cult items survived the fire."

"I don't want anything to do with those things," said Heather.

"If we don't find them, the cult will and they'll use them in their ceremonies. They're just pieces of metal, but they're symbols of evil, too. We have to find anything that's left in the rubble and destroy it."

Kent grabbed shovels and a pick from Heather's garage and the three climbed into Uncle George's light blue sedan. Soon they were sorting through the rubble of the burned-down house. Heather located the spot in the basement where the ceremony took place. Kent moved a number of charred beams and Uncle George dug into the ashes. It took three sweat-filled hours to hit the basement floor. Kent found a beat-up bronze dish—it was unusable, so they left it and searched for other items. Finally Uncle George found the first of the gold bars. By pacing off the triangle, they uncovered the remaining two. Heather carried the bars to the front yard and set the sooty gold on the trampled grass. Uncle George wiped them off with an old rag and the gold shone brightly. Heather stared at each bar. Something looked different—the evil words were gone. What happened to them? Maybe they were scratched out or melted away by the fire. Heather didn't care. She was just glad they had disappeared.

"Let's get back to the basement and see what else we can find," said Uncle George.

Two glowing eyes peered from the black debris. The great horned goat watched Heather dig through the charcoal and rubble. It was badly damaged—a large beam had fallen on its head. Heather moved closer to the golden idol; its horns were broken off and several of its gems had fallen out, leaving gaping wounds. Heather's shovel hit metal and she cleared away the ashes from around the baphomet. It was dirty and misshapen but no longer frightening. Heather picked up the twelve-inch-tall image, carried it from the debris, and set it in the front yard beside the gold bars. It looked pathetic. She pried out the remaining jewels and studied its half-melted wings.

Uncle George found a sledgehammer in the tool shed behind the devastated house and handed it to Heather. She raised the heavy instrument over her head and drove it down onto the satanic image, smashing it into a flattened lump of sooty metal.

Uncle George placed the loose jewels, the three gold bars, and the flattened baphomet into an old burlap bag. He then reached into his pocket and threw in the Gnostic ring. Tossing the bag in the trunk of his car, he said, "Let's get rid of this wickedness once and for all."

The threesome drove to the Bridge of the Gods, where Heather had tossed the Ouija board three weeks earlier. They wanted to take these items as far away as possible. They parked the car on the Oregon side of the bridge and walked to the center of the span. Kent handed the bag to Heather. "You may have the honor."

The wind rustled through the trees and the sun glistened on the water. Heather took the bag, swung it over the pedestrian rail, and let loose. It fell quickly, hitting the waves with a restrained splash, and was gone. The water swallowed the bag instantly. As the brown burlap disappeared, so did Heather's fears. In the darkness of the muddy silt, at the floor of the Columbia, the bag and its demonic contents would rest. Heather was ecstatic. She hugged Uncle George, thanking him for everything he'd done. Then she hugged Kent and kissed him passionately on the lips. He picked her up, whirled her around and said, "I love you. I really love you."

"Are you sure?" she said. "Even after all the hell I've put you through?"

"Nothing that's happened in the past three weeks changes how much I care about you."

Heather kissed him again. Tears sparkled on her cheeks. "You're just too good to be true."

Chapter 26

The three returned to the car. Uncle George led the way while Kent and Heather followed hand in hand. Looking back at them he said, "I hate to rush us, but I'd like to get back to the rectory for vespers. I'll drop the two of you off at Heather's place and be on my way."

"Are you sure you can't stay awhile?" Heather asked as they climbed into the car. "We can go to my house and unwind."

"No, thanks. You kids need some time alone. An old priest would just be in the way."

"Uncle George, I bet under that calm, cool exterior you're a real romantic. Mother said when you first entered the priesthood every eligible woman in the parish had her eye on you, along with a few who weren't so eligible."

"I don't know, I never noticed. Academics always had my attention. Well, almost always."

"You mean you've never been in love?"

"Priests are married to the church."

"But priests are human. There must have been at least one love along the way."

"Maybe one—a long time ago."

"Please tell us about it."

"Her name was Maggie. She was tall and thin with the most beautiful red hair I'd ever seen—thick and wild and hanging halfway down her back. I was twenty-two and had just entered the priesthood. She was eighteen and lived a mile or so down the hill from the rectory complex. I often made excuses to pass by her house, hoping to bump into her. Whenever we met we talked politely of God and the Church. She was an avid reader and frequently borrowed books from me and we'd later discuss them. It was an emotional time in my life, and the only time I've regretted my vows. We fell in love, but I was a priest and she respected my calling. Two years later she married a stock broker and moved to San Francisco. We still exchange Christmas cards and she calls whenever she's in town. Sometimes I wonder what might have been, but . . ." He ran his fingers through his hair and for a moment seemed lost in pleasant memories. "But I'm a priest. That's where God has called me to serve and that's where I serve."

Uncle George parked in Heather's driveway and they all said goodbye. Kent decided to go home to shower and change clothes. Heather went next door to pick up Jennifer.

She watched for a moment as Jennifer and Brittany played in the living room with their dolls—feeding them, rocking them, lecturing them when they misbehaved. They had built a blanket fort between the sofa and coffee table, and had furnished it with pillow beds, laundry baskets, and a badly crumpled cardboard box. The two girls finally settled down beneath the blanket to read a picture book by flashlight to their dolls. Heather hated to break up the party.

"Jennifer, it's time to go home."

"Oh, hi Mommy. Can't I please stay a little longer? We have to put our babies to bed."

"No, we need to go home and eat dinner."

At home, Heather fixed Jennifer a dinner of peanut-butter sandwich, apple slices, and milk while Jennifer relayed the highlights of her day. Heather left Jennifer in the kitchen eating her dinner and went upstairs to get ready for Kent's return. She stepped into the shower and quickly soaped herself. She looked forward to the evening alone with Kent and thought about what to wear. As she toweled off she decided on the gauze turquoise-print skirt and white silk blouse. Standing before the bathroom mirror, she pulled her hair back and carefully did her make-up. She slipped into light-brown sandals and added the finishing touches—a breath mint, perfume, silver earrings, an ankle bracelet, and a double-check in the mirror. Everything was in place.

She peeked into Jennifer's room. Jennifer was asleep on the bed, fully dressed with a book clutched in her hand. Heather removed her daughter's shoes, covered her with a light blanket, kissed her cheek, and tip-toed out.

When the doorbell rang a moment later, Heather rushed to answer it. Kent was right on time. His face was freshly scrubbed, his hair combed, and his clothes crisp. Heather wondered if he did his own laundry. He wore a chambray shirt with sleeves rolled up to just above the elbows, Levi's, a thick leather belt, and the cowhide boots she had given him last week. In one hand was a bag of Chinese food, in the other a simple bouquet of three red roses.

"Oh, they're beautiful. Thank you." Heather took Kent's free hand and led him inside. "And thanks for bringing dinner." She placed the bag on the kitchen table and the flowers in a vase. "Would you like to eat now or sit on the back porch for a while?"

"Let's sit outside; we can eat later."

It was still hot and humid with a slight breeze. Sitting on the back porch, they drank Diet Cokes from ice-filled glasses. They were quiet, lost in private thoughts, and comfortable in each other's company. Heather felt contented, strangely contented. The yard was framed by a newly-painted white picket fence. A giant oak tree sheltered half the yard and an old wooden swing hung from one of its lower branches. The yard was mostly grass, the smell of its recent mowing permeated the air. The last rays of sunset shone through the oak and splashed the sky orange with a touch of purple. The sun disappeared, but the colors lingered. Heather watched Kent soak in the final light: his skin glowed and his hair took on the sun's golden hue. Heather was transfixed, and an old-fashioned word came to her—winsome. Kent was winsome. She moved closer to him and night settled on the back porch.

She reached out her hand and rested it on his shoulder. "What about dinner?"

"I'm ready," he said.

Within a few minutes they were sitting face to face across the table eating Chinese food out of white cartons by candle-light. Crickets chirped in the background and a large moth tried to force its way through the screen door. They spoke in whispers of feelings and dreams. She loved to listen to him; a certain quality in his voice exuded softness and confidence. Heather asked questions just to watch his face and listen to that voice.

"What sort of hobbies do you have?"

"I like basketball . . . and reading, especially literature such as Hawthorne, Dickens, and Fitzgerald. I like hiking and working out. Then there's writing. I'm not very good at it, but I enjoy trying to capture a thought or feeling with the perfect phrase."

"Have you written any more poetry lately?"

"As a matter of fact, I have. Today when I went home to shower I put together a poem, but I haven't written it down yet."

"Do you remember it? Can you quote it?"

"I think I remember it. But I'll recite it only if you keep in mind it's still rough, okay?"

"Okay."

"Let's see. It goes something like . . .

"Thank God for the stormy clouds,
And thank Him for the sun.
Thank Him for the stars above
When each crazy day is done.

"Thank God for His shelter
When those stars break loose and fall.
Thank Him for His sword and shield
When the demons come to call.

"Thank God for this lady,
Who's slipped into my heart;
Earnestly, I ask of Thee,
That we'll never be apart."

"Kent, that's beautiful," Heather said. "I wouldn't change one word. It's like a prayer. I like it just the way it is. May I have a copy?"

"Sure, as soon as I write it down."

Heather took Kent's hand, weaving her fingers into his. He squeezed gently, pulled her out of her chair, and led her into the living room. She turned on the radio to a slow country song and they met in the middle of the room. Hand in hand, cheek to cheek, he led her around the hardwood floors, in and out of the shadows. The songs changed and the wax dripped down the candlesticks. Gazing into Kent's blue eyes, she rested her arms around his neck and ran her fingers through the hair at the back of his head. He placed his arms around her waist; he was strong, yet gentle. Heather closed her eyes and buried her face in his shoulder. Her perfume mingled with his aftershave as they danced on and on.

"This is perfect," Heather whispered. "I wish it could last forever."

"It could."

"If only you were right."

"All you need to do is marry me."

"Don't play with me." Heather pulled away from Kent. "Nobody would want to marry someone who's gone through everything I have."

"Heather, would you be my wife?"

"I mean it. Don't talk about marriage unless you're serious."

"I wouldn't propose unless I meant it," Kent insisted. "I love you and would like to spend the rest of my life with you."

"But my family. Why would you want to marry into a family like mine?"

"I want to marry you, not your family. Besides you're a new person. You're free from your family and you've renounced their demons. You're sweet and kind and beautiful and the best little dancer I've ever met."

Heather laughed. "Are you sure you want me?"

"I'm positive. And Jennifer, too. How can I prove that I love you? Tell me and I'll do it."

"Just hold me," she said softly.

He wrapped his arms around her and pulled her to him. She sighed and whispered to herself, "This is too good to be true. It must be a dream." Kent gently pinched her arm and they both laughed. So the evening passed—touching, dancing, whispering, laughing—until the candles on the kitchen table flickered out.

The night was late, but neither wanted to say goodbye. They moved to the front porch where they stood under the light in a final embrace, not wanting to let go for fear the perfection of the evening might somehow be shattered.

"Tomorrow," Kent said, "I'll see you tomorrow." He kissed her lightly and strolled toward his car.

"Thank you," she called after him. "Thank you for everything."

He turned, smiled a deep I'm-madly-in-love-with-you smile, climbed into his car, and left. Heather stood motionless on the porch, happier than she'd ever been in her life, and watched the glowing tail lights of Kent's car fade into the distance.

Chapter 27

Early the next morning the phone rang.

"Hello this is Dr. Spires at Eastside Hospital. Is this Heather Davis?"

"Yes."

"We were trying to contact your brother. Would you know how we could find him?"

"I don't have a brother," Heather said.

"Our records indicate that your brother took your father out on a two hour pass yesterday, but they never returned."

"I thought there was to be a commitment hearing yesterday."

"It was rescheduled for this afternoon," said Dr. Spires, "but he's missing. A man by the name of James told the nursing staff he was the patient's son and that he was taking your father out for a walk. He showed up at a change of shifts and was somehow able to get a pass. He should've never been allowed off the ward."

"James isn't my brother; I'm an only child. I know James, the man you're talking about. He's an impostor."

"Oh, my," Dr. Spires said. "I apologize for this inconvenience. Have you seen your father at any time during the past eighteen hours?"

"No. Am I in any danger?"

"We've reported his disappearance to the Portland police. If you hear from your father, please notify us immediately. I'm sure we'll have him back on the ward in no time. I'm sorry for interrupting your day."

Heather hung up the phone. What was James up to? What was he doing with her father? Where did they go? The more she thought about it, the more she thought she knew where her father might be. Maybe it was simply intuition, but she was sure he was either at his burnt house or Stonehenge. Heather called Kent and told him about her phone conversation with Dr. Spires. "I'll be right there," Kent said. "We can go to your parents' house and check it out. If your father isn't there, we'll drive to Stonehenge."

Heather agreed and an hour later, the two approached the ruins of the old house.

"There he is." Heather pointed to the black debris.

In the middle of the burned-out basement was a cloud of dirt. Crouched in the center of the cloud was a solitary figure with disheveled hair and striped pajamas. What was he doing? And where was James?

Kent and Heather cautiously walked across the front yard. Her father sat in the ashes, half buried by soot. James was nowhere to be found, but Heather saw someone in the shadows of a nearby Fotenia hedge—someone big and old, dressed in a black robe. She blinked and he was gone. Maybe he'd never been there. Heather found it difficult to look at her father. Black smudges covered his face and bed clothes. There was a crazed look in his eyes, as he knelt in the dirt and frantically dug through the debris, throwing dust into the air and babbling. Heather stared at this strange scene in disbelief. Tears filled her eyes. "What's wrong with him?" she asked, not expecting an answer. Absorbed in his search, her father was unaware he was being watched. Drawn by his odd behavior, the couple slowly moved forward and tried to hear what he was saying.

"I must obey Vincent. Vincent loves his vow. The white cub must keep the vow. The vow to the baphomet. The baphomet hides in the ashes." He threw a handful of soot into the air and grabbed at it as it rained down on him. Saliva drooled from the corners of his mouth as he broke into excited singing: "Ring around the rosies, pocket full of posies, ashes, ashes . . ."

He laughed wickedly and continued his babbling. "The knights are dust. Ipsissimus is ashes. I must find his ashes. I must find the baphomet. I must find my insanity." Again he threw soot into the air and broke into song. "Ashes, ashes, we all fall down."

Then he returned to his digging with renewed vigor; his fingers were bleeding and his hands were red.

Heather's stomach turned and her eyes stung. It was too much for her to deal with. She took Kent's arm and they moved a few feet away. "I'm sorry you had to see him this way," Kent said.

"It's hard for me to even believe that's my father," Heather said. "I wish I'd never seen him like this. Now the image of him sitting in the ashes is embedded in my mind. I'll never be able to forget it. I wish there was something I could do . . ."

Suddenly Heather's ears perked and she whirled around; her muscles tensed as she scanned the Fotenia hedge. Kent started to say something, but she quickly quieted him.

"Listen!" she whispered

Faintly, from deep in the hedge, came a strange eerie voice. "Faster, dig faster."

Heather motioned Kent to move down the sidewalk. They hid behind a neighbor's car, watching and listening. It was Grandfather Vincent.

"What should we do?" Heather asked.

"Do you want to confront your grandfather?"

"No, it wouldn't do any good."

"Then let's just ignore him," Kent said. "But we need to

call the police so they can get your father to his commitment hearing this afternoon."

"I know, but I wish we could do more. I wish . . ." Her chin quivered and she buried her face in Kent's shoulder.

The couple climbed into Kent's car, drove to the nearest phone booth, and made their call. Fifteen minutes later, the police transported Heather's father back to the hospital.

The following evening Kent and Heather went to a romantic movie. Afterward they ate chocolate cheesecake at a quaint little cafe where the waiters sang love songs by candlelight. About 10:00 P.M. a thunderstorm broke. Kent and Heather raced through the rain to her house. The sky was gloomy as lightning zigzagged to the earth and thunder rumbled. Heather toweled her hair dry, while Kent lit the logs in the fireplace. The two huddled around the crackling heat and glowed in each other's company.

Kent held Heather closely. "The only thing that could make this evening better is if you'd slip this on your finger." Kent handed her a simple diamond solitaire; it was clear and flawless and fit her perfectly.

Heather threw her arms around him. "I love you," she cried. "I love you more than I ever thought possible."

"If you'd like to exchange it for something else, I wouldn't be offended."

"No, I want this one!" She hugged Kent again. "This is exactly what I want."

During the next few weeks Kent and Heather spent nearly every day together; sometimes with Jennifer and sometimes alone. They hiked, attended a concert, rollerbladed, went to dinner, played tennis, saw a movie, and visited Kent's parents on several occasions. Yet most of their time was spent in conversation talking of everything imaginable: their hopes and fears, their beliefs and opinions. They didn't always agree, but they decided that didn't matter. What they did have in common was a mature love for each other and an old-fashioned faith that could overcome any obstacle.

On August 31st, Heather awoke with a start. It was just before dawn and the house was silent. Her body was tense and her palms wet. Something was wrong. She jumped out of bed and checked Jennifer. The little girl slept peacefully with her dolly snuggled close.

Heather breathed freely. "Everything's fine," she said to herself. "I don't know why I'm still nervous."

She walked down the stairs to the kitchen and fixed a cup of coffee. Sitting at the breakfast table, she watched the first rays catch the hills on fire. Then she opened the front door to get the morning paper. No, it couldn't be.

Driven deeply into the wood of her front door was the cat knife. Its golden handle gleamed in the dawn. Its blade pinned a parchment note to the door: *Today is the eve of Lammas. BEWARE!*

Her body shook uncontrollably. "Oh, God, protect us." She slammed the door and double locked it, then broke down and wept. Her head swirled. Images of Templestowe, Stonehenge, and the caves of the Yucatan flooded her brain. Red hands and Grandfather's 1929 vow followed. Demons in her bedroom . . . black cats . . . coiling snakes . . . the baphomet . . . the fire at her parents' house: all this and more sent her reeling. Was she going crazy? "I don't need to be afraid," she said to herself. "God is stronger than the cult." She picked up the phone and called Kent. He listened to her, told her to call the police, and promised he'd be there immediately. After she hung up, Heather called the police.

A few minutes later, two officers were at her door. They looked around the premises and asked a lot of questions. Heather asked a few of her own.

"I thought the police had this knife in their possession," she asked.

"We did, but it was reported missing from the evidence room three days ago," one of the officers said.

"How is that possible?"

" I don't know."

"How can you simply not know? Wasn't it locked up or something?"

"It appears it was stolen."

"So somebody broke into the police station and stole the knife," Heather said. "That gives me a lot of confidence in the police department."

"I probably shouldn't be saying anything," the officer whispered, "but it's impossible to break into the station."

"So what are you saying?"

"I'm saying it had to be an inside job. That's the only logical explanation. The police chief has called for an internal investigation and hopefully we'll have some solid information in a week or two."

"A week or two? That does me a lot of good. I'm worried about tonight."

Heather was shocked. The cult must have infiltrated the police department. How could that happen? If she couldn't trust the police, who could she trust? Heather decided not to say anything more, at least not until she could figure out what was happening.

Several minutes later, Kent arrived. Heather showed him the knife and told him how nervous she felt. They decided to escape to the beach for the day. They woke up Jennifer and packed a picnic lunch. By 9:30 the three were headed west toward the ocean.

At the beach, a light mist hung over the shore until noon, shrouding the rocks and keeping the temperature cool. The threesome strolled through the art galleries of Cannon Beach waiting for the sun to break. When it did, they spread out a blanket and ate lunch.

The rhythm of the waves splashing on the warm sand was almost enough to cause Heather to forget it was the eve of Lammas. Jennifer and Kent built a sand castle, while Heather lay in the sun. Then Kent pulled out his camera and began snapping pictures; one of Jennifer in front of Haystack Rock looking at starfish and sea anemones in the tide pools, one of Heather in her bikini telling Kent that if he snapped a picture he was in "real trouble," one of Heather and Jennifer in Seaside laughing as they rode the bumper cars. It was a wonderful escape for a day, but Heather knew she couldn't run away forever. She wanted to return and face whatever the cult might do. If the cult was going to try anything, they'd wait until after twilight. Heather was determined to be ready for them.

Three sun-burned beachcombers arrived home in the early evening hours. Heather froze when she saw the black Cadillac parked in front of her house. The car was empty, of course; James was lurking about somewhere. Kent walked quickly around the house, looking for him, Heather right behind. The doors and windows were still secure. They searched the backyard, especially the area around the giant oak tree. Nothing looked out of the ordinary. Heather walked cautiously to the front porch, looking in both directions. She stood at the door and stared at the knife scar in the wood. She placed the key in the lock and turned the knob. What if James was inside? The name alone made her queasy. Her mind played tricks on her. She saw his unshaven face with his bushy eyebrows hiding in the shadows and heard his warning about Lammas.

"Let me go in first and make sure everything's safe." Kent must have sensed her fear.

A few minutes later, Kent returned to the front door. "Everything looks okay." Heather was still anxious. Did Kent check carefully enough? She walked slowly into the house, listening for any unusual sound. She looked behind each door and in every corner. Then she walked through once more, just to make sure. Jennifer was outside looking for her kitty and Kent was unloading the car. Heather went to the kitchen and tried to fix something for dinner, but her mind wasn't on cooking. She decided she'd better keep it simple so she threw together hamburgers and a fruit salad.

"This is delicious," Kent said as the three sat around the dining room table.

"Thank you," Heather said quietly. "That black Cadillac—James's car. As long as it's out there, I can't relax. James is somewhere near—waiting, watching, plotting his next move."

"I'm not sure what this guy is up to, but I'm not going to let anybody hurt you or Jennifer."

"First the cat knife and now James's car. The cult is up to something."

"Didn't the police say they'd keep an eye on the place tonight?"

"Yes," Heather said, "but that's not very reassuring since somebody in the police bureau stole the knife from the evidence room and is probably cult related."

"Nobody's going to hurt you as long as I'm around. I'll stay here until . . ."

"Kent's strong," Jennifer broke in. "He won't let James get us."

"You're right, Sweetheart," Heather said. "We're going to be okay."

"I know something else," Jennifer said.

"What?"

"God is with us and he won't let James hurt us either."

After eating, Kent and Jennifer cleared the dishes. They laughed and joked and sang. But Heather was in a more serious mood. She stood in the living room and stared outside at the black Cadillac. The light shifted and darkness collected in the room's corners.

As the sun began to go down, Heather turned on all the lights to chase away the shadows. But it didn't help; the house still felt dark. James was watching them, she could feel it. When it was least expected, he'd sneak in and kidnap Jennifer. Heather looked out the front window; the Cadillac seemed closer.

Soon all three were huddled in the living room. Jennifer fell asleep on the sofa wrapped in her favorite blanket with four stuffed animals keeping her company. Kent turned on the television, but Heather couldn't concentrate. Every noise set her on edge. She watched the front door, she watched Jennifer, she watched the black Cadillac, she watched the clock. Ten o'clock . . . eleven o'clock . . . midnight. The two sat on the floor, played gin rummy, and talked of their future together. Kent looked drowsy, but Heather was determined to keep watch.

Suddenly someone pounded violently on the front door. Both Kent and Heather jumped as it sounded like the whole house was tumbling down. Kent flung open the door and demanded, "What do you want?"

It was James. His face was red and he reeked of alcohol. He looked past Kent, right into Heather's eyes, and pointed at her. She hid behind her fiancé and trembled. "You killed him. It's all your fault. He's dead and I hope you're happy."

"What are you talking about?" Heather said.

"Your father, of course," he blurted out.

"You're drunk," she said gathering her courage. "Daddy's been in the state mental hospital the past few weeks."

"You don't get it, you stupid ungrateful little . . ."

"Now that's enough," Kent burst in. "I want you to leave Heather alone and if . . ."

"It's okay, Kent." Heather turned back to James. "What don't I get?"

"He's dead. When it hit midnight, he realized there was no way to keep Vincent's vow. So he shot himself in the head. It's all over." James looked at the ground.

Heather was shaking. "Even if that were true, how would

you know? You've been stalking somewhere around my house for the past six hours." She caught her breath. "Besides, they don't allow guns in mental hospitals."

"You can smuggle anything in, if you're smart enough." James leaned on the door frame and started crying. "I wasn't here. I parked my car out front this afternoon and caught a taxi to the hospital. I don't know why I did it. He asked for a small gun. I shouldn't have given it to him, but it's too late now."

"How do you know he used it on himself?"

"I was there. I watched him from across the street. He stood at his window and pulled the trigger. It was terrible."

Heather turned to Kent. "If he's right, wouldn't the hospital let . . ."

The phone rang.

Epilogue

Another Vow
(August 20, 1995)

Heather stood in the foyer of the sanctuary—waiting, watching. Colored light from the great stained-glass windows danced on the heads of two hundred guests. Violins played in the background and the scent of sweet flowers lofted through the wooden pews. Jennifer was adorable in her ribbons and bows as she scattered rose petals down the center aisle. Heather smoothed out her wedding dress and leaned on Uncle George. He stood sturdy beside her, ready to give her away. He was a good father-figure, but she missed her real father.

It had been a year ago now since Heather's father had committed suicide. That night Kent had comforted her and even written her another poem. The words ran though her mind as she waited for the ceremony to begin.

This is a song for your morning,
When the dawn spreads its warmth out to you;
A poem from a friend to brighten your day
As you struggle with all you must do.

This is a thought when you're fearful
And old walls steal the light from the sun.
Just remember the battle is over—
You've fought a good fight and you've won.

245

She had won the battle and now she felt free: both her parents were dead, Vincent was dying at Templestowe, the coven had dispersed, and even James had disappeared. Heather and Kent had made it through Halloween, Oimlc, and Beltain with no word from the cult. Heather was thankful, but she was not so naive as to believe that satanic ceremonies had ceased altogether. Many covens were still out there; they had simply moved to more fertile ground where other families were attacked and other children were threatened. Heather prayed each night that the forces of good would overcome the forces of evil. She had memorized Bible verses. Two of her favorites were: "The Lord is faithful, and he will strengthen and protect you from the evil one," and "Those who hope in the Lord will renew their strength. They will soar on wings like eagles; they will run and not grow weary, they will walk and not be faint."

The organ reverberated throughout the sanctuary as the wedding march began. Heather refocused on the present. The room was beautifully decorated with pink roses and baby's breath. She looked down the long aisle and Kent smiled at her, a joyful twinkle in his eyes. She gripped Uncle George's arm and they made their way to the front of the church. It was a fairy-tale wedding with traditional vows: "For better or worse; richer or poorer; in sickness and in health, 'til death do you part . . ."

Then together the couple knelt, held hands, and prayed in unison: "Heavenly Father, we commit ourselves and our marriage to you. Guide us, protect us, and help us. During the pressures of each day give us love and unity, wisdom and humility, sensitivity and compassion. Amen"

When they looked up, the newly-married couple saw Noah, Moses, David, and Daniel illuminated by the glow of the sunset. The moment was magical. They looked into each other's eyes and smiled. They knew they were safe. Just as God had guided these ancient saints through troubled times, so He had guided Heather and Kent. Their escape seemed complete with their wedding vows to God, replacing Vincent's old vows to Satan.

After the wedding, the couple went to the home of Kent's parents to open wedding gifts. Mrs. Thomas welcomed each guest at the front door. It was a joyful gathering with crowded rooms and delicious hors d'oeuvres. Kent was beaming, Heather was more peaceful than she ever remembered being, and Jennifer was showing off like a typical five-year-old.

The living room was a quarter filled with a mountain of elegant-looking presents. The guests watched politely as the newlyweds opened their first gift. It was a large flat package from Carolyn and Dale. Kent held it as Heather cut the ribbon and tore open the silver wedding wrap.

"What is it? What is it?" Jennifer jumped up and down.

It was a painting. Heather smiled brightly. Before her stood Daniel in the lions' den.

"I knew how much you liked the stained-glass window at church," Carolyn said. "We also thought it might remind you of where the two of you first met."

Heather gave her a big hug and said, "Thank you so much. This means more to me than you'll ever know."

Among the other gifts there were dishes, towels, and everything else one would expect to be given at a wedding. At last came the final gift. It had been specifically set aside for the end because of a small note that read "open me last." Heather shook the long narrow package and heard something move. She carefully undid the gold foil wrapping and the guests leaned forward in anticipation.

Lifting the lid of the box, she rustled through several sheets of pink tissue paper. Suddenly two glowing eyes glared at her from the inside of the package. Heather shrieked and shoved the gift away from her. Falling to the floor, the gift spilled from the box. The crowd gasped. It was the cat-knife.

Kent was by Heather's side in an instant. "This is just a trick. They want you to think they still have control, but it's a lie." Heather couldn't move; her total being was fixed on the cat and its shining blade. "No matter what happens," Kent continued, "I'm here and, with God's help, I'm not going to let anything happen to you or Jennifer."

He took Heather's hand and lightly kissed it. Carolyn brought her a glass of cold water and she took a sip. Her hand trembled as she set down the glass and said, "I'm okay." Embracing Kent, she whispered in his ear, "With you and God on my side, I don't think this cult has a chance."

After the guests left, Kent grabbed the cat-knife and led Heather to his father's workshop.

"What are you up to?" Heather asked.

"Just watch."

Kent placed the knife in a vice, tightened it on the cat's head and plugged in a hand-held rock saw. He slipped on a pair of protective goggles and motioned Heather to stand back. The machine screamed as it bit into the knife and showered sparks to the floor. The cat glowed red as the saw made its cut. Again and again Kent ran the machine through the knife, slicing off chunks of metal, until all that was left was seven or eight small pieces of silver.

Heather sighed and a smile stretched her face. The cat-knife was useless, its power was gone. The broken pieces looked gray and dead. Kent dumped them into a can of murky water and let them cool.

"Nobody will ever use that weapon again." Kent picked up the pieces. "There's just one more thing." He walked through the backdoor to the patio with Heather close behind. The air was hot and the view of Portland was magnificent.

"What are you doing?" Heather asked.

"Making a statement." Kent held the pieces tightly in his right hand and threw them high into the air, over the roses and brick wall, to the thick overgrowth of the vacant lot next door. The silver sparkled in the sunlight as the pieces flew in different directions, never to be used again.

About the Author

Steve James is a successful businessman, teacher, seminar speaker, and writer. He enjoys playing basketball, traveling, and encouraging people to think. The rough drafts of this book were written in Jamaica and Grand Cayman.